T0123700

Adriatic Allure

An International Mystery

JANE GOLDEN

iUniverse®

ADRIATIC ALLURE
AN INTERNATIONAL MYSTERY

Author Credits: Patti Golden

iUniverse Star
an iUniverse LLC imprint

iUniverse books may be ordered through booksellers or by contacting:

iUniverse
1663 Liberty Drive
Bloomington, IN 47403
www.iuniverse.com
1-800-Authors (1-800-288-4677)

ISBN: 978-1-5320-7646-6 (sc)
ISBN: 978-1-5320-7714-2 (hc)
ISBN: 978-1-5320-7647-3 (e)

Library of Congress Control Number: 2018907165

Print information available on the last page.

iUniverse rev. date: 06/20/2019

SLOVENIA
HUNGARY
CROATIA
ROMANIA
BOSNIA
AND
HERZEGOVINA
SERBIA
MONTENEGRO
KOSOVO
BULG.
MACEDONIA
ALBANIA
ITALY
GREECE
Adriatic
Sea
Nagykanizsa
Kaposvár
Szekszárd
Hódmezővásárhely
Szeged
Arad
Pécs
Subotica
Celje
Varaždin
Sesvete
Zagreb
Bjelovar
Velika Gorica
Karlovac
Sisak
Sombor
Kikinda
Timișoara
Deva
Hunedoara
Osijek
Zrenjanin
Petroșani
Vukovar
Vinkovci
Novi Sad
Reșița
Slavonski
Brod
Bosanski
Brod
Prijedor
Ruma
Vrsac
Târgu Jiu
Bihać
Banja
Luka
Brcko
Pancevo
Belgrade
Doboj
Bijeljina
Šabac
Drobeta-Turnu
Severin
Udbina
Ključ
Tuzla
Smede revo
Travnik
Zenica
Valjevo
Knin
Glamoc
Srebrenica
Bor
Kragujevac
Vidin
Calafat
Čačak
Paračin
Šibenik
Sarajevo
Pale
Užice
Kraljevo
Goražde
Split
Priboj
Kruševac
Foča
Montana
Mostar
Pljevlja
Niš
Novi Pazar
Bijelo
Polje
Mitrovicë/
Kosovska
Mitrovica
Leskovac
Berane
Herceg-
Novi
Nikšić
Pristina
Pernick
Pejë/
Peć
Gjilan/
Gnjilane
Vranje
Podgorica
Gjakovë/
Đakovica
Ferizaj/
Urosevac
Tivat
Cetinje
Budva
Kyustendil
Prizren/Prizren
Kumanovo
Bar
Shkodër
Kukës
Tetovo
Skopje
Gostivar
Veles
Štip
Manfredonia
Peshkopi
Kicevo
Kavadarci
Strumica
Cerignola
Tirana
Prilep
Andria
Kavajë
Elbasan
Bari
Ohrid
Bitola
Lushnjë
Altamura
Pogradec
Édessa
Fier
Berat
Flórina
Thessaloníki
Brindisi
Korçë
Taranto
Kastoriá
Véroia
Vlorë
Lecce
Kozáni
Kateríni
Otranto
Gjirokastër
Sarandë
Ioánnina
Lárisa
PANNONIAN BASIN
BANAT
TRANSYLVANIAN ALPS
DINARIC ALPS
BALKAN MTS
PINDUS MTS

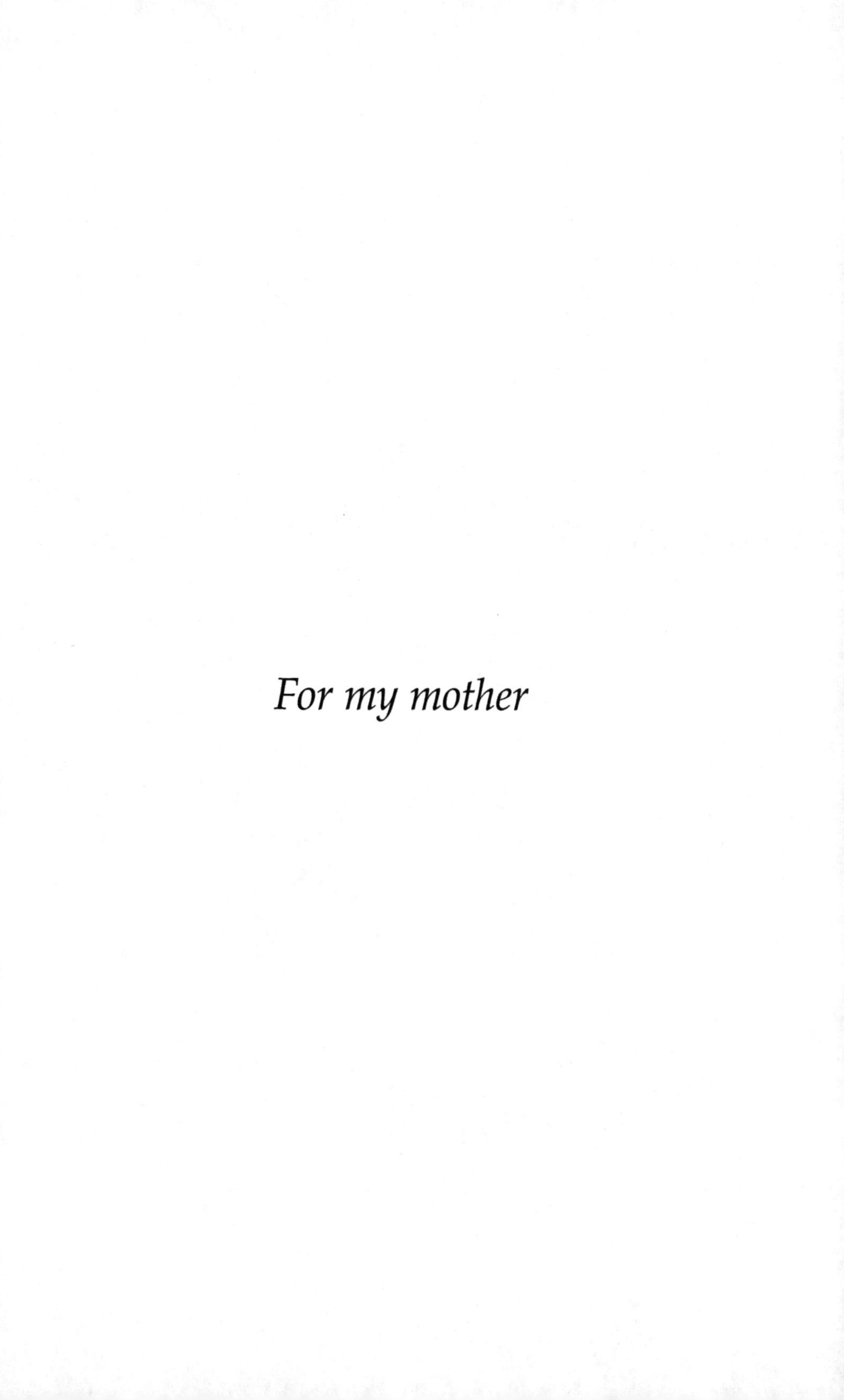

For my mother

Never trust the calm sea when she shows her false alluring smile.

—Titus Lucretius, Roman poet and philosopher (ca. 99 BC–ca. 55 BC), *De Rerum Natura*

Preface

I AM COMPELLED by common sense and the law to point out that *Adriatic Allure* is a work of fiction; all the characters and the plot are creatures of my imagination. However, the Adriatic Sea and the amazing coastlines of Croatia, Montenegro, and Albania could never be adequately described in words. It is my hope that this mystery whets your appetite and compels you to visit the ancient villages and islands that serve as the authentic backdrop to this story. Nothing would please me more than for the people of this region, citizens of nascent democracies, to benefit, even slightly, from the money you spend as tourists exploring these unique places and cultures.

Adriatic Allure would not have been possible without the time my husband and I spent sailing in the Adriatic with Kim and Dragos, our dear friends from Romania. Nor would it have been possible without the experiences gained from a lifetime on the water aboard every conceivable kind of vessel, from summer days as a child drifting and playing in simple rowboats to an adult fascination with the world of yachts.

No words magically appear on the pages of a book. Many people have helped with the production of this one. Thank you to my readers Jay, Jennie, Patrick, and Karen. To Kristina Mullenix, who read and edited, and advised, encouraged, and assisted me, at every step of the publication process—special thanks. Your professional advice and friendship were invaluable.

I also deeply appreciate the contributions of Jennifer Fisher, who read my finished manuscript and then proceeded to make it the best book it could be.

Most of all, I thank my readers. You are the ones who keep Jeni alive and ready to tackle new adventures in faraway places. Stay tuned.

Chapter One

SHE WAS UNMISTAKABLE in her faded green T-shirt with the words Tulane Golf barely legible, her long reddish-blonde ponytail, and her tan legs topped by very short white shorts. Her attire screamed American in a sea of European black—black tops, tiny black skirts, black heels, and black hair. Although I had not seen her in a year, Candi looked like an elongated version of the ten-year-old who had occasionally visited me in summers past, even down to the few freckles that remained on her nose.

Each time the modern opaque glass doors slid open—those teasing doors that separated people waiting for arriving passengers from the exhausted new arrivals impatiently looking for their luggage on the baggage carousel—I caught sight of Candi hugging what I presumed to be her seatmates, and each of them returning her hugs with tenderness, as if they were at a family reunion. One little lady even stroked her hair, brushing a wayward lock from her cheek as if she were a small child. I was so tired that perhaps I was hallucinating. How had she worked her way so far into their hearts on a mere overnight cross-Atlantic flight? It was well past 1:05 a.m. I was ready to head home and fall into my bed.

Though I was excited to see my niece, the email early that same morning had put me on edge about being responsible for a barely legal college graduate in eastern Europe.

> Sis, I just put Candace on a plane to Bucharest. She will arrive tonight at 1:05 a.m. I don't have time to explain it all—Bob and I have to rush to meet our plane and take a quick tour of the outback. I'll write in about a week when we board the cruise ship. Candace will tell you everything when you see her. Thanks for always being there.
>
> I love you,
> Sue

"Who does something like that?" I'd muttered to myself as I read the morning email that had been written in a time zone eight hours away. Last I had heard, Candi, as we usually called her, was finishing with college and in the process of "finding herself." Just what I needed was for her to find herself in Bucharest with my husband, Zach, and me. A little over a year ago I had left my career as a lawyer in a small city outside New Orleans when Zach accepted a Department of Justice position in Romania as a diplomat. We were just settling into our new lives and were still in the honeymoon period most expats experience.

How, I wondered, *is this going to work?*

Candi's one-year-older sister, Kate, was just fine—perfect in just about every way—but Candi had always been a roller-coaster ride. Sometimes she was on top of the world winning golf tournaments, and other times she was on some collegiate sports TV channel flaming out in reverse epic proportion, with the flameouts generally coinciding with the demise of her love du jour. Sue did not like any disorder in her life, and Candi, the one I was now observing with her unruly hair spilling out of the ponytail, challenged her country club mother.

The worst part was that Sue was twelve years older than me and Candi was less than ten years younger than me and Zach. I suddenly became anxious. What was I going to do with an overly dramatic niece? I could barely handle navigating this new home of mine. How would I help Candi do so as well?

I waited and waited, watching the doors open and close, thinking perhaps customs had snagged her. It was just as I was ready to either call security or fall asleep on the ground that she emerged, smiling brightly despite obvious red eyes swollen from crying. We looked more alike than my sister Sue liked to believe. Candi and I shared the green eyes predominant in our genetic line and the same tint of color in our hair, which turned to blonde in the summer. We resembled sisters separated by less than a decade, rather than a conventional aunt and niece.

"Hey, Aunt Jeni, I'm so sorry. I had to get Scout," she said. It was then that my bleary eyes focused on the animal crate she was carrying.

"Scout?" I was confused. In retrospect, I am sure she thought I scowled.

Immediately Candi's eyes teared up, and her cheeks flushed. I could sense the drama begin.

"You're mad, aren't you? I didn't want to come here, so Mom said I could bring Scout if I came, but she didn't tell you, did she?" Knowing her mother well, Candi didn't wait for a response. Instead, the tears began to fall.

"This is so awful. My life is falling apart, and now you're mad. You couldn't have expected me to leave Scout and stay with you alone for two months, could you? Oh my gosh, Mom has dumped me on you, and you don't want me! How could she?" Soon her sniffling and wailing were joined by the sympathetic barking and whining of Scout.

Throughout this sobbing soliloquy, I just stood there, not knowing what to do.

This was not a good beginning.

Now we were the center of attention for those people still waiting for arriving passengers. Maybe it is a better description to say we had become late-night entertainment for the tired and bored masses. A pretty young woman begging to keep her dog was of great interest even to those who knew no English. Romanians love dogs without reservation. What to do with all the dogs roaming the streets of Romania is a constant political issue that runs from failed (because of corruption) spay-and-neuter plans, to relocation projects of dubious means causing many conspiracy theories, and even once to a euthanasia program that had more protestors than a sixties' war movement.

All eyes were on me, and I knew whose side everyone would take if I objected—Candi's. I was acting like a heel, yet I was no heel. I was just *very* tired. Despite any reservations I might have harbored, Scout was going home with us.

"No, no. I just don't know Scout. I'm sure I'll love him."

I reached toward the cage to show my sincerity. Scout just looked back at me with utter confusion. Poor thing. It was easy enough to tell that he was a nonpedigree dog of some sort that most likely came from a dog shelter. He was a small dog but not one of those fancy small dogs that you carry in a purse or a carry-on bag. He was just an everyday kind of dog. I had to admit he was a bit cute, in an odd way, with his short black hair and random white spots, one of which surrounded his right eye. It was a plus that he had so far refrained from barking and growling at me.

"Okay," Candi murmured. I helped her gather her suitcase and dog. Without saying much, she followed me to the car. We both agreed that we needed sleep. Any real conversations would have to wait for tomorrow. In the meantime, I wondered how I was going to tell Zach that she had said something about staying two months. Had I really heard that?

It was at five thirty in the morning when I heard the first bark. Zach nudged me.

"It appears that you're on dog-walking duty," he said before he rolled over to get a few minutes' more sleep.

Five floors down and two blocks to the park and then five floors back up—thirty minutes minimum. After securing Scout to the leash, which I found after a ten-minute search of suitcases while Sleeping Beauty never awakened, I endured Scout's leisurely walk around the park with all its new smells in the cool and dark early morning. It was twenty more minutes before he was satisfied that it was time to perform, and by then an hour had passed. Zach was up and ready for work when we finally made it back up the stairs.

Despite my lack of income and my scant savings, we had settled nicely into our life abroad in a modern spacious apartment near Herastrau Park. Zach worked long hours while I spent my time as a European wife, complete with coffees and social events. I had few responsibilities other than planning meals, doing household chores, and helping with charities. Working was not an option for me, as I had no license to practice law in Romania and didn't read or write the language.

We didn't have a goldfish, much less a feline or canine pet. Even after almost ten years of marriage, we also didn't have children. Now, without warning or any informed consent, we had adopted a twenty-two-year-old college graduate in the midst of an emotional breakdown. Or at least it seemed as if she were being adopted. Two months is a long time. Plus, there was the dog.

"Two months?" Zach had been quiet that morning up until that moment.

"I think it's coinciding with the cruise around the world that Sue and Bob are taking, but I don't have any idea why a college graduate needs a babysitter. Plus, a dog? I can't believe she brought her dog!"

"I'll see if there's anything she can do with the embassy, and you can check to see if any of your charity friends can use her. Let's just take it one day at a time." With that, he kissed me goodbye and smiled. "Don't worry—it's just a new adventure. How bad can it get?"

Chapter Two

"IT WAS AWFUL," Candi wailed at breakfast after I'd gently broached the subject of a sudden visit. "A text—it was a text—'We're over.' He said he needed to concentrate on his own stupid golf game and that I was a distraction! How could he do this? Who's that mean?"

All I could think was how many times she must have said the same words to her fellow passengers on the plane, who then felt compelled to listen to, comfort, and pray for her. They deserved extra frequent-flier miles for their efforts.

"Well," I said, "if I recall correctly, the news said that Rory McIlroy infamously made a ten-minute call to his fiancée to end their engagement so he could go on and win lots of money. It worked for him. Maybe it's a new trend."

I could tell from Candi's face what was coming next. I prepared myself for the breakdown.

"And *I was winning* the tournament that weekend until I got the text, and it was just awful—just awful!" Her eyes welled up with more tears after she'd registered anew the horror of her most recent humiliation.

Just as I suspected, it had been another spectacular loss after the text that caused this latest meltdown. I had witnessed her choking on golf matches after breakups enough to know that the phrase "just awful" was probably the best description of her game in a meltdown. I had seen her walk down the fairway slumped over with her club behind her neck as if a piece of iron were strapped across her shoulders, shuffling her feet, looking intermittently at the sky under the brim of her cap, and then occasionally stopping to tap imaginary mud off her shoes with her club—all signs of a loss of confidence.

I had often thought that perhaps Candi just didn't have the level of concentration that a winner needed to do well consistently, but I smartly decided that it was not the right time to share with her this little piece of insight. In any event, she was not through with her story.

"I told Kate that I was going to go backpacking in India. Graduate school wasn't going to start for a while, and I wanted to go to some unknown place and find myself—you know, like those books written by women who do that and find love and the meaning of life."

"Really?" I said. I almost laughed, but I held myself together.

"Yes, it happens. Anyway, Kate called Mom and tattled before I could get plane tickets. So now I'm stuck here somewhere in eastern Europe."

It was, even after a cup of coffee and more efforts on Candi's behalf to explain herself, a preposterous plan. *Really?* A single, young, naive American traveling alone in the midst of almost a billion people in a country lit up with State Department travel warnings? Of course Sue panicked.

"Mom offered a compromise—spend some time with you. For good measure, she told me that she would cancel my credit card in the event that I didn't accept the offer. Since I have no money, I had no choice." She slumped farther down into her chair to emphasize her seemingly dismal situation.

I gleaned that Scout was only included at the last minute by my desperate sister. It proved once again to me that Sue could have been a ruthless military general. It mattered to her not whether I wanted my niece and her dog or whether the niece and dog wanted to see me. That was irrelevant. This was the only plan she had up her sleeve, and it would have to work.

"Now that you are here, what do you want to do?" I asked.

I looked at a startled and blank face. Candi was momentarily puzzled.

"Play golf?" she posed.

It was my first real laugh of the day.

"I think you would get bored. The only option is a six-hole course that you play three times to make it an eighteen-hole round." The Diplomat Golf Course by our house was beautiful and stately with its grand clubhouse of white stone, its deep brown Brâncovenesc pitched roof, its heavy wooden trim, and its large verandas. It was known for its perseverance throughout Communism and its architectural beauty, but the course that sloped from the clubhouse to Lake Herastrau was also famous for its lack of holes. It was so short that there were no golf carts, and any wayward shot on some tees landed on the walking path around the lake. Still, it was peaceful.

Candi, on the other hand, was anything but peaceful.

"No way!"

"Way. You won't be playing much golf here, even if you could afford it. Which reminds me—do you have any money?"

"Not much, but I have a credit card."

This was not good news. It would take a while for that complication to sink into her mind. Her credit card was worthless since she had neither a chip in the card nor a PIN. Nor was it compatible in any way with the Romanian banking system. I had been in her shoes before—without any money and holding only worthless cards. ATM cards worked well to get cash, but don't even try to buy shoes with an ordinary American Express. MasterCard may be "priceless," as the commercial says, but without a PIN, it was useless for groceries. Before I understood the issue, I would argue at length with sales clerks, repeatedly making them reswipe the card. At some point the clerk would become convinced I was trying to defraud the store and call security.

"Candi, this is hard to explain, but what you need in Romania is cold hard cash in every denomination. That means in your wallet you must have lots of one-, five-, and twenty-leu notes. Exact change is mandatory. If you only have hundred-leu notes and you are buying something for fifty leu, the sales clerk will shake their head and send you away. If you have twenty and the cab fare is five, be ready to forfeit the rest."

She looked at me in dismay as I spoke.

"Sometimes hoping to make a sale, the store clerks will conspicuously look in your open purse or wallet to see if you missed the right note, pointing out that you do, indeed, have a five-leu note tucked in a pocket of the wallet."

"Why is it that way?" she asked.

"I think that this happens because banks don't give change freely. In fact, the banks charge dearly for everything," I said.

It was a lesson I'd learned the hard way when I unwittingly was elected the president of the International Ladies of Bucharest. This large group of women, primarily expats, was similar to other groups around the world that were organized in country capitals to fulfill the need for friendship and some meaningful existence for a lonely spouse immersed in a new life. Most of the members were like me, educated but unable to work without licenses or the local language skills.

"I'm not sure I told you, but I'm president of the International Ladies of Bucharest. I just call it ILB sometimes," I said.

"That's insane. You've only been here like a year or two," she said.

"It turns out the women had a big disagreement over finances right before I arrived. They were having a hard time finding a member willing to take over as president of a group of strong-willed women from almost fifty different countries and cultures who were infighting. I got tagged before I knew any better."

"Do you do the banking too?"

"Yes, and that was a surprise to me as well. I have to approve bank deposits and withdrawals, and I can't read a thing in Romanian. Thank goodness I appointed a great treasurer who can. I just stand next to her and sign exactly where she puts her finger."

I explained to her that I'd quickly discovered each time the board went to the bank that the bank charged us—to look at our documents, to make a deposit, to let us withdraw, and for just about anything else. An account with euros, dollars, and leu was nothing but a bundle of fees.

And there are the Romanian coins as well. I learned about their value when I noticed them accumulating in large piles on my dresser and going nowhere. I noticed that people left them at grocery checkouts and waved them off if you tried to use them. It is even poor taste to give change to a beggar, as they have no means to convert them into paper money, which is necessary for real shopping.

"I know it sounds complicated, but once you get the hang of it, you will feel very superior to the ordinary tourist." I finished my international monetary lesson just as I saw Candi stifle a yawn.

"Right now I have no money at all, so I don't feel so superior," she said.

I pondered what to do with Candi and her finances. She was not prepared to be let loose in Bucharest.

I had a monthly coffee meeting with the International Ladies of Bucharest that day at the Hotel Intercontinental. The problem was Candi's clothes. The 150 women who might attend had already planned out their outfits well in advance and would be perfectly groomed. I didn't have much time to make Candi presentable.

"Candi, I'll tell you what. Today, you can go with me to a meeting and we'll get you some money from the ATM in the hotel. It's safe. You'll enjoy the coffee. What did you bring to wear to a coffee?"

"Coffee? What do you mean—like Starbucks?"

"No, a coffee where people meet and talk—like a social club."

"I don't know. I wasn't in a sorority; I played golf. What should I wear?"

We walked upstairs to her room for clothing inspiration. I looked inside her suitcase. Four bikinis—parts of them at least—five sets of short shorts, four T-shirt-type tops, six pairs of sandals, two pairs of tennis shoes, one pair of golf shoes, a tiny sundress, two pairs of jeans, and miscellaneous skimpy undergarments. Nothing would do.

Against Candi's will, and while she intermittently whined that she would prefer to stay in the apartment all day, we went to my closet and found the least offensive thing that she would consider wearing—a plain black knit dress devoid of any decoration. Although Candi wore it well and she looked every bit the long-legged American with her shiny hair now brushed, it was barely acceptable for coffee at the Hotel Intercontinental. I begged her to wear some jewelry, but I only persuaded her to don some simple dangly silver earrings.

While I waited on Candi's hour-long shower and for her to get dressed, I watched a bit of the local news. It had few channels, but there was one good Romanian news channel that I enjoyed watching. Much of my Romanian vocabulary had been picked up from the rows of scrolling words at the bottom of the screen. On this channel the news was always "breaking," and the reporting news segments were repeated throughout the day.

Today's news was about a murder. This death was the first of its kind that I had heard about since arriving in Bucharest, a city of two million where random violence almost never occurred. I was intrigued by a drawing of a woman whose body had been found in the thick wooded area in Herastrau Park near the train trestle that crossed over the dam separating Lake Herastrau from another body of water. I knew the area well. The wooded area that the TV anchor referenced was part of the meditative one-third of the park defined by natural beauty and lack of entertainment or buildings.

Having often climbed up and walked across the elevated train tracks at the furthest edge in order to get to the other side of the lake, I wondered how no one had ever been killed by a speeding train.

"I wonder if she was hit by a train," I said out loud. Before Candi's arrival, talking to myself had almost become normal since I was on my own so much of the time. "No, she couldn't have been hit by a train. They would have said it on the news if that was how she died."

What made the death all the more unsettling was the discovery of the body so near my home.

The serious anchorman in his dark suit and tie ended his report by saying, "The *polizia* are searching for the woman's identity."

The artist's rendering of her face repeatedly flashed on the screen. Something began to tug at me the more I concentrated on her likeness. The dead woman did not look Romanian. I guessed that she was from a nearby eastern European country and probably quite beautiful.

I began to believe I had seen her face somewhere before, but it made no sense. Where could we possibly have met? I knew for sure I had not seen her walking a dog or jogging in the park. Each time her pencil-sketched wide eyes peered at me from the screen, I felt like she was speaking to me. It was creepy. I had seen that look somewhere before, and not on a dead body.

Eventually Candi emerged, ready to leave. I stood up and shook my head to forget the images. Whether I had seen the woman or not really didn't matter, because I knew nothing about her. I decided that Zach would think I was crazy if I mentioned that I might know a random dead person. He would tell me not to sit and watch the news all day. In any event, surely the body of the poor girl would be identified by day's end.

Chapter Three

WHEN I CHECKED my cell phone for the time, I realized we were already too late to walk through the park to the underground metro, which was my usual routine, and still make it to the meeting before it started.

"We'll have to drive today, which will be crazy in the midday traffic," I told Candi. We headed to the elevator and down to the underground parking garage to my old but trustworthy BMW X5, the car of choice for many Europeans.

"On the other hand, it's probably a good thing, as it will allow you to see a bit of the city," I added.

It was always a chore to navigate the car's gray hulk out of the underground garage. And it was always a challenge for me to remember the ever-changing exit code and then lean out of the driver's-side window to punch it in accurately. Once the door swung open and the second iron gate lifted, the exit ramp still frightened me. It was almost straight up, until it flattened out right in the middle of the busy sidewalk next to a kindergarten school. For those pedestrians ambling by the garage and not paying close attention, the SUV seemed as if it were shooting out of the earth like a missile. Except for snowy days when I had to gun the car to make it up the steep incline, I drove slowly and tried to be extra cautious.

Today there were no worries; most of the cars and residents in the area had cleared out early for work. We quickly emerged from the dark and into the bright morning sun, where Candi caught her first view of the 462-acre Herastrau Park.

"Oh!" She gasped as she took in its sheer beauty.

The surface of the park's large lake was visible beyond a row of slim trees, shimmering like reflective glass in the morning sun and only occasionally rippling with the movement of some kayakers. Joggers, bikers, and nannies pushing strollers were beginning to fill the three-and-a-half-mile-long path alongside the water's edge. Soon enough they would be joined by professionals seeking to have lunch at one of the outdoor cafés.

We did not talk much as I drove to the city center, the two of us still delicately feeling our way around each other as our new cohabitation relationship developed. It was fine. I could tell idle talk was not necessary since Candi was mesmerized by the activity and the sights around her.

"That's Romania's own Arc de Triomphe," I told her as we drove past an arched monument sitting majestically in the middle of a roundabout and connecting several wide boulevards, one of which led to the impressive outdoor Peasant Village Museum, and another of which led past the estates and embassies on Kisseleff Boulevard to the winged statue honoring Romania's pioneering pilots on the famous Aviatorilor Boulevard.

I drove past one park after another filled with playgrounds, benches, and outdoor sculptures, until we reached the city center. It was then that Candi could no longer contain herself.

"Wow, those clothes are *amazing*! I wasn't expecting high fashion in Bucharest," she said as we moved past the windows of designer clothing shops in old buildings lining the tight corridor of Boulevard Calea Victorie.

Candi drank in everything, rolling down the window and craning her neck to see as much as she could. I could see her smile at something, and then a few minutes later her face filled with a look of confusion at the nameless tall concrete structures built by the dictator Ceaușescu that housed families relocated during Communism.

The historical importance of the apartments was far too complicated a discussion for that moment. Once again silence filled the air.

Ancient domed cathedrals sat amid shiny new malls and apartment buildings. Restaurants, fountains, and parks tied everything together with Romanian flair.

"I can't believe all the people walking everywhere," she said as we navigated the heart of the city. As usual, it was vibrant and humming with activity.

The last building on the random tour was the ubiquitous Palace of the Parliament that towered above the entire city—white, ornate, and controversial. It was made even more impressive by the blooms of roses, pansies, and marigolds spread out along its vast green space in whimsical beds.

"This is where Zach works, on the top floor," I said. "This should interest you: I watched Lady Gaga's concert from the tiny top balcony."

"Seriously?" she said, suddenly impressed with me, straining her neck and shielding her eyes from the sun in order to see the top of the building from our close vantage point.

I smiled.

"Yes. The building was the brainchild of Romania's former dictator Ceauşescu, and was constructed by the people at their own expense—both in money and lives. You'll have to take a tour and learn about the massive amount of money and labor it consumed, leaving the people starving. The opulence is almost mind-numbing. The revolution started before the building was finished or occupied. They later decided to finish it, and now members of parliament, the government authorities, and regional law enforcement offices like Zach's are in the building. Another interesting fact is that it's the largest office building in the world after the Pentagon. Maybe there's one in Dubai that is larger now. I'm not sure."

When I felt Candi had taken in enough, I parked the car near the poignant sculptures in Revolutionary Square just outside the hotel. This area marked the pivotal spot in the 1989 revolution when many Romanians risked their lives, with some losing their lives, seeking freedom from Ceauşescu. Once the car was turned off, Candi sat back in her seat and sighed as she removed her seat belt.

"I didn't know what to expect," she said.

"I know how you feel. Everywhere I look in Bucharest evokes a different emotion in me," I responded.

It was true. My new home was a cacophony of sights and sounds—some harsh, but most of them wonderful. Here beside me was a young woman whose carefully laid out life had revolved around closely cut fairways, manicured sand traps, and hamburgers in the clubhouse. Now she was seeing a world she never knew existed.

It had taken less than a day, but old boyfriends were far away and Candi was already embracing something new.

When we arrived in the historic lobby of the Hotel Intercontinental with its cubist décor, many of the members of the International Ladies of Bucharest were already there. Although English was the common language of ILB, most members conversed with each other in whichever language best suited the group at the moment.

"Don't feel overwhelmed by these women. I was shy and awkward when I first got here—even intimidated—and now I'm the president of the group. They'll be nice."

She turned to look at me in disbelief. I saw her eyeing the exit toward the car lot.

It was just when I was beginning to reconsider the decision to bring Candi to the meeting that my two closest friends, Anna and Julia, appeared. Anna, petite and stylish, was an Israeli American married to a Romanian. Julia was the quintessential beautiful Romanian who had dual citizenship with the United States and was part owner of a family winery. Both women were active in women's and children's charities.

I introduced the three of them. "Come with us," Anna told Candi. They headed to a table.

I left to go to the podium to start the meeting, happy that Candi was otherwise occupied.

Despite having been elected president of the ILB by an almost unanimous vote, I remained anxious hosting the meetings. I had quickly realized that *almost* meant that there were members in my midst who had cast secret nay votes against me—six of them. It shocked me at first.

"Who would do that when I was the only candidate on the ballot?" I asked my friends. They said to just ignore it. I couldn't.

Plus, I felt sure that it would be way more than six nay votes if the women voted again. I had discovered that there were so many cultural and personality divides that I felt I was constantly treading through a minefield. It seemed a new controversy arose each time a woman lifted her hand to ask a question. More likely than not, I figured, something would pop up today to bite me right in front of my niece.

It did.

This time the problem emerged immediately after the luncheon speaker finished.

It came from a woman who was born somewhere in Eastern Asia but who grew up in Romania. Moira had returned to Romania after three years of living in Spain. She made a grand appearance reeking of new money and now seemed determined to become the next president of ILB—the sooner the better, I thought. Her hair was pulled back in a tight black bun, and her designer knit dress hugged each of her sharp curves. Her nails and lips were the same color of red. The fake smile she wore made her look a lot like Cruella de Vil. Of course, that isn't a kind thing for me to say. But my perspective was likely linked to some hurtful personal things she had disclosed about two sweet members of the group.

In the short time I had known her, Moira had become a problem on all fronts, enjoying any chaos she could create that would make me look bad. She had made it perfectly clear to me that I was old news as president and she wanted control of the organization. I had been told by other members to be wary of her. Although I might have fallen into the presidency, I had no plans to acquiesce to someone like her.

Her slim fingers danced in the air, multiple gold bracelets tinkling with the movement, as soon as I asked if anyone had anything further to say.

"Yes, Moira?"

"I just want to tell the ladies that I have spoken to the Diplomat Club and I have the most wonderful news! This year, for the first time ever, we will be helping with the annual Diplomat Games! Isn't that great? I just knew everyone would be so excited. They have asked me to be on the committee! Who else wants to be on it?" she asked, turning to look at me with a fake smile.

The room erupted with clapping and expressions of joy, although not many in the room other than me had any idea what this meant. The last thing ILB needed was to be dragged into the political jostling of the annual Diplomat Games, a sports competition among all of the city's embassies. It could be controversial enough without our intervention. I had learned the year before that they were best enjoyed by those who were not in charge of anything.

The games, which were hosted by the Romanian Foreign Ministry, were scheduled for a weekend later in the summer.

I was stuck standing uncomfortably like a politician who had just been one-upped by his competitor. If I had worn a tie, I would have grabbed the knot and pulled it from side to side to loosen it. I could feel my cheeks begin to burn and turn a bright red. It was time to think fast, or else we'd be running the entire event.

"Of course, I'll head the committee," I rushed to say. "The board will discuss the other members to invite next week." That, at least, stopped her from stacking the Diplomat Games committee with women she could manipulate.

Moira was momentarily shocked by her lack of control over the situation, but she recovered enough to say she would be happy to wait and hear from us.

Everyone smiled back at her but me. All I wanted was for the meeting to end.

When I finally adjourned the meeting, I went to find Candi. By then I had gathered my wits about me and lowered my frustration level. Even so, I was caught off guard by what I saw. Candi was deeply involved in a conversation with a new member whom I didn't know. Anna and Julia were nowhere nearby. The woman, who did not look much older than Candi, had thick black hair pulled into a loose ponytail and wore a colorful native dress. *Perhaps,* I thought, *she is Moroccan or maybe from Southern France.* Her exotic looks took me aback, even in a room full of women from around the world.

"Hey, Aunt Jeni. Do you know Tina?"

Tina smiled and held her hand out American style for a handshake. She seemed nice enough, but it was strange we had never met. I decided I would have to speak to Anna about her.

"Nice to meet you," she said with a thick French accent. "'Tina' is short for my real name, which can be hard for some people to pronounce. I'm really excited about joining the group. And, I love your niece! We'll have to get together."

I nodded in agreement and apologized for having to leave, saying that my car was already waiting in valet. Tina smiled and passed her card to Candi, offering it with both hands as is often done in Asia.

"We'll keep in touch," she said. With that she turned and left.

"How did you like Anna and Julia?" I asked Candi once we were alone.

"They're nice, but they're like five or ten years older. Anna wants me to help with her charity for human trafficking victims. I told her to let me wait a few weeks and I would visit her place. But for now I think I might hang out with Tina."

"Tina?"

"Yeah, she's great. Oh, and I forgot to tell you that when I went to find the restroom, I ran into the nicest guy. I accidentally bumped into him, and we started talking! He's from Moldova and staying here at the hotel."

"Moldova?" I was beginning to have trouble keeping up with her new slate of friends.

"Yeah, I barely know anything about Moldova. Anyway, he asked me to go clubbing tonight, but I told him I was too tired. Maybe I'll see him tomorrow night. He asked for my phone number, but I don't have a phone yet. Can we get it soon?"

"I don't know. You just got here." I started stammering, unprepared for Candi's newfound confidence and for what was to me disturbing information.

"Don't worry, Tina said if I went clubbing, she'd go with me to make sure I'm okay." With that she turned and almost skipped with joy toward the car.

So, things really could get worse. *Clubbing with strangers?* I wanted to throttle my sister.

Chapter Four

WHEN WE REACHED the apartment, Candi's jet lag hit with full force. As much as I hated to assume dog duties, I felt sorry for her and offered to take a very anxious Scout for a long walk. I needed to get some fresh air as well.

"How far do you usually walk with Scout?" I asked.

"Oh, he walks forever. No worries."

Scout stood patiently as I clipped on the leash, but it was clear from his whining that he preferred to be with Candi. It was only with reluctance that he left her room.

Scout and I were slowly forming a bond. It was like he'd decided that I was his nanny. I walked him and fed him, and once I disciplined him when he felt compelled to gnaw on one of Zach's leather dress shoes. But in the end, I was the hired help who only existed to make his life pleasant. His unabashed love was for Candi. When we arrived home in the morning after his bathroom break and he jumped into her arms to lick her, I could see him glance my way as if to remind me just who I was and where I ranked in his life.

We walked to the path and struck out in the direction of the train tracks. My curiosity was killing me. I wanted to see where the dead woman had been found. Scout was constantly stopping and sniffing, or growling at much larger dogs, but he was otherwise social with others strolling along the lake's grassy banks.

I could tell easily enough where the woman had been found, because the grounds were trampled, some branches were broken, and a bit of leftover crime scene tape was still attached to a thin tree trunk. It was about a hundred feet from the train tracks and off a dirt area sometimes used by people to train their dogs. I couldn't figure out why anyone would walk alone to that part of the park.

Having satisfied myself that there was not much else to learn, I turned to walk with Scout back to our apartment.

Scout, on the other hand, decided it was time to take a rest. He stopped and laid his stomach on the ground, paws stretched out to the front and back. I tugged. He didn't move. I called his name, tugged harder, begged, and then threatened some vague consequence if he did not get up. He still didn't move. I began to realize he wasn't going anywhere without a rest—and he was too large for me to carry very far.

I sat on the grass beside him and waited for him to gather his strength and resume our walk. It was then that I realized how tired I was. I reclined into a more comfortable position. But after what seemed like just a minute or two, I heard, "Doamna? Doamna?"

I sat up quickly, totally disoriented.

I had fallen asleep. The realization was embarrassing. The voice was from a teenage boy trying to get my attention. Evidently not able to speak English, he pointed to the train tracks, where Scout was prancing away from me, dragging his leash behind.

Trains barrel down this track so fast that Scout wouldn't stand a chance if I didn't catch him. I did what I had to do—I scampered as fast as I could up the steep hill toward the tracks and then ran across the railroad ties, praying a train would not appear.

"Scout! Scout!" I cried frantically at the dog, but he paid me no attention.

I only began to make headway because his short legs were slowed down by the wooden railroad ties. When he was close enough, I jumped with both feet onto the end of the leash, dragging behind him, stopping the escapee dead in his tracks.

It was then that I was able to stop and see the entire area of the crime scene from an elevated view. The land around the tracks was scruffy and unkempt with the occasional stacks of dead tree limbs that collected windblown litter. There were no buildings, no park benches—nothing at all that might entice anyone, much less a pretty woman, to walk alone. Farther away from the tracks and at the beginning of the woods, I saw the entrance to yet another path. It was no more inviting than the general surrounding area and had no discernable end. I shook my head. The park was full of wonderful places. Why had the murdered woman come to this remote area?

"We'll never know," I told Scout as we wandered back to the apartment.

Zach was home when I returned from our walk, foraging in the refrigerator for some food. I was exhausted from the tug-of-war that had transpired when Scout ran away and offered to make tomato and cucumber sandwiches rather than a full meal.

"What about Candi?" Zach said.

With that Scout wagged his short tail at Zach and ran to the door of Candi's room. I opened it gently and saw her fast asleep. It was a good time to talk to Zach about the day.

"Of course, she wants to go out," Zach said. "You would too if you were her. We just need to keep her busy and help her meet some people we trust to take her out. I don't want her to get too involved with people we don't know. A pretty young American girl alone in eastern Europe could be trouble."

We both thought for a few minutes about options. Zach was the first to come up with a plan. He told me he'd invite some of the young guys from the consular section over for barbecue and a wine club meeting. We hoped they could introduce Candi to other diplomat children and employees her age. In the meantime, I found out that she could volunteer at the embassy library once we obtained all her clearances as a member of our household, which could easily take the full two months.

"Have you considered her helping at Anna's charity?" Zach asked.

"Candi didn't seem overly excited about it, but I'm going to plan something with Anna that might get her interested."

Anna had a house in Bran and sometimes volunteers to help a few women from that area. It was the number one tourist destination in Romania.

"Maybe I'll invite Anna and some other friends to the barbecue. That might help," I said.

The next morning's local television station had even more breaking news on the dead woman in the park. She had been identified as a waitress from eastern Moldova. A photo of her from when she was alive flashed on the screen—a pretty young woman, probably of Hungarian descent, with light brown hair and blue eyes. I couldn't tell much else. I got the sense that the police now considered her death accidental.

Surely, I thought, *there must be more to the story if they originally assumed murder.*

This disinterest exhibited by the police and the lack of motivation to follow leads was unusual in a place that rarely had murders and, when it did, always made it into a hot topic.

Although the picture of the woman's face was only momentarily on the news and I had no time to study it, the more I sat on the couch, the more I became convinced that I had seen the victim sometime recently. For some reason I thought it had to do with the park. The blue eyes were unnerving to me.

Before I could pull up a memory, the news moved on to other topics. Scout was anxious to take a walk.

This time I decided to see if I could make more sense of the woman's death. My connection to her had to be somewhere in the park. I couldn't think of any other possibility. Perhaps something would jog my memory this time.

Instead of taking the paved lakeside walkway over the train tracks and toward the Diplomat Club, I took the narrow, worn footpath in the opposite direction. It led past the area where dogs were trained and toward the entrance of the remote path that led into the densest part of the woods. It was little used, and littered with paper and objects. It was near where the woman had been found, but it was almost hidden from the average park visitor by a thin stand of woods. It was not intended as a place to picnic.

Scout was intrigued by the change of plans and took the opportunity to explore pungent new scents from previous canine visitors. Once he encountered them, he refused to leave the apparently irresistible aromas without a firm tug on the leash. I tried to let him enjoy each new sensory experience, but ultimately I became impatient.

"Come on, Scout. You're wasting time." I tugged at the leash to no avail. It was then that I looked around and noticed that it had been more than twenty minutes and I hadn't seen anyone head off the lakeside path in my direction. In this huge park in this large city, I suddenly felt terribly alone and vulnerable. I shared Scout's apprehension about my plans.

"You know, Scout, you might be right to hesitate. This may not be such a good idea." I liked to talk to myself when I was with Scout. Of course, if I were alone and talked to myself, then I would look crazy, but because people all over the world talk to their dogs, no one noticed when I chatted with Scout about complicated subjects. Plus, he never casted any doubt on my conclusions the way Zach often did.

Eventually I decided we had wasted enough time. I'd tried to retrace my walks from the last few weeks, hoping to recall where I had seen the woman. When I finally got up and pulled Scout toward the overgrown and unkempt path, he looked at me with frustration. Even he knew a bad idea when he saw one.

"You know, something tells me that we need to head this way," I told him. He stood his ground.

"Sorry—we're committed," I said. This time he relented and followed me.

Almost immediately, the topography changed when we stepped onto the path. Trees in this area were so dense that the sunlight did not filter through. The ground alternated from rocky to almost muddy where old rain spots could not get enough light to dry out. The soft land underfoot and the trees overhead muffled the sounds from anything other than an occasional bird or the drifting bark of a dog. I could tell it would be impenetrable at night, even with light from my cell phone.

"No intelligent woman would dare take this trek alone in the dark," I told Scout, as if to warn him of the dangers to dogs as well.

I gingerly walked across the roots of old trees, dead limbs, and sharp rocks that randomly obstructed the path. It must have been a useful shortcut to someone. But for whom? It wasn't even straight.

After navigating the path for a distance, I considered turning back. I knew that I shouldn't be doing this alone. There was no indication where I would end up or of how tired Scout and I would be at that point. On the other hand, I didn't like the idea of quitting before I could find where it led, and the thought of returning to where I'd begun was even less appealing. It was just at that moment of indecision that I heard the distant sound of a car in the direction we were headed. Scout perked his little head up and ran ahead to the end of his leash, pulling me with him.

The sound of a car was good news. I figured we could get to a road and hail a cab if Scout refused to cooperate again. Quickening my pace to keep up with Scout, I tripped over some dead limbs. My arms flailed in the air for something to stop the fall, but instead I landed face-first in the dirt, scraping my bare knees. I wasn't hurt badly, but I was definitely aggravated. I sat on the ground for a few minutes to regain my composure. Even a dog knows when his nanny needs a bit of love. Scout came over to lick me like a Popsicle. I smiled.

I hopped up, dusted off some dirt and leaves, and proceeded down the path until the tree canopy thinned. At first I found it difficult to acclimate my eyes to the sun. The smell of something rotting seemed to linger in the air. I winced at the horrible odor.

Maybe it's a dead body, I instinctively thought. I didn't know what one smelled like, but my heart began to race. I readied my phone to call 211 (Romania's 911) if a lifeless body appeared on the path before me.

Before I could embarrass myself with a call to the police, I discovered that the walk had ended right at a bank of large trash bins full of restaurant waste. These were at the back of a paved parking lot for a restaurant, which I immediately recognized as one I had visited with some friends. It was a simple outdoor café on a remote outcropping of the park. At some point it had been a full indoor restaurant, but that part of the establishment had been abandoned and boarded up, probably because of its remote location far away from the lake.

Several of my friends and I had been at the restaurant only a couple of weeks before to meet two Romanian women who'd started a neighborhood business. They were earnest young entrepreneurs on a budget, and showed us their new inventions for making the average woman happier. I only half listened to the talk and mostly surveyed the restaurant while the other two guests asked questions. The day I went with my friends, we sat on the outdoor patio, sipping lemonade with honey and snacking on cheese and crackers. It should have been a good memory, but I recalled that it wasn't. The cheese was old, the waiters were surly, and something else was off.

Based upon that past experience, I ordinarily would have avoided the restaurant at all costs, but I didn't today for the simple reason that both Scout and I were thirsty.

I tied Scout's leash to a pole near an outside table where a dog's watering bowl already sat. He thirstily lapped up what was left in the bowl and then lay down to have a nap. I selected the table next to Scout, which happened to be right next to one I'd sat at on my earlier visit.

"Limonada cu miere, va rog," I politely ordered from the waitress. My eyes followed her as she left to prepare the drink, real lemonade with local honey.

It was when the waitress reached the swinging door to the kitchen that I noticed a mirror fastened behind the adjacent outdoor bar. *That is where I saw the dead woman!* She had been, like me, sitting at another table facing the bar. I remembered that I could see her clearly and had studied her reflection in the mirror. Her looks and demeanor were so unsettling that I could not help but gaze at her—a vision of beauty and ice. Her hair was not brown that day; it was very blonde. The picture on the news must have been from an earlier, innocent time in her life, before she colored her hair.

She was heavily made up in a tight white dress that was cut into a risqué wide V down the front, all the way to her navel; it was held together only with an insert of some sheer lace. Although quite tall and thin, she wore strappy sandals with four-inch heels. Her tanned arms and legs had no visible imperfections. She was every man's dream, but that was for nighttime dreams. Even in Bucharest she was way over the top for the middle of the day.

Still it was not her dress that had intrigued me—it was her blue eyes. They were almost dead to the world. Even when we made eye contact through the mirror, it was as if she looked right through me. She made no sound, never changed her expression, and only occasionally moved her salad around her plate. She took a sip of her wine when nudged by her closest companion and smiled when she was prompted to do so by the laughter at the table. Even then it was not a real smile. It was melancholy, not happy. I wasn't sure she spoke Romanian, as I never heard her interact with the waiter for their table at any point. Even if she was a rich snob, a Romanian *always* said *mulţumesc*, "thank you."

The two men with her, on the other hand, were anything but reserved. They were drinking expensive liquor. They were loud and vulgar. The man sitting next to her, with his hand on her thigh, appeared to be the leader. He stood out in his brightly colored cheap Italian clothes. Well, they were probably not cheap, but they looked very silly on his big belly and heavy legs. His patterned knit shirt was sleeveless, revealing muscular biceps. But for the fact the shirt was Italian, we at home would call it a "wifebeater." His loose jersey shorts matched the shirt.

Some salon must have shaved his head and then shined it up with oil. Finally, gold necklaces around his neck rounded out his ensemble. I grew disgusted by him when he occasionally ran his hand over the woman's arms.

I could only see a bit of his companion, as he was behind a stand of plants, but he too was dressed similarly to the leader and had the same physique, but none of the gold necklaces. He was not as flashy. There was an indecipherable tattoo on his upper arm, the kind that was badly drawn and had no real meaning except to the wearer. The more I'd watched the men and woman, the more I felt sure I was witnessing a bad scene.

"Anna," I'd whispered. "Look at that woman. Isn't something off about her?"

She had to turn in her chair to look at the woman, and then she'd turned back.

"Yes, but I think it might be drugs. Those guys look like they're the type."

"I don't know, I think it's something else. Why would someone like her be with those thugs?"

"Who knows? Money? A job? A job is the most likely answer. They probably promised her something."

We both were quiet as we considered the woman's situation.

"She doesn't smile back to me," I'd said. "She's not happy."

"Hmm," Anna had said, obviously thinking more about the possibilities. "There is the chance that she's being held against her will, but we have no evidence of that. The men look like they are OC, and those men deal in drugs and women. Unless she follows us to the restroom or gives us a signal, I don't know how we could help. That tells me that she probably doesn't want to be helped. It's more likely that she is on drugs and just out of it."

Although I never understood a word the men had said, Anna was right. Everything about the leader had screamed OC, as in organized crime, and to an American that usually included drugs. No matter what the reason, I had to believe that no woman like the one I saw that day would be with those men for a minute, much less a meal, unless she was forced to be there.

Anna and I had looked around for a security guard or some nearby park police to alert, but the restaurant was too far off the beaten track.

I remembered feeling sick that day and pretty certain of my deductions. A battle had brewed within as I felt torn about what to do. *Should I say something to her? What if I am wrong and I insult them? What if I am right and they hurt her or me? Should I just tell Zach?*

In the end, neither Anna nor I had done anything.

"Don't plan anything else here again—it's awful," I'd said as we left the restaurant. Anna had agreed.

Chapter Five

A WAVE OF nausea hit me as I thought about my past indecision and the fact that I had so readily forgotten about that day.

The waitress caught me lost in those thoughts when she came back with a frosted glass of real lemonade. Looking down at the tray and cool drink, I realized I'd forgotten to ask for ice, but I was not going to send it back now. She had also brought me a cotton cloth and a bowl of water to clean my dirty knees. How thoughtful.

"Mulţumesc," I thanked her.

"Cu plăcere," she responded with a genuine smile. I loved the way Romanians always said "with pleasure." It is so civilized.

"Do you speak English?" I asked.

"Yes, a little." That usually means "a lot."

"I was wondering—I came in here a couple of weeks ago and saw a young lady with two men sitting at that table," I said, identifying it with my hand. "I am trying to remember her name. I wrote it down, but I can't find the paper. Do you know who she might be?" I lied to her in my effort to fish for more information.

She shook her head no.

"Do you know if anyone is here today who might have been working lunch last month?" I asked.

"No, I'm sorry, but there were only two waiters then, and they aren't working here right now. They left at the same time when someone offered them a summer job. I'm a university student and just started here, so I don't even know the owner's name." She lowered her voice. "The manager is not so nice, so I don't ask too many questions." With that she gave a furtive glance toward the back and whispered, "I am leaving next week for another job."

"Ah, I think I remember the waiters. They looked like twins. They weren't too friendly," I said, lowering my voice to match hers.

"Yes, the cook said they were twins. I think they left last Wednesday because I was hired the next day. The manager was desperate to fill the positions and was forced to hire me and another college student. He let me know he doesn't like to deal with students and that the job is temporary."

I slumped into my chair upon realizing that the discovery of the young woman's dead body must have occurred immediately after the restaurant's small workforce had evaporated.

That night I couldn't wait to talk to Zach about the day's experiences.

"That's quite a story, Jeni."

Zach had changed out of his suit. We were alone for a few minutes, having a glass of wine on the terrace. I felt anxious and was watering the plants to keep busy while we talked.

"I know. What should I have done? What should I do now?"

Zach was a US representative in an advisory position, attached to an organization known as the Southeastern European Law Enforcement Center, based in Bucharest. It was comprised of representatives from thirteen eastern European countries and was created in part to combat cross-border transnational crime. Human trafficking was one of its top priorities. I needed his advice.

"I'm not sure what you could have done. It's frustrating. I hear the agents who work those kinds of cases talk about it a lot. Too often the women leave home voluntarily, thinking they're going to obtain great employment, and when they realize they've been taken for prostitution or slave labor, it's too late to change course. It is complicated because they weren't really kidnapped—just deceived. They're stuck, or at least they feel that way."

"What a terrible situation," I said.

"I know. We also know that they are the most vulnerable during the transport."

Zach explained that the victims have no money and most of the time they make the mistake of giving their passports and papers to the traffickers to "hold" for them—and then they can't get them back. It makes it easy for the bad guys to scare them about their status. They threaten to report them as illegals and criminals if they try to run. Even worse, if they don't cooperate with the traffickers, then they may be locked away with no food to eat.

"You know that we all have seen the news about what occurs to the locked victims when the boat sinks or the truck breaks down," he said, his voice by then almost at a whisper.

"Oh, it is so dreadful."

"Yes, it's unbelievably cruel," Zach continued. "The saddest thing is when we get someone out of the situation and they believe that they have made so many poor decisions that they have no other means of support or their families disown them. Then they head back into it.

"I guess what I'm telling you, Jeni, is that I'm not sure you could've ever done anything. There is nothing you can do now either. You don't know the circumstances of why she was with those men. Maybe she was on drugs."

"I don't think so. I mean, she might have been on drugs, but there was something else. I know you look at this in a law enforcement practical way, but it's emotional to me. *What if I could have saved her?"*

"It's unlikely that you could have done anything at the time other than make things worse for her," he said. "Remember that you aren't even sure the murder victim is the same person. I'm sure the police did a thorough job of interviewing everyone, so they'll find out the truth."

"I hope so," I said.

"I'll also talk to some of the agents at work and give them your information. It might be helpful one day. In the meantime, I'm more worried about you. *Please* don't walk alone down deserted paths, especially one near where a woman was recently murdered. *Please*?"

"I promise. That walk was unnerving enough." I smiled at Zach to convince him of my sincerity. I involuntarily shook at the thought of another walk through the woods.

"Thanks. Then I only have one more question for you, Jeni. You didn't actually consider Scout your guard dog, did you?"

He looked down and tousled the short black hair on Scout's head. The contented canine looked up and wagged his tail. I gave the two of them a rueful smile and decided to change the topic.

"I forgot to tell you that the International Ladies are helping with the Diplomat Games this year. I think we're just handling food or registration. I'm going to head up the committee for our group," I said.

"Sounds like a lot of work."

"Maybe, but it made me think. Remember last year when all the games were ones we couldn't win? Well, this year I'm going to insist on golf. Think about it."

Zach knew that the way they set up the games is ridiculous. It was like a conspiracy against the United States. We couldn't win in Ping-Pong with the Chinese, tennis with the Romanians, soccer with any European, or even volleyball with the Norwegians. We were lucky to win anything. And I *hated* to lose.

"So, here's my plan. They have a golf course—why not a game of golf? You can play with Candi. And I know just how good you two are. Plus, it'll give her something to do," I said.

Zach thought for a second or two before I saw a slight smile cross his face. He was tired of losing at tennis, too.

"You know, I think that would be fun. The Chinese and Japanese diplomats play golf there, and that might make it a bit challenging. Still, we'd have a good chance at actually winning. Do you think you can pull it off?"

I smiled back and bent down to kiss him.

"Remember—I am *el presidente* of ILB, and I declare *we will have golf*!"

I was on a roll and spontaneously decided to announce my own entry into the auspicious games.

"I think this year I'll play women's doubles in tennis. I hated it when we forfeited last year because no one wanted to play against the Romanian women. We looked like cowards. Anyway, I know the Foreign Ministry Office brings in ringers, but we might have a chance for the American women to at least place if I can find a good partner."

"Better than you, I hope."

"What is that supposed to mean, *better than me*?"

"Jeni, I've played with you. Have you seen the tennis players on the courts around here? They live for tennis in eastern Europe. I want you to do well, but it's unlikely. *And* I know you hate to lose. I just want you to be realistic. These games aren't like the ones at the tennis courts back home."

As he felt my eyes bearing down upon him, he began to backpedal.

"But sure, it's a great idea. If you really want to do this, I'm with you—if you can be a good sport. Remember even if you lose in the Diplomat Games, it should still be fun to participate—you know, get to know some of the diplomats from other embassies."

Pfft. He sounded like a grade school coach.

"You'll see. I won't lose." Even as I said it, deep down inside I knew it wasn't true. I would probably lose, and in an ugly way. But what if I didn't? What if we got a second or third place? It was worth a try to put another point on the scoreboard for Team USA.

I began supper and went to wake up a napping Candi before she could get too far off schedule. As we were setting the table, I asked her if she might be willing to play in the golf tournament.

"Sure, if Kate will send my clubs to the embassy."

"Great. I'll send her an email with the directions. We are also having a barbecue Friday so you can meet some people."

"What? Are you serious?" she said, her forehead furrowing and her eyes narrowing in annoyance. "I've already made plans to go clubbing and you want me to meet people from the embassy? I mean, who are they? Why would they even join us here?" She surveyed the room with a critical eye as she continued her run-on questions, just as she had as a child, giving the listener little time to respond.

I patiently told her this had been in the works for a while (not so true) and that she would enjoy it. I knew that two of the guys who would likely show up were about her age and worked together in the consular section, where visas are issued. One was an American, Collin. He was one of those smart young men who passed the tough foreign service exam and was starting from the bottom. It was hard not to like Collin; he was deferential, funny, and sincere. Plus, he was cute in a puppyish kind of way, and Candi liked dogs.

The other young man was his friend and colleague, Victor, a Romanian who also worked in the consular section. In State Department lingo, Victor was referred to as a foreign service national, or FSN. He was aligned with the United States in the sense that he was an employee and paid by the United States, but he was still a Romanian. Victor took his job as a real honor and was a serious young man. It's a little-known fact that most of the people who work at US embassies are foreign nationals. The terms of their employment are dictated by whatever agreement was made to allow the embassy to hire them in the first place.

"You pronounce *Victor* as 'Veector,'" I told her. In Romania, the *i*'s sound like our long *e*'s.

It had taken little effort to plan a spontaneous "wine club" meeting at our apartment for that Friday night. We all knew the drill, and it was easy. Years ago a small group of embassy employees, neighbors, and friends conceived the idea of wine parties in order to make friends and explore all the Romanian wines on the market. Everyone in attendance had to introduce the wine they brought. Over time the parties expanded to trivia contests, wine tasting competitions, and long evenings of fun. It was no surprise that I immediately received twenty-four yesses to my admittedly last-minute invitation.

I decided to serve the traditional appetizers—devilled eggs, *vinete de salata* (eggplant salad), sliced prosciutto, sausage, olives, fresh bread, and a platter of Romanian cheeses. Others would bring homemade pastries and perhaps a dish from their home country. Between the food and wine, it was certainly not for the diet-conscious. How Europeans stayed so thin was a complete mystery to me.

The next day Candi accompanied me to the neighborhood grocery store, Mega Image—pronounced "may-ga-masch"—as in one long mash of letters. When I first arrived in Bucharest, I was constantly told to shop for special items at the *may-ga-masch*. When I became frustrated and asked what in the world was a may-ga-masch, Anna was stumped as to how I could not read the large sign on the store two blocks away. I was equally stumped as to why they couldn't pronounce the simple words "Mega Image."

Finding the store was just the beginning of my confusion. I also couldn't figure out the system of depositing a coin in a slot to free the grocery store cart to shop around in the big stores or how to retrieve the coin upon returning the cart. I never seemed to have the right coin and had to wait for some lost cart in the parking lot. Even worse, it was a nightmare to weigh and print out the prices of vegetables whose names I didn't know. I was right only 50 percent of the time, not exactly endearing me to the store clerks when I clogged up the customer line. In fact, I couldn't read but a few labels other than Coca-Cola. And Jack Daniel's.

As I learned more and lessened my mistakes, I eventually gained some hard-earned affection from some of the checkout ladies. I decided to teach Candi what little I knew.

"I don't buy much of our food at the grocery store," I told her as she surveyed all the products labeled in everything but English. "Most of the time I find fresh vegetables from the outdoor markets, meat from the meat market, and bread from the baker on the street. I just buy tomato sauces, pasta, milk, baking supplies, and paper products in the grocery store. Plus Coke Zero. By the way, they don't sell Diet Coke. If you find it anywhere, they call it Coca-Cola Light. I also buy cheese here sometimes, but only if it has a picture of the animal on top from whence it came—like a goat or a cow for example. I've made some expensive mistakes on cheese."

Candi dutifully and uninterestingly followed me around as the clerks looked on in amusement at their least-knowledgeable customer doling out instructions.

The next day was a series of trips to banks, stores, the metro, and a small museum, but it was tense. Candi made it known to me that she was still not happy about my lack of enthusiasm for her "clubbing" idea. She wanted to be with single exciting new friends and not with me 100 percent of the time, but I worried about the friends she would chose given her poor choices in past boyfriends. My continued excitement about the upcoming wine club party only made her more sullen. Finally, to keep peace and be a good hostess, I decided we had to strike a deal, which Candi begrudgingly accepted.

"Okay, so we agree. There will be no going out with strangers until you have been here over ten days. That'll give you time to become acclimated, get a cell phone, and obtain access to money. Until then, we'll stick together and I'll continue to show you Bucharest—the museums, churches, parks and, shopping—all on my dime." I had reached out to Sue by email and hoped that before ten days ended, I would be able to get her advice on how to handle Candi.

"Whatever," she said before she could stop herself. Then her good upbringing took over and she corrected herself as best she could muster. "I mean, whatever you say is fine."

We both knew what she meant, but I was just happy we had struck a deal. And I hoped her attitude would improve a little.

Chapter Six

"HEY, ARE WE early?" Victor asked. He'd arrived with three other foreign nationals from Bucharest who also worked at the embassy. Being early in Europe was a huge faux paus.

"Of course not. I'm glad you brought friends," I said. That meant there were more people to meet Candi.

Two of his guests were women, and one definitely had her eye on Victor, periodically touching his arm to tell him something while gazing into his eyes. I had met her before in the passport division, and she was quite stunning. I imagined that she knew precisely how to tag poor Victor. He wouldn't even see it happen but would likely enjoy when it occurred.

I was surprised to see that Victor was awkward when introduced to Candi. He only mumbled hello—in Romanian no less. It was then that I realized how he'd probably met few young American women his age his short career at the embassy. His position dealt primarily with Romanians asking for visas to the United States.

It didn't help that Candi also had little to say. She gave me a withering look to let me know she thought it was a setup, when that was not my intention at all. The Romanian beauty queen accompanying Victor also sensed a potential setup. She narrowed her eyes and gave Candi a glare that could only be interpreted to mean "back off."

Collin was the last to arrive at our apartment. I immediately sized him up and found him seriously deficient in appearance. What had formerly seemed cute and puppyish to me now looked ridiculous. Here before me was a grown man, at a party no less, with broken glasses held together by masking tape and with a large fresh bruise across his face. And his clothes—his wrinkled shirt, old jeans, and muddy Top-Siders—made him appear more homeless than chic.

As he entered the room, he said to the group, "Sorry I'm late," and cheerily waved a hello to everyone.

I was momentarily caught off-balance when the whole room erupted into cheers and he was welcomed like a conquering hero. Some of the guys began slapping him on his back so hard that his broken glasses kept falling down his face. Other guests were pouring their favorite wine into his glass each time he took a sip.

"Did you hear?" Anna said, turning to me. "He got involved in a pickup game of soccer and it got ugly. A Serbian soccer player intentionally downed a local boy, and Collin went after the Serb. I heard the guy was a brute. Anyway, the security guards came over and stopped them before Collin got killed, but they were all so mad that they decided to play the game out to the bitter end. Collin scored two goals, one a header off a corner kick. His team won; ergo, he is a hero tonight."

It was clear he was the star. The more the story was retold, the more people crowded around him. In fact, the other young woman who had come with Victor had already run to Collin's side, gazing intently into his crooked eyeglasses and offering to bring him a glass from her bottle—a special reserve Fetească Neagră (a deep ruby-red wine from Romania).

"Is Candi meeting new friends yet?" Zach had wandered over to me with a fresh glass of white wine. We both stood to the side and watched as Collin was reenacting his last goal, his foot almost kicking down my new lamp.

"This is a disaster," I confided. "Victor apparently is taken by someone who doesn't look like she would appreciate him having more friends. Even if he weren't, he couldn't get a word out of his mouth when he met Candi.

Collin looks like a rock star who drank too much and fell down a flight of stairs."

Zach laughed and nodded in agreement. "And it doesn't matter anyway. I can't get close enough to him to even introduce Candi. Plus, Candi doesn't look in the right mood to try to force her to talk to him."

I sighed as I looked at Candi, who by then was sitting alone flipping through pages of a Romanian fashion magazine.

"You're right. Just so you know, I think Collin has a girlfriend in the States."

"*What*? I can't believe you're just telling me this. So there are no single friends at all?" I was whispering so as to not be overheard, but Zach could feel the force of my frustration.

"I just found that out a few minutes ago. She was supposed to come with him when he arrived several months ago, but she got some PR contract work and had to stay in DC for another month. I'm sorry. We'll just have to figure out another plan."

I took a deep breath and began to survey the room for other prospective friends—suitable single embassy workers in their twenties. Heck, I would accept midthirties. But there were none at the party, either male or female. It was time for plan B.

Plan B was to tell Victor and Collin that although they might be taken, they still had the responsibility of entertaining Candi and keeping her company around town. After all, it was their diplomatic duty. I would tell them that it would help their careers. If that didn't work, I would beg them. My last resort would be threats. I had learned a lot from my older sister.

By then, the party was lively with talk of wine, politics, and travel. It was a cool, clear night, so most of the guests hung out on the wide veranda that ran the length of the apartment and looked out over the Chinese Embassy and Herastrau Lake. Many smoked. It was a surprise to me that ashtrays came with the living quarters, but I'd learned that many eastern Europeans smoked. My early concession was to permit the use of the ashtrays outside.

Around midnight the guests began to straggle out. Collin and Victor were among the last to leave. Zach had managed to introduce Collin to Candi earlier in the evening, but he told me it was just as brief as the Victor encounter. That was why I was shocked to hear Collin mention her name.

"You know, if your niece Candi is bored, she can come to the embassy swimming pool or lending library. We can show her around when you get her security clearance," Collin said as he pushed his glasses over his nose once again.

"Thanks. She'll love that. I'll have her call you," I said gratefully, even though I knew that Candi would never call. By then, she had already left the apartment to walk Scout and then head to bed. Worse yet, I didn't have the energy to handle Candi if she began to like either of these two guys, who were definitely off the market. One meltdown was enough.

Chapter Seven

THE NEXT DAY I set out to execute my plan to win a trophy for the United States in women's double tennis. To help reach my goal, I decided I needed a new tennis skirt. I felt sure it would divert attention from my lack of a good first serve. I invited Candi to join me. The new Mega Mall was right by the new US Embassy. I wasn't sure which came first, the embassy or the mall, but it made life easier for me. On the way there, I stopped by the embassy in order to cash a check on my credit union at home—one of those slips of paper that couldn't be cashed anywhere but at the embassy. Even the embassy cashiers were sometimes suspicious. Candi said she would wait in the car since she still did not have full embassy privileges.

"Hi, Victor," I said, noticing him in front of me in the tiny bank's customer line.

"Good morning, Ms. Jeni. How are you?" he said. We exchanged pleasantries as he cashed a travel check and I did my business. But as I was leaving, I sensed Victor had hung around waiting for me and had something more to say.

"I saw Zach on the way in this morning, and he told me that you were planning on playing in the women's double tennis team for the Diplomat Games."

"Yes, but I don't have a partner yet. There are no tennis courts at the embassy, so I don't know who plays. Maybe I'll post a notice somewhere."

"Well, you can do that, but *do you want to win*?" Victor now had my full attention. I looked around to see if anyone was listening.

"Of course I do."

"Then I might know a good partner."

"Who?"

"My mother. She played professionally for the country when she was young. She still gives lessons periodically. She fits the criterion—a member of the embassy staff's direct family. It's not like we are just hiring her to work for the month of the matches. It's legit."

I smiled. This was really good news.

"Do you think she'll do it?"

"I know she will. She has her own reasons for wanting to get back on the courts. I'll have her call you. Her name is Nadia."

I almost skipped out of the bank. A former pro player was simply too good to be true. Now all I had to do was pick out the perfect tennis skirt, preferably red, white, and blue. I wanted to make sure everyone knew that the Americans weren't going to be losers this year.

That afternoon I left Candi taking a nap while I met with the new International Ladies of Bucharest Committee at the Diplomat Club to discuss the details of the ILB's involvement in the games. As we counted out the necessary food booths, I casually mentioned food for the golfing event.

"I don't remember a golfing event," Moira said.

"Well, I'm not sure it has been done in the last couple of years, but I know that it was discussed. In fact, I bet the Asian men who play here regularly assume we'll have a tournament this year."

"It makes sense to me. Why have a golf course and not use it?" Cathy from Canada enthusiastically interjected. I loved to call her "Cathy from Canada" and was always was happy to get her support. Still, her enthusiasm concerned me. She had agreed way too fast. It made me wonder if she had some ringer in the Canadian Embassy, maybe an ex-pro. As the slippery slope of self-doubt began, so did the chatter among the group.

Almost immediately many of the Western women agreed that golf made sense.

"It is such a civilized sport," the Scottish member said—she who came from the land of golf. I had forgotten that the Scots might be a serious contender as well.

"Who is going to tell the Romanian foreign minister? He might be mad," Moira interjected.

Moira was beginning to turn red at this change of events. She knew the Romanians didn't play golf; they played tennis. If there were to be a golf match and the Americans won, then it would increase our cumulative points at the end of the day. There might be a possibility that the United States could even win the entire event, something that had never happened.

The truth was that Moira and I had a lot in common. Competitiveness is in every Romanian's blood, and it coursed through my veins, too. I began to see this event as more than friendly games played by diplomats and politicians all over the world.

"I think that we'll just tell the minister where the golf food booth will be in a letter with all the other details. We can point out to him that we know that there are many golfers excited about playing. Then we'll thank him. If he says that there is no golf—and he won't—we'll tell him that we're sorry but it's too late to delete it. Some of the diplomats have already ordered their clubs to be sent here and will be very angry at a change in plans."

Everyone agreed, except for Moira, who was pondering what looked to be my strategic golf victory. All eyes were on her.

"Okay," she finally said. Then she quickly added, "How about rowing?"

"Huh?"

"Rowing. If golf is added, then we should suggest rowing—after all, we're on a lake." Moira had recovered nicely and smirked with an arrogant glare. Rowing is when each person in the boat uses one paddle, as opposed to sculling, which is when there are two oars used backward. It took me a year to figure that out, and I'm not sure I got it right even now.

Every day I watched rowing clubs slicing through the waters of Lake Herastrau. Each morning they ritually polished their boats' sleek hulls and later emerged from buildings hidden behind trees and gates along the water's edge in order to begin a fierce training regimen. Coaches sat in small rowboats in the middle of the lake, periodically barking out orders that needed no translation. For hours and hours, the quiet and determined rowers competed with each other and themselves, barely making a ripple in the water. As a result of the training, over the decades

Romanian rowers have accumulated not just Olympic gold medals but also worldwide respect.

Sadly, I could not recall any American in or on the lake other than the diplomat who'd jumped in to retrieve her errant dog. I sighed as once again all eyes were on me. I could feel our chances for an overall win once again slipping.

Still, what could I say? Moira was right.

"Of course, we should suggest that they add rowing," I said.

Chapter Eight

TEN DAYS CAN go by quickly when you don't want time to pass. I had tried to get Candi her State Department family member credentials in time for her to spend more free time at the embassy, but they still weren't ready. Although she had visited Victor and Collin a few times for lunch at the embassy and taken the standard tour, she wasn't yet able to volunteer in the library or roam around on her own. She seemed fine with the embassy ban and was nonplussed about both young men. She told me they probably did not like her anyway.

"Why would you think that?" I asked.

"Well, they were talking at lunch, and it was clear that I got confused about where Serbia was and why World War I really started. And that's just for starters. Don't even get me going on the ethnic makeup of Sarajevo. I could see by their faces that they thought I was stupid or something. They're just know-it-alls."

"You have to remember this is their job—diplomacy. Plus, Victor would know those details for sure. Serbia shares a border with Romania. I'm sure they didn't intend to hurt your feelings."

"Well, I don't like to feel stupid, so they can have lunch without me in the future." With that she glowered and began to cross her arms as if to pout like a child, but she caught herself before she did so. Instead, she raised her hand and flipped her hair back as if to compose herself. I said nothing further.

I knew what she was going through. It took a while to untangle the complex web of eastern European political relations, especially when you were newly arrived. I know how stupid I often felt. Sometimes I had wanted to crawl under the table when I heard a person sitting next to me speak several languages—fluently. It was easier to be alone and walk in the park than to stumble through a conversation about international affairs.

I hoped Candi's summer vacation would change all that for her. By the end of two months' time, the names and locations of cities like Sarajevo, Belgrade, and Sofia would be as familiar as Baton Rouge and Mobile. Her bit of French from her school days would be enhanced by TV Monde, the French channel, and the myriad of people around her. Her knowledge of world affairs would grow exponentially. One day Candi would look back and realize that she wasn't seeing the world as a tourist, but actually living the life. Those are experiences she would never forget. Maybe she would one day thank me for her current "prisoner" status.

When we were through talking, I heard her new phone beep as a text message came through. It was just a cheap pay-by-the-month phone, but when she'd unwrapped the gift from me earlier that morning, she was ecstatic.

"Who is already sending you a text?"

"Tina. She's agreed to take me clubbing. I sent her an email last week about the ten-day rule and told her you said I had to have a phone, blah, blah, blah. And then I sent her a text today telling her the ten days were up. She agreed to go with me tonight. This is so great! I thought ten days would never come."

"I don't know ..."

"You promised you wouldn't treat me like a child, and I've lived by your rules. Now our agreement means that I'm going out. Thanks!"

She reached over to give me a quick hug, more to punctuate her excitement than to show real affection.

"Don't wait up!" Then, in a flash, all I saw were legs running up the stairs.

I ran to the study, where Zach was reading some papers, to register my complaint. He listened as I rapidly told him about the drama on floor 1.

"Plus, I didn't tell her I wouldn't treat her like a child! She made that up!"

This mothering thing had become a nightmare. I was beginning to lose control. Why couldn't she just sit around and read books? Or maybe not be a recluse, but do whatever I told her to do? Why did she have to go *clubbing* in a city that is internationally recognized as the world leader in the pastime?

"Jeni, you aren't her mother, and I don't think you're supposed to take on that role now. She's a college graduate. We can't keep her in lockup. I'm sure she'll be fine, or at least use good sense. She has money, a phone, metro tickets, and a brain, and I don't think she drinks much. She told me she never got in the habit because of golf, and she's of age anyway. In fact, I think she's probably far better equipped to be here than most kids her age. Come on, she parties in the French Quarter … You're overreacting."

I stood still looking at him, the traitor. There was nothing left for me to say.

"Okay. I'll still worry, but I won't complain. I'll just kill my sister when I see her."

"That's actually a good idea, but you probably need some lessons in murder. Speaking of which, how are the tennis lessons going?"

"I haven't started real lessons yet, but I will next week. For now I'm just doing some exercises for tennis I saw on the computer, like throwing the ball in the air."

Zach laughed as I pretended to throw a ball in the air and slam my racquet through it.

"Ace!" he cried, putting his arms in the air. He pulled them down only to wrap them around me in a gentle hug. He knew I was still concerned about my niece. "Jeni, Candi will be fine. It's her life. You have done all you can to help her make good decisions while she's here. Let's go and see her off for her first night out in Bucharest."

I did as he suggested, and in a small way I enjoyed watching Candi preen for just a bit. Makeup was not her forte, and neither was fashion, but she pulled together nicely with a black sundress and a bit of gloss and mascara. She was a pretty young woman when she wanted to be, although I always thought she was the cutest when she dressed like an American college student on the way to class. I realized how much I missed my sister when I observed a very happy Candi checking herself out in the mirror. I knew Sue would have enjoyed watching her youngest prepare for her first eastern European night out.

"I hope you have fun tonight. I can't wait to hear about it tomorrow morning," I said, secretly and pettily wishing it would be a disaster, one she would not want to repeat.

Zach and I took advantage of the now rare opportunity of being together without Candi. We went to eat at our favorite local restaurant on the corner. Its red cushions and checkered tablecloths on the outside terrace, complete with a pitcher of wine, were just how I wanted to spend the evening.

"I think I'm just getting old and ugly. That's why we don't go clubbing."

Zach rolled his eyes and smiled at my assertion. "Jeni, you are neither old nor ugly, and we don't go clubbing now because of my job. And even when we did go, we didn't stay long enough to make it worthwhile. Plus, you're always worried about fires and checking for extinguishers and exits. I'm always confused as to whether you're a fire marshal in high heels or my date." With that he pretended to be me pointing out blocked doors and windows.

"I forgot to tell her about that! She needs to know that they have a lot of fires here!" One of my first intense experiences in Bucharest was the night my next-door neighbors' apartment caught on fire and they almost died. They got frostbite from the snow while standing outside in their bare feet waiting for help. It didn't help my unease when it was discovered that none of the fire alarms in their apartment worked. Just recently, the hottest club in town had caught fire, injuring over forty people. Then there was the restaurant a block away, and another one five blocks away …

"What should I do? Maybe I should text her."

"She'll be fine. I told you she is smart and wary. Don't start texting less than an hour into her evening."

When we arrived home, I left Zach reading some papers and went to check my email. Finally, I had heard from Sue.

> Dear Jeni,
>
> I'm sorry this has taken so long. We are just now settled into our cabin. The cruise ship is amazing. I'm *so* sorry about sending Candi to Bucharest without talking to you first, but I had less than a day to make a decision and was too worried about what she would do if we left her on her own. I know she will be safe with you. I hope you aren't too upset. I think staying with you and Zach will be good for her. Whether you realize it or not, she really looks up to

you. She tells all her friends about her aunt Jeni and uncle Zach living in Europe as diplomats.

She's incredibly smart, as you well know, but now that she's graduated from college she's floundering. You remember what it's like. She's agonizing about what she should do. It hurts that all her best friends are getting married, or going to medical school, or landing dream jobs, at least from her perspective. I'm not sure Bob and I would be all that happy for her to work in Colorado on a ski slope, but something like that would appeal to her right now. The only planning she has ever done is to plan to play golf.

Look, I'm glad her boyfriend is gone—he bordered on abusive—but their breakup will probably mean that Candi will fall for the next guy she meets, no matter how bad, whether she stays home, heads to India, or spends time with you!

Please keep in touch and let me know how things go. Keep a close eye on her.

If it means anything, we are having a great time. I will try to take a lot of pictures. I had no idea how much we needed this trip and time away! Thanks for everything and for being there for me!

Hugs and kisses,
Sue

I had to agree that Sue needed a break. Although she looked like she had a country club life, it wasn't always that easy for her. It had hit her hard when our parents died many years ago in a freak car accident. She was a mother of two daughters and had been left with a younger sister who was still in college. Sue not only handled all the details of the deaths and shouldered everyone's grief but also went back to work as a teacher to help with my tuition. She even paid for Zach's and my wedding. She was the glue that held us all together.

I didn't need to complain about Candi. Sue and Bob deserved a stress-free retirement cruise.

Dear Sue,

Got your email! Glad it is all going well there. Candi is having a blast here, and we are having a great time.

Keep in touch, and send pics!

Love,
Jeni

Chapter Nine

I BEGAN TO doubt Zach's assessment of Candi's smarts the next day when she woke up and came downstairs. It was almost noon, and Scout and I were on the terrace. He was napping, and I was reading or at least trying to. I couldn't sit idle, as my curiosity was in overdrive.

"How did it go?"

"It was incredible. I never imagined it would be so cool. I met lots of people my age, plus the guy I told you about. He's amazing."

"Really? Who is he? How again did you meet him?" She seemed in a talkative mood for a change, so I put the book aside while she practically threw herself down on a chaise lounge.

"His name is Dimitri ... I think. I had a hard time understanding him. He's from Moldova. Remember when I told you I bumped into a man at your ILB coffee at the Hotel Intercontinental?"

I nodded nervously.

"It was Dimitri! I introduced him to Tina. Anyway, he's really good-looking and so smart. I couldn't believe he was interested in me, but he bought me some Moldovan wine. He wanted to talk about my life and what I was doing here ..."

"What did you say?" I asked, more anxiously than I'd intended.

"I said what we agreed on—that I'm here in Europe on my own. I admitted staying at a relative's house, but I didn't give your full name or tell them what Uncle Zach did. Actually, Tina might know your name from ILB. Anyway, I told them you weren't a teacher but that you did something in education for embassy kids."

"Thanks for that." We had been taught that divulging too much information about Zach's job to the wrong person could put us at risk.

"I also told Dimitri that I was planning on taking the train around Europe—you know, kind of roam around by myself. He was super interested in my plans and said he might could help me plan parts of the trip." She continued to divulge even more troubling details of her night out with her new friend, including how he liked that she was independent and pretty much free to do anything she wanted.

"You know, he's right—I can do *anything* I want. And before you even ask, he didn't try anything, although I'm not so sure I would have fended him off if he had."

She told me he was a gentleman and that she'd been invited to join him at the Mango Lounge on Saturday. It took every ounce of self-control I possessed not to say anything negative about the Mango Lounge, although I knew a lot about it. Criminal owners, shady investors, and lots of loud music, drink, and naive young kids. It was a bad mix.

"It is *the* place to be seen. I think I might want to get a new dress—something a bit more European," she said.

I didn't know what to say that would change her mind, although nothing she said sounded good to me. Not a single word. Not even the new dress. I couldn't for the life of me zero in on just what it was that made me so uneasy. And was she serious? *Did she really intend to roam around Europe?*

I went to bed with a headache, wondering if I should write Sue with the truth—that I was beginning to worry about Candi—but I shook off the idea, postponing it for the next morning.

"There's nothing to report," I convinced myself as I tried to fall asleep. "It's all fine."

The next day I had my first meeting with Victor's mother, Nadia, at the tennis courts by our apartment. Not only were they manicured clay courts, but also they were in the middle of Herastrau Park, surrounded by roses and with stunning views across the lake. Beautiful people played perfect tennis all day, even in the winter when the courts were covered with white plastic domes. Because I was not a member of the park's tennis club, I played the back practice courts with no view, where those less proficient at tennis could camouflage their inadequacies. It was easy to convince myself I was far better than those around me when they were primarily beginners. What I failed to consider was that my play was far worse than that of the real members on the middle courts.

Victor's mother, Nadia, was about my height and was youthful-looking, with a short haircut that made her dark eyes stand out. I don't know what I expected, but to me she resembled a compact and very fit gymnast, rather than the lanky Romanian tennis players I had observed on the courts. She was pleasant but matter-of-fact about getting down to business and playing tennis.

We decided to start with hitting some balls so she could assess my game. She jogged to the opposite court, deftly put several balls in her tiny skirt pockets, and lobbed an easy ball my way.

It didn't take long for her to reach one obvious conclusion: I was unable to consistently connect with the ball, no matter how furiously I swung my racquet through the air.

"Sorry. Lobs are not the best part of my game."

She nodded in agreement and said, "Yes, they can be tricky." Then she suggested I practice some serves. After a series of double faults, which were always accompanied by me saying "My bad," I could see her lose a bit of her bounce. At one point I told her that the lack of good pockets on my skirt was not helping my game.

"I also think I'm just rusty," I said as I went to retrieve a ball that had bounced all the way onto the neighboring court.

"Perhaps," Nadia replied. "When is this match?"

"Not for a while—a couple of weeks or so. I'll be much better by then."

"Perhaps. Why don't you try to return my serves, and then we'll volley?"

I told her that was fine and ran back to the baseline, bending my knees, balancing on the balls of my feet, ready to shift in a hurry to the left or right. I lifted my racquet up high with both hands, just like I'd seen pros do on TV. I'm sure I looked good, but the first serve whizzed by me so fast that I never even moved my racquet. It was the same with the second serve, then the third, and then the fourth …

It was awful. She didn't give me time to get ready. It was unfair. Most of my effort was looking backward after the ball passed by me to see if I could find it. Zach was right: this was definitely not the Volvo ladies' league back home, and I was wholly unprepared. These people were serious.

Finally, Nadia could take no more. "Let's have a lemonade."

We didn't say much as we waited for the drinks and watched the graceful game on the adjoining court. It looked more like a ballet than a competitive match, as both women appeared to be close friends dressed in almost matching outfits.

"They're good, aren't they?" I said.

"Yes, but not all that good. They just like to get dressed up and hit the ball back and forth for some exercise. It is not too difficult what they are doing."

I realized that was me at home—just a happy, gentle hitter. I was the golden retriever of tennis.

Then she got to the heart of the matter.

"Are you sure you want to play in this match? *Really sure*? I know one of the women who will most likely be playing against us. She is quite good. I played her in school. She works for the foreign minister now." She paused. "We are not friends."

The last line took me by surprise. I got the sense that they were enemies, not just "not friends," perhaps "frenemies." But she didn't volunteer more.

"Yes, I want to play, but mostly I have to play. I already signed up. It is too humiliating to back out."

"Okay. Then I think we need to have a plan. I know how our competition will play. They will always hit to the weakest player."

"Me?" I asked lamely, although I knew the answer.

"Perhaps. So, we need a plan to work as a team. My thought is that you could work on your serve. Just get it in the right court, nothing too fancy, and then we will work on you returning serves. I will do the rest. You will just need to know how to duck and get out of my way. Okay?"

"Sure," I said, although I didn't mean it. I hated serving, which was why I was so bad at it. Returning serves was not as bad, but only if the server was really awful. But to just duck and run? That was humiliating.

After we'd finished our drinks, we returned to the court, where Nadia gave me some lessons in the fundamentals of serving like a pro. Number one was to learn the toss.

I was still tossing a tennis ball in the air when Zach came home that night. Scout enjoyed jumping up as if he could catch it and then running after those balls I dropped.

Zach agreed that Nadia's plan was good and that it would eliminate much of the stress for me. I told him my only problem was controlling myself every time she said the word *perhaps*. He laughed and held out his hand for me to toss the tennis ball to him. Scout jumped up for the ball and missed, which turned into a game for us, while Zach and I talked about our day. Candi joined us while we were throwing the ball back and forth for fun, with a happy Scout jumping between us.

"I wish I had a video of you two and Scout!" she said. I could tell she was in a good mood.

"How are things with you?" Zach asked.

"Awesome. I am going to Bran tomorrow with my new friends. Now you don't have to take me to Dracula's castle. They'll do it. I'm so excited." As she talked, she pulled her hair back into a ponytail and began to swing it back and forth as if to punctuate her enthusiasm.

"Why are they taking you to Bran?" I asked.

"I don't know. I didn't interrogate them. Dimitri said he had to meet two men there to do some business. I'm not sure if Tina is going or not. But the bottom line is that he said he was going, told me I would have fun, and asked if I would like to go. I said yes."

"But what do you know about him?"

"Enough to know that he is safer than a bus driver or some random taxi. Don't overreact."

That made me really mad. I *never* overreacted.

"Fine. Can I join you? I want to see a friend there."

"No," she said, looking at me incredulously. "Are you serious about tagging along with me?"

Zach had said nothing, but he could clearly sense things were getting ugly, so he leaned forward and held up his hand to interrupt us.

"Jeni's right—she does have a friend there, and it would save on gas, which is expensive in Europe. Still, if you don't want her to go, she won't. Just make certain to take your phone and some money." He was finished with the discussion.

Candi knew she had been dismissed and turned on her heels to head to her room.

I was still angry.

"I don't like this. Why Bran? It's my fault. I should've taken her there first thing and gotten it out of the way."

Bran Castle, built in the 1300s, was just over an hour's drive from Bucharest. Perched on the side of a craggy Carpathian ridge, it overlooked a broad plain near one of my favorite towns, Brasov. The castle literally loomed over the valley's choke point. It's an old stone castle with walls at least four feet thick. The steep gray walls cast a perfect background for Bram Stoker's 1897 book, *Dracula*. Outside its entrance were booths of every kind selling Romanian wares as well as cheap and tawdry Dracula-type memorabilia. The castle is often the first stop on every visitor's Romanian tour, and it had been a priority destination for me when I first arrived.

But now I was completely over it. Every official guest visiting Zach from the States expected a tour of the place if their visit to Romania lasted long enough to accommodate a daylong tourist excursion.

Several of my friends grew up in the picturesque land that surrounded the castle. As with all other privately held land, the dictator seized it in the mid-1950s and later, after the revolution in 1989, the land began to be returned to the local families like Anna's. The best I could tell, the castle was now owned by an archduke who is an heir of the former royals. I read somewhere that it was on the market for a cool $60 million to the right person.

"Why don't you go anyway?" Zach asked. "You can visit Anna while she is at their summer place. That way, if Candi needs you, you'll be close by. Plus, I'm working really late tomorrow."

"I don't know. Who'll watch Scout?"

"Take him with you. It'll be more fun."

"What do you say, Scout?" I asked, peering into his dark eyes. Predictably, with Zach in the room, he refused to comment.

Chapter Ten

CANDI WAS UP and dressed for Bran before nine the next morning—a new personal best for her.

"I'm going to take the metro and meet Dimitri in the middle of the city," she said.

"He's not picking you up here?"

"No, of course not. It's out of the way. I didn't even suggest it."

"How about if I drop you off? I don't mind."

"No, I like to ride the metro, and he's expecting me at the stop by Unirii Mall. I can get there faster by metro than a car at this time of day. I do appreciate what you do for me, but remember—you aren't my mother."

She was right on all points, but it bothered me that I wouldn't see the car or her companions. However, I let her comments pass without a fight.

"No problem," I said. "Just be safe."

The Unirii Mall was a huge rambling building with large European stores like H&M and Zara. It was, as Candi said, right in the middle of the city near the Old Town, and the metro stop was at its front door. There would be a thousand people around her if she needed help.

Scout and I waited until she was safely on her way to the bus stop before I loaded the car with some water and food for him and snacks for me. He clearly knew the drill. He curled up on the back floorboard and promptly went to sleep.

The route to Brasov, a city not far away from Bran and Dracula's castle, was a bit circuitous from our apartment. It meant that I had to drive some busy and confusing roads. However, once out of the city, the road was easier to navigate. I didn't need a map or GPS to guide me in the direction of the mountains looming on the horizon. It was that time of the year when roadsides were populated with vegetable stands and when fields of sunflowers extended for miles on either side. It was the perfect day for a trip to the mountains, even if it wasn't originally my idea. I wished I could see Candi's happy face as she surveyed the landscape. I felt a bit down that I was not with her, Scout being a poor substitute asleep on the floor.

My original plan had been to meet my friend Anna at her house near the castle and have coffee, but she was actually in Brasov that day, just a short hop and a skip away from Bran. We made plans to meet for an afternoon snack at the pastry shop across from the massive Black Church, a cathedral built in the fourteenth century and known for a fire in 1689 that gave it its current name.

The little German-looking shop with its café table in the front window was a perfect place to rendezvous with a friend. The shop was downhill from a massive citadel from the sixteenth century that towered over the walled city, and our outdoor table had a wonderful view of medieval churches, shops, and homes with their unique Transylvanian architecture.

This trip to Brasov, like all of them, put me in a great mood. Scout and I leisurely roamed the streets for an hour or more, waiting for the appointed time to meet Anna.

As planned, at two o'clock she was at the pastry shop at a café table right outside the front door. Scout and I exited the car. I waved a cheery hello as soon as I was near.

"Bună ziua," she said as she stood to exchange the Romanian kiss on each side of my cheek.

"I see you have something to eat already, but let me run inside to get a pastry and coffee. I'll be right back," I said. I passed Scout's leash to Anna to hold while I went inside. I was glad to see Scout was compliant. He crouched down at her feet.

I returned with an éclair and coffee and plopped down on my bistro chair, eager to bite into the pastry. Scout, happy to be out of the car, moved closer to my feet, hoping I might drop a morsel of food. Instead, as I was instructed by Candi, he got a dog treat.

"No human food," I told him.

"How is it going with your niece?" Anna asked.

"I don't know. Okay, I guess. It's odd because we are closer in age than most aunts and nieces. I think she really sees me as her former free babysitter more than an aunt. She doesn't want my advice all that much—well, frankly, not at all."

"I'm sure she does. You just need to give her space. Isn't she old enough to be on her own? Weren't you at her age?"

"Yes, but I think she can be quite naive. She's led a pretty sheltered life. By the way, what do you know about Tina, the new member who showed up at the last coffee morning?"

"I met her at the coffee morning. She seemed nice enough. She listed her occupation as an employment recruiter. Why?"

"Candi is hanging out with her."

"Well, that might be a good thing. Candi needs some career guidance from what you told me. But it's weird that I've never heard of Tina before. I thought I knew most international women in that field. They often help me find work for the women in the shelter."

I thought about that bit of information. I didn't say it, but we both knew it was also odd to have someone randomly appear at a meeting and not first be introduced.

"I wish I knew more about her. I wonder why she latched onto my niece as opposed to any one of the other hundred women there," I said, mulling the possibilities.

"I wouldn't worry. She looked okay," Anna said. Then she smiled broadly to cheer me up and let me know she was on my side.

"You're right. I worry way too much. It's probably because I feel like I have a responsibility for Candi while Sue is on her cruise. This is the first time that Sue has asked me to help her in a meaningful way; it's always been the other way around since Mom and Dad died. I know she's trusting me to protect Candi. I really don't want to disappoint her."

I returned my attention to my pastry, dropping bits of crust around me, no matter how delicately I tried to eat it. It was as I stood up to brush the crumbs from my lap and looked into a café mirror that I remembered the second pressing issue on my mind. I sat back down and leaned toward Anna.

"Anna, remember that day we went to meet the two girls about their inventions? At the outside café?" I almost whispered.

"Yes. We decided never to go there again." I could tell she knew some important information was to come, as she ceased to eat and placed her fork back down on the table.

"Something has been bothering me. Do you remember that there was a woman there with some men and she looked to be either on drugs or under their control in some way?"

"Yes, of course I do. Why?" Anna asked, using her feet to move her chair closer to me so as not to miss a word.

"I think she might be the woman that they found dead in the park."

"Oh no!" she said. Her usually happy expression crumbled. "I heard about them finding a dead body on the news, but I only saw the drawing—and it was all in pencil—just for a second." She paused. "Are you sure?"

"Yes. I also only saw her real photo for a few seconds at a time, but it was her eyes. I'm sure they are the same."

"Oh, I hope not, but you were the one watching her throughout that day, not me," Anna said. She thought it through and evidently realized that I might be right. I could almost see her mind reeling. "How did she die? Did they ever say anything?"

"That she was from Moldova and they think it was drugs."

"Then it was probably her. For sure she looked Moldovan, and the timing is right," Anna said, her shoulders suddenly slumping so much that one dress strap fell to the side.

"Shouldn't we have done something?" I asked Anna directly, looking straight into her eyes.

She thought for a second before responding. "No, not if she was on drugs and with drug dealers. It would have been too dangerous. Plus, she didn't ask for help. I know you are upset, but even looking back I don't see what we could have done to help."

"You're sure?" I trusted Anna's judgment more than my own, but I needed more reassurance.

"Yes, I'm positive." Anna gave me a quick smile to show she had regained her confidence in our actions. Then she took up her fork to resume eating.

With that definitive response, I resigned myself to moving on to a happier subject and began to entertain her with my tennis adventures. We talked about the Diplomat Games and new shops in Bucharest for far longer than I had intended.

"Oh, it's getting late. I probably need to leave now," I said.

"What are you going to do now?" Anna asked as we prepared to leave.

"It's a pretty day. I want to get another tablecloth. I found a stall with items I liked the last time I was in Bran, so I'm going to drive to Bran, buy a tablecloth, and then take a shortcut road through the mountains back to our apartment."

"What a great idea. I hope Scout doesn't get carsick in the mountains."

I hadn't thought about that, but he had looked a bit out of sorts on the way to Brasov. I decided right then that I would take him on a long walk around Bran so he could get some fresh air and new dog smells before the long ride home.

Chapter Eleven

DESPITE THE BEAUTIFUL scenery along the higher mountainous road, I took the lower, more direct route to Bran. It meant I wouldn't pass near the famous Poiana Brasov skiing area. I had only visited the resort once, and that was in the summer. Given the way Romanians drove, they probably skied the same way. I wasn't anxious for that experience anytime soon.

Built in the 1950s by the Communists in order to dazzle the dictator's friends and visitors, Poiana Brasov is a completely over-the-top rustic ski lodge. Our "room" for the weekend that we stayed there had actually been four giant rooms with a dining table for ten, a sauna, a full living room, and lots of heavy Victorian-type furniture with gold accents. There were four TVs, but we had lacked the skills to operate even one. The suite was huge—at least two thousand square feet. It might not have been modern and fashionable, but during off-season, it was affordable—about the same per night as the Holiday Inn Express on Interstate 10 back home. I peeked in through the open doors on our floor and found that most rooms appeared almost as spacious as ours. The views of the mountains were spectacular.

Of course, we didn't eat in our room since we had no food. Instead, we ate in the original dining hall, with walls still festooned with a wide range of previously alive animals from decades past.

We had enjoyed Poiana Brasov in the summer season. It was a fun place to be with its three heated pools and hiking trails. I could see its appeal to the high and mighty. I made a mental note to take Candi there the next week.

When taking the lower road to Bran, the imposing walls of the Rasnov Citadel, built in the 1300s, are visible for miles. It is perched high above much of the surrounding countryside and boasts of great summer festivals. When I encountered it, it always signaled to me that Bran was right around the corner.

I entered the village just as many visitors were beginning to leave. It was later than I thought. The good news was that I knew the exact location of the tablecloth I wanted to buy. I steeled myself to begin the negotiations to purchase it. I had seen it before, a creamy white homespun fabric with hand-embroidered lace edges. I'd waited patiently until I was sure of the size I wanted, and now I was ready to make my purchase. After haggling over the price and agreeing to a fair sum, I took my prized possession to the car. Then Scout and I walked along the park surrounding the Bran Castle.

Soon enough Scout was back to his normal happy self, tugging on his leash and stopping to sniff the bottoms of light poles. It was a surprise to me when I saw him stop and gaze into the distance, almost pointing like a pedigree hunting dog.

He was the first one of us to see Candi at the castle entrance with a man I guessed was the Dimitri guy from Moldova. They were talking to two men whom I couldn't quite make out. Scout started to bark, but I pulled him behind a tree and gave him a treat to be quiet. I knew Candi would be furious if she saw me there, especially after she had been so clear in telling me to stay away.

After a few moments, Candi and her escort left the other two men and began to move away from the castle and walk toward the main visitor parking lots. I decided to follow and observe them, stopping in the afternoon shadows of buildings so as to not be seen. I felt like the helicopter mother hovering over her kindergartner on the first day of school. I had to admit that the man was a gentleman to her, appropriately helping her over wobbly cobblestones. I even saw them laugh about something in a collegial way. Maybe I had judged him too harshly.

Eventually I lost track of Candi, but I was no longer as worried about her. It was getting late; even the tour busses were starting to leave town and head back to Bucharest. Scout and I reluctantly walked back to my car, which was in a remote parking space on the opposite side of the castle—a free one I'd discovered on an earlier visit. It was farther than I remembered, so I anxiously began to walk faster and paid little attention to anything other than locating my car.

"Ouch!" I yelled, as I felt my arm being pulled back behind me just as I was within sight of the car. It shocked me so much that I turned too quickly, twisting my ankle. I tried to get loose, but the hand dug in tighter.

"Con-dee?" the man said, beginning to loosen his grip.

"Huh? Who are you? What are you doing?" I jerked my arm once more, but he kept hold.

Once I spoke and we locked eyes, the man seemed to know immediately that he had made a mistake. *Did he think I was Candi?* Although she and I had similar hair, were of similar size, and had worn sundresses that day, up close I couldn't be mistaken for Candi.

I was right—he had made a mistake. He mumbled something incoherent and let me go, but I was angry—really angry. He started to walk away.

I glared at his retreating back and then audibly gasped as I saw the tattoo on the back of his bicep. Now I knew where I had seen him. It was his crummy tattoo that prompted my memory—and those Italian clothes. Before I could stop myself, I said, "I know you! You were at the restaurant. You were one of the men with that dead woman!"

He turned and came back toward me a fierce look on his face.

Why, oh why, do I always say what is on the top of my mind?

He was still close enough to grab for my arm once again. It shocked me. I pulled away quickly, unbalancing him. I screamed for help, but I knew no one was close enough to hear me. He said something under his breath and seemed to grow angry with me.

He was determined to grab my flailing arms and take me with him somewhere I didn't want to go.

It was then that docile Scout sensed that something was wrong and became a vicious junkyard guard dog. He stopped, turned around, and lunged at the man's thick calf, which extended beneath his odd-fitting shorts. The meaty white flesh was an easy mark for Scout's sharp teeth. The dog managed to take a hunk, leaving a gaping wound and bloody mess behind.

The man screamed some obscenity in Romanian and jumped away from Scout just long enough for me to hit the Open button on the remote keyless entry for my car, which was a few feet ahead. The headlights flashed, signaling a successful unlocking. However, before I could hit the alarm button, the man once again was grabbing for me.

With a dexterity I didn't think he had, my pursuer lunged for the key ring, intending to rip it from my hand.

With no other option, I turned away from my him and made a final mad move to the car door as fast as I could, fumbling around the bundle of keys for the panic button.

Scout knew that the danger wasn't over. He went after my attacker again. This time he used his diminutive size to evade the man kicking at him. He took another bite at the man's leg, a bit lower this time and not quite as powerful. Still, Scout's second attack gave me enough time to open the door and leap into the front seat. I held out my arms for Scout to jump in, which he instinctively did. But in doing so he knocked the bulky key out of my hand, sending it flying somewhere between the seats.

I couldn't believe my bad luck.

I tried to slam the door after Scout joined me in the front seat, but I couldn't. The man jammed his foot in the doorway, blocking my effort to escape and leaving me open to his reach. I felt my heart explode as he inserted his hand around the doorframe and grabbed for me once again. I knew how the dead woman in the park must have felt at the end. It was terrifying. I had no way out.

It was then I realized that even though I might consider capitulating, Scout had no intention of letting me surrender without inflicting more pain. He lunged with his teeth bared and attacked the man's hand. Scout bit so hard that the man wailed in pain. I could see his right index finger was almost severed. Blood gushed everywhere. Satisfied with his efforts, Scout retreated toward the console. In doing so, he stepped on the dropped key and set off the alarm.

It was so loud that it shocked the man. He momentarily loosened his grip and, without thinking, stood up, just for a second, and looked around the car to see if anyone was responding to the alarm. One second and a bit of space was all I needed. I kicked his foot away with all my might, slammed the door shut, and pressed the door lock.

My hands were shaking, but I grasped the key and shoved it into the ignition to start the car. The enraged man banged on my window with his left hand and cursed. I saw him pick up something in order to break the window. I looked away and tried to block his face and words out of my mind. The BMW's ignition turned over on its first try, I threw the transmission in reverse and spun out of the parking space. Undeterred, the now bloody man tried to block me, thinking I wouldn't run him over. He didn't know me very well.

In the end I must have only run over his foot, but it was still satisfying to see him through my rearview mirror hopping around in pain.

I took a deep breath and tried to regain my composure as the castle became smaller in the distance behind me. Within minutes Scout was licking his paws contentedly, curled up on the back seat of the car.

Even though I finally felt safe, I was still confused. My mind was reeling.

Why was he trying to stop me? What did they do to the woman in the park? What had I stumbled upon? Did this guy really mean to hurt Candi? Could he be coming after me?

It was then that I realized that the man knew what my car looked like. He might try to follow me. I decided that I better step on it.

As soon as I could, I tried to reach Zach to see if I should call the police. More questions flowed through my mind. Was it just a random event? What should I tell them? Would they believe me? I didn't have anything but a bruise on me. How could I explain that the blood on my door was from when Scout attacked my mysterious attacker? What would be the charges? I kept dialing Zach over and over again like a stalker until I realized he had told me he would be at a meeting until late. It only made me more agitated. I knew I shouldn't do it, but I had to speak with someone.

"Hey, Candi, just checking in. How are you?" I think I managed a normal voice. I tried to anyway.

"I'm fine," she answered cheerfully, but then she lowered her voice. "But why are you checking in on me? I thought we agreed that I'd call you if I needed you. How embarrassing. I'll see you later tonight." End of conversation. *Click.*

I sighed and looked at my companion in the back seat, now fast asleep. Scout—my hero. Who would have thought? No one but me and the man with a severed finger would ever know the damage we'd inflicted.

Chapter Twelve

"JENI, THIS STORY is absurd," Zach said later that night when he returned from work and had listened to my detailed version of the attack earlier in the day. "And, really, how did you do all that and still manage to make it home with a tablecloth and nothing but a bruise on your left arm?"

I was speechless. *How can he not believe me?*

"The man was not out for my purse—it was me that he'd wanted. Or maybe Candi. He didn't want a tablecloth."

Scout lay exhausted at my feet, not much inclined to help me. Before I began supper, I had bathed him and then cleaned the blood from around the doorframe. When finished, I wanted to kick myself. I realized I no longer had proof of my harrowing experience.

Zach, seeing how dismayed I was, softened his approach. He knew I wasn't an outright liar.

"I imagine you did see someone who frightened you, but I'm equally sure it was a communication issue or language barrier. I'm glad you weren't hurt. As for Scout, if he did bite someone, then I'm not so happy. I sure hope we aren't sued. Has he had his rabies shots?"

I was momentarily at a loss for words. Rabies shots?

Just then Candi arrived home and strode through the door. She offered no greeting, but stood in front of us, hands on her hips and eyes flaming with anger.

"I'm so embarrassed. How could you check up on me? I saw you and Scout walking behind us."

It took me longer than it should have to gather up a good response. Candi wasn't in the mood to wait for me to concoct one.

"I know you didn't want me to come, and now it's all messed up. I can't stay here as your prisoner or pet or whatever. I don't know what I'm going to do, but I have to get out of here as soon as I can figure out where to go!" Then she turned on her heels to leave the room.

"Candi, wait, we *do* want you ..." I called out to her, but she ignored me and ran upstairs to her room, with Scout trailing as fast as he could on his short legs.

I didn't know what to do. I had a lot of diplomacy skills, but I wasn't prepared for this type of conflict.

"Is this how it's going to be for the whole summer?" Zach asked a few minutes later. It was obviously a rhetorical question.

I decided to pour myself a glass of wine and then curled into the big overstuffed chair in the corner of the living room. I looked around the apartment, taking in the bright blue Romanian dishes in the embassy-issued cabinets, my pretty new tablecloth, and the prints of two Nicolae Grigescu sunlit paintings hanging on the white walls. *How did I ever get into this situation?* All of a sudden I felt so alone. I just wanted to go home—home to the United States.

But then I shook my head.

"No. I'll make it right," I said to Zach, but exactly how I would do that was the million-dollar question.

The next morning after taking Scout for our regularly scheduled walk, I waited for Candi to wake up. I decided to check the English version of the Romanian news on the internet to see if there was any more information about the dead woman. It was always hard to understand because it was not professionally translated, but it confirmed that a woman was found in the park dead from an overdose of drugs. The article then went on to talk about how few drug cases there are in Romania, which was true. I gave up searching for more when Candi arrived downstairs.

She was remarkably cheerful, and even more so when I apologized to her again. I decided against asking her if she knew anything about the man whom Scout had attacked.

"It's okay. I shouldn't have been so surprised. I overreacted. At least you aren't Mom; she would've hired a private eye and dropped a tracking device into my purse!"

"Thanks," I said, genuinely grateful. "I'm going to the mall. Do you want to go?"

"Not shopping, but can you drop me off for lunch with Collin and Victor? Apparently, Collin's girlfriend isn't coming to Romania after all and he's sulking. Victor asked if I could join them so we could try to cheer him up. I think they're only inviting me because I have more experience in being dumped than anyone they know."

"I'm sure that isn't true," I said.

"Nah, we compared notes and it's true. But they did admit that the guys I described are jerks, so they don't really count."

I smiled. It was true. She just needed to be more selective. I was glad they had become friends.

That afternoon, after dropping her off at the embassy, I went to tennis practice. This time Nadia had chosen a court even farther in the back, far away from other players. I tried to believe it meant we were some secret force to be reckoned with more than the possibility that I was an embarrassment, but I knew better.

It did not help that when I attempted to return her first serve, I was so overly anxious that I misjudged the distance and ran too far. I tried to slow down, which only caused me to trip over my right foot and fall forward, my now useless racquet stretched out in front of me. The graphite rim hit the ground, bouncing slightly, before the palms of my hands and knees made contact with the clay court. *Ouch!* There is nothing worse than a court scrape, but I was too proud to cry.

Immediately, I jumped up and pretended nothing had happened. After checking my racquet strings, I jumped back and forth on my feet and then took my stance as if prepared to return her next serve. I must have looked insane.

I looked across the net. Nadia was standing there looking at me with a horrified face. I'm not sure she had ever seen anything quite like it.

"Are you okay?" she asked.

"Sure," I said. "No problem."

"But your knee is bleeding."

"Oh," I said and looked down. I winced, as much from embarrassment as from the pain. "I guess I need a Band-Aid. I'll get one from my purse." I jogged to the courtside bench, cleaned the scrape with water, and covered it with eight tiny crisscrossed Band-Aids that were really intended for blisters on toes. They failed to cover the red scraped flesh, but the more it stung, the more I smiled gamely like it was a minor scratch.

While we were sitting at the restaurant waiting and finishing our drinks, I took the opportunity to talk to Nadia about the restaurant where I had seen the now dead woman. Despite Anna's assurances, I still couldn't forget the face on the news. I needed some closure, some answers as to what had really happened, so that my guilt about doing nothing would go away.

"What do you think? You know the area. Have you ever been to that restaurant?" I asked.

"I know it is one of those places that goes in and out of business. It's a bad location. It is far from the lake and near the train tracks. Usually it caters to a bad crowd, especially on weekends. Why?"

"Nothing. I just went to it and was wondering. The food wasn't good."

"That doesn't surprise me," she said.

I didn't ask anything else. By then we were finished and ready to get back to the courts.

Once my knee was dressed, Nadia suggested we stop playing tennis for the day, but I told her we needed to practice.

"Perhaps," I said, picking up on her use of the word, "you could just start a bit slower for me right now and then move up to your normal serves."

"I think perhaps you are right," she responded, and smiled sweetly. "I don't think I have been going at this the right way. I'm impressed. If you can take a fall like that and keep playing as if nothing happened, then for sure you have the determination to play in the tournament! I'm not saying we will win, but we'll give it a try."

With that, we took our positions once again and practiced our Diplomat Games strategy for an hour. I managed to remain on my feet until we finished.

I left the tennis courts, and then ran a few errands before going home. I was in the kitchen preparing dinner when Candi texted that she had decided to go shopping at the mall with friends and would be home late. I was actually able to enjoy the process of cooking a full meal. There were no "cream of" soups, prepared pastry crusts, or inviting frozen foods at the local grocery store. Each time I cooked I felt like Julia Child, learning to create amazing dishes the old-fashioned way. I was in such a good mood that after I added some red wine to the sauce I was making on my tiny stove, I poured a glass for me.

I was still in the midst of cooking supper when Candi arrived, her arms full of packages from the mall.

"Wow, you really bought a lot!" I said.

"I know! It was so much fun. I got some new dresses and some high-heeled sandals, plus some earrings. I'm gonna look so European!"

"Those bags look like they're from expensive stores," I said, trying not to sound overly critical. "I didn't know you had that much money."

"It's not all that much. I had people helping me pick out things—you know, so I'm sure I got a good deal," she said. Then she turned away, effectively ending the conversation. "I'm going to go upstairs and put them away. Can I help with dinner?"

Instinctively, I knew not to delve further about the money. Instead, I was grateful she was in a good mood. Perhaps, I reasoned, she had gotten the clothes on sale.

"Sure, get organized and then you can make the salad. I'd love the company."

Dinner that night was fun and light, with all the family banter that I had missed. Candi was really a smart and intelligent young woman. All she needed was some life experience to broaden her worldview. Suddenly things seemed to be going in the right direction.

Chapter Thirteen

Dear Aunt Jeni,

Don't get mad at me, but …

IT WAS NOT until midmorning that I noticed the note propped up on the counter where I kept the car keys. Candi must have planned it that way, putting it in a place where I would see the note, but not too early in the day that I'd be able to stop her.

Previously I had assumed she was still asleep in her room.

"Oh, Scout! What has Candi done?" He looked up with a worried expression, like he knew what she had done and that I was going to be very unhappy.

> I am leaving for a while. I've been offered a job modeling in Italy! I'm so excited! I knew you wouldn't let me go without Mom's approval, and that would take too long. They told me that I had to go now or never! Please don't hate me! I'll come get Scout when I make some money. I know he loves you the *best* now!
>
> Hugs,
> Candi
> XOXO

"That's it?" I yelled loud. "Scout, what is your mother thinking? Modeling? Who is she with, and where is she going? What kind of note is this?"

I tried to call Candi on the cell phone. Predictably, it went to voice mail, so I texted for her to call me immediately. No response. Next I sent a quick email on the off chance that she might respond to that.

Once again, I was in a *What to do? What to do?* panic mode.

I called Zach and told him what had happened. "We have to go to the police! She's left without real money and, oh my gosh, my sister is going to kill me!"

"I'll come home and we can work through it together. Don't call anyone yet." This time I knew Zach was just as worried as I was. Candi had done something very foolish.

I turned off the TV to help calm my mind, curled up on the couch with a glass of hot peppermint tea, and sat in the quiet contemplating options. I even patted the cushion to my side, signaling to Scout that he was free to jump up next to me. He needed comforting as well.

Zach was home in a hurry, having forgone the Metro and instead opted for a taxi.

He sat opposite me and read the note several times.

"I take it she's never modeled before?"

"Not to my knowledge. And she's not a natural model, unless it's for sports clothes. She's not tall enough."

"Do you have any idea who she went with?"

"Maybe this Tina girl. She supposedly is an employment specialist. They went shopping yesterday and Candi bought clothes. Maybe Tina hired her. But why the secrecy? Why not tell me the truth?"

"Would you have said yes?" Zach inquired, looking at me for a truthful answer.

"No, of course not ... not off the bat. But maybe if I knew enough about it I would have at least considered it."

"It sounds to me like she was hitching a ride with someone and didn't have time to get into a battle with you. Kids do this all the time. They backpack all over eastern Europe. And she's going to Italy, so she should be okay."

"What about calling the police?" I knew the answer, but I had to hear it out loud from Zach.

"She's over twenty-one, left a happy note, and doesn't sound incapacitated or as if she's being held hostage. She's decided to get out of Bucharest and spend her summer vacation in sunny Italy. What do you think they'll say?"

"I'm crazy?"

"'Fraid so."

I sighed.

"Is there anything I can do?" I asked. I wanted to think everything would be fine, but I knew better.

"The only thing I can suggest is that you try to find this Tina woman. She might know something more about where Candi is going. In the meantime, your sister will eventually call to check in and you can tell her what happened."

"She's gonna kill me."

"I doubt it. Italy is far safer than rural India. She knows that. Plus, I'm sure we'll know more by the time she calls. That reminds me—you should call Kate in New Orleans and talk to her. Maybe Candi told Kate something that will be useful."

I had forgotten about Candi's sister Kate. It was the middle of the night in the United States, so I needed to wait a few more hours before I called.

Zach and I both sat quietly for a while. My mind was reeling with images of Sue in a flowered sarong and floppy sun hat calling me using a satellite phone under a lone scrubby tree on a remote island. I could hear her screaming the sentence "Modeling in Italy?" over and over again. Zach may not have known it, but we women do. When dressed up, the women in our family can certainly turn an eye or two, but what we don't do, and are unlikely ever to do, is produce international models.

Zach left to return to work. I called Anna in the hope that she had seen Tina lately. She told me that at the coffee morning Tina had signed up to attend a gallery opening that was to occur later in the day. She offered to call me if Tina was there. It was near my house. I could get a cab and join them, she suggested.

It seemed like endless hours before I could call Kate without risking waking her up. Kate listened to my story without comment until I was finished.

"Well, I talked to her once and she did say she had met some cool international friends. I think one was from Moldova—maybe—and there was a French woman. She seemed so happy and finally over her crummy ex-boyfriend. We hated him so much that even if she's off on some wild-goose chase to be an international model, I'm happy that she isn't still crying over a selfish golfer with a bad slice.

"Anyway, Aunt Jeni, I wouldn't worry about this. Italy isn't that far from Romania. She'll call when she needs money."

"It's not all that close by car, but thanks for making me feel better. I hope Sue feels the same way," I said.

"Just email Mom. She won't care. Maybe she already heard from Candi."

That was a tough decision. If Sue was blissfully ignorant of Candi's departure and happily cruising, then I might mess up her trip. But if I didn't call and something was really wrong …

I agonized over what to do, until I finally bit the proverbial bullet. Sue was Candi's mother. She would want to know, and deserved to be made aware of, the current situation.

> Dear Sue,
>
> I hope you are still having fun on your trip. We are all fine here, but I wanted to send a note to tell you that Candi has left with some friends to go to Italy and perhaps do some modeling. I'm not sure whether she told you or not, but I didn't want you out of the loop. As soon as I hear something from her, I'll let you know!
>
> She seemed very excited to go.
>
> Love,
> Jeni

The phone rang just as I hit Send on the computer.

"Tina didn't show," Anna whispered into the phone from the gallery. "No one knows where she is. One person told me that she thought Tina might have some legal issues because she saw her going into some government offices a few days ago. Maybe her work visa ended or something like that.

Visa issues arise all the time. It doesn't mean she did anything wrong. Don't worry for now. We can talk tomorrow."

"Thanks."

There was nothing left for me to do other than run a Google search on Tina and her company, but nothing appeared on the screen when I did so. There was no website for Tina's international employment agency that she entered as her employment on the ILB application or any mention of it on social media. There was no Instagram or Twitter—nothing. I tried to find her picture or information on the ILB website, but she seemed to be camera shy. Only once did I see her image, and it was of her facing away from the camera.

This lack of a footprint was just another bad sign to me, especially given the fact that the normal employment specialist is obsessed with reputation and publicity.

When Zach returned home that afternoon, I could tell he was anxious as well.

"Any news from the model?" He tried to be lighthearted, but it was hard.

"No," I said and told him about my conversations with Anna and Kate.

"What about her social media, her and her business—you know, Facebook and Twitter and LinkedIn?" he asked.

"Nothing."

"Nothing?" Zach was shocked.

With that my eyes teared up and Zach's face became tense with concern. We both knew that in today's world, no news is not necessarily good news.

Chapter Fourteen

THE NEXT DAY I spent cleaning Candi's room, hoping to find something that would help allay my fears or provide some clue as to where she'd gone.

The first bit of information I found didn't exactly put my mind at ease—in fact, it was simply shocking. As soon as I entered her room, I almost tripped over an empty shopping bag that had held some of her recent purchases from the mall. When I went to put the bag and its overflowing tissue paper into the trash, I saw a cash receipt crumpled up near the top. I'm not sure what I'd expected to see when I looked at the white slip of paper, but it sure wasn't that she had paid over $1,000 for two new dresses.

I don't call that a good deal, like she'd told me the previous evening. On top of that, the new sandals were from some Italian designer and cost almost half that amount. She'd also left on the bedside table a wad of receipts for purchases of makeup and expensive costume jewelry. I mentally added them up; the total was over $300. I stopped counting when it dawned on me to look around the room for her old luggage. It was still there, with a receipt for a new bag on a nearby dresser.

Where in the world had she gotten that kind of money? And in cash? I knew she couldn't use checks and she had no debit account. Or at least I thought she didn't.

I sat on the bed to think. The Candi I knew had never been the type of girl to spend a lot of money on anything, much less clothes. What was going on?

My mind began to spin with questions. When did Candi decide that she wanted to wear high-end makeup—and lots of it? And designer high-heeled sandals instead of flip-flops? It was like she had been beamed up and was going to be replaced with an Italian Barbie doll.

But then I realized that I hadn't spent much time with her in years. Perhaps she had changed a long time ago. And, if she had no money, then she would have to look to other sources to fund pretty things. The answer had to be that someone was luring Candi with riches. What I didn't know was if it was for romance, or because she might actually become famous as a model, or for some nefarious reason.

In the end, the only thing I knew was that the receipts and new clothes confirmed Zach's assessment: Candi had not been forced to do anything. She was no hostage. She had seen European women, liked what she saw, and decided to become one.

Maybe it was a good sign. Candi was taking a risk and going on a new adventure. She was in control of her destiny. I needed to give up worrying and imagining horrific things and just wait for her to call. It wasn't like I wouldn't have done the same thing right out of college. Summer in Italy? Why not? It sounded so enticing.

With those mental gymnastics over, I slapped my hands on my thighs and bounced off the bed. There would be no Italian dreams for me; I needed to go to tennis practice.

This time my service return was slightly better. I only stumbled once and avoided falling on the ground. Nadia and I both agreed that I showed some improvement. Staying out of the emergency room had become the third goal of our plans for the Diplomat Games.

In a great mood when I returned to the apartment, I threw my racquet in the closet.

The phone began ringing as soon as I took off my shoes.

"Candi?" I immediately answered.

"No," the sweet voice said. "It's me, Anna. I was wondering if we could meet for coffee first thing tomorrow morning."

"Sure. How about the French Bakery?" I said, but something in her voice made me wonder about the call for a meeting. "Is anything wrong?"

"I don't know. We can talk tomorrow. Nine?"

"Great. See you then."

After I hung up, I wished I had asked more questions, but if it was about some ILB controversy, I wasn't in the mood to hear about it right then. If anything, Anna's call had reminded me once again of Candi and made me wonder why she hadn't yet contacted me. That nagging worry was the one thing I was unable to shed.

When I arrived at the French Bakery the next day, the sun was already high in the sky, its light filtering through the leaves on the trees that surrounded the outside deck of the small coffee shop. I immediately succumbed to temptation and picked out a chocolate croissant from the glass cabinet holding a row of pastries fresh from the oven in the adjacent kitchen.

When the waiter brought my cappuccino and croissant, he opened the large green-and-white umbrella over my head in order to provide total shade from the sun. It was such a nice hideaway. This coffee shop was tucked behind a white stucco wall in the midst of old trees and amid an equally historic neighborhood. When life seemed to be unraveling, a peaceful coffee in a serene setting always brought me back to my senses.

Anna had trouble finding a parking space. I watched her through the front gate as she hurriedly circled the shop, until she appeared to be reconciled to parking illegally. At that point she popped her front wheels up and over the sidewalk curb, half in and half out of the street. It was not like her to just drive up on a sidewalk and park, although on this day she was merely following the example set by the other drivers. Still, I knew Anna well and had never seen her drive erratically or park illegally. She appeared to be in a great hurry to meet me.

Some people walk into a room and own it. Anna, although diminutive, was one of those people. She wore a smart sheath dress in beige with a tiny Chanel-type jacket in light pink—almost a rose color—and matching shoes. Cute but classic. It caused me to glance at my reflection in the windows. To my dismay what I saw was a black jersey sundress topped off by oversized black sunglasses covering much of my face.

I made a mental note that I was blah looking. I really did need to go shopping and work harder on my style.

"Sorry I'm late," she said.

"No problem. I was trying to think about what has you so concerned. I'm sorry I didn't ask. Is it ILB?"

"No. Yes. I mean, there are all kinds of things wrong with ILB, but that isn't why I wanted to see you." She waved off the waiter and then proceeded to lean toward me.

"I think there is something bad about Tina. I feel horrible that I told you not to worry, but now I'm very concerned. Last night after we talked, I casually mentioned her name to Camellia, and she told me that Tina's name is not really Tina."

"Oh, I knew that. It is short for something else. Either she or Candi told me that."

"No, it's not what you think. She's not the Tina we thought or anything close to it. It's a totally made-up name—at least her last name is."

I felt a frisson of concern.

"You know how Camellia works for Banca Transylvania?"

I nodded.

"Well, Camellia said that Tina came to the bank to make a large cash withdrawal, and when Camellia went to talk to her, she saw that the name on the withdrawal slip was not Tina's. It is Camellia's job to make sure that the name on the slip is right, so she required Tina's identification. I asked about Tina's real name, and Camellia said she didn't recall, saying that even if she actually knew it, she couldn't tell me. All Camellia would say is that Tina was very uncomfortable about the entire incident."

"I guess it makes sense that Tina was withdrawing money for their trip to Italy. I'm not sure that has any great meaning at this point." I had been a lawyer long enough to know to be wary of "negative" information that could be reasonably explained.

"But there's more. This morning I found out that last week a woman who had a French accent and the same hair and looks as Tina tried to befriend one of my volunteers at the shelter."

Anna then told me that the woman asked her questions about two women from Ukraine, sisters who were brought here months ago. Anna helped get them trained and on their feet.

"Unfortunately, they left when I was on vacation, so I don't know where they went," she said. "I assumed they had been offered jobs."

She paused and took a breath.

"Jeni, I think the French woman who was asking questions is the Tina woman."

I still wanted to be rational about the news. It was my training.

"Well, again, Anna, I really appreciate the information, but I'm not sure that it means anything. Tina said she was an employment specialist."

"My volunteer swears Tina said she was a magazine publisher in Italy—not a recruiter. But that's not the real issue. My real problem is, what was Tina doing at my shelter? Something is wrong. I feel it."

For a few minutes we sat quietly. I nibbled on my croissant, not sure what to make of this information. Anna was right. The shelter was way off the beaten track in a remote area of town. It didn't make sense. My worries over Candi's disappearance began to reemerge and flood over me.

Anna sat back in her chair and looked around the café as if to make sure we weren't heard. Once she had finished telling me what she had felt compelled to divulge, she seemed to still be on edge. I watched her intently. One part of me said that Anna failed to provide any real proof that something was wrong, but the other side reminded me that Anna was a smart and perceptive woman who knows the dangers that a young woman could encounter. I had always trusted her judgment; why would I change now? Her instincts were telling her that something was wrong.

I wondered if I should panic or stay patient and wait for Candi to call.

"Do you have any suggestions as to what you would do if you were me?" I finally asked Anna.

"I thought you would ask that. I wish I knew what to do. Maybe Zach will know someone who can check out Tina's identity, or whoever she really is. I tried to find a picture of her at our last meeting to help you, but she always was turned away from the camera. How often does that happen? The women run over each other to be in a picture."

"I guess I could check with Zach, but he has to be very careful about these kinds of things. And Candi is a grown girl who left on her own. He can't just decide to direct a search of Tina's or Dimitri's background. It might not be legal, and he won't break the law, not even to find Candi."

It was frustrating. In the end, we agreed on one thing: that I wouldn't panic—yet. I would just wait for more news.

Chapter Fifteen

INSTEAD OF SITTING at home and waiting for news from Candi, I went to the embassy later in the morning to pick up some Jiffy peanut butter from the commissary. I needed to be there before lunch because it was Saturday and they closed at noon. This embassy store was seriously small, about the size of a child's bedroom, and was lined along the walls with narrow shelves and a deep freezer, with a stack of back-to-back shelves in the middle.

Once every four or five months the commissary received a shipment of American food products from Ramstein Air Base. But almost immediately after a shipment, there were slim pickings on the shelves. Usually it was the stuff no one wanted, like sugarless cookies or cans of beets. The shipment had just been unpacked; I knew to get there fast before the best foods left the shelves, in particular Jiffy peanut butter.

Europeans ate Nutella, which is made with hazelnuts. I was sure it probably tasted good given the amount of Nutella sold in Bucharest, but Zach and I preferred Jiffy. It was one of those days when a good peanut butter and jelly sandwich might sooth my soul.

As I left the commissary with a plastic bag containing two jars of creamy peanut butter and equally valuable Ritz crackers, I saw Collin and Victor leaving the cafeteria with to-go cups of coffee, dressed as if they were headed to play soccer.

"Hey there," I said.

"Hello, Jeni," Collin responded. "How are you today? I haven't seen Zach lately."

"Oh, fine. I guess. Did Zach tell you that Candi has left to go to Italy for a while?"

"Oh, she did decide to leave?" Victor said. He took a swig of his coffee.

"Yes," I said before it dawned on me that this was not shocking news to either of them.

"Wait a second. Did she talk to you guys about this? Why didn't you tell me?" I tried to remain calm, but my voice increased by at least an octave. I couldn't believe they supported her romp in Italy with a strange man I had never met.

Victor sensed my anger and wisely turned to Collin to let him answer my question.

"She had lunch with us the other day and she said she'd been offered a chance to work in Italy with that guy from Moldova she's been seeing and his friends. I asked her some questions about where in Italy and what she was going to do, but she didn't seem to know much other than the possibility that she might make a lot of money. Truthfully, I thought her lack of details meant she wasn't serious about going," he said before he could tell that the news was upsetting me even more.

"I'm really sorry. I guess I should have said something, but I thought she was too smart just to leave like that. But no worries. International kids are always flying here and there. I am sure she'll be fine. She'll be back soon."

I took a deep breath to keep from exploding. Their flippancy was annoying and I needed reassurance, not banter.

"Well, I'm not so sure I agree that she'll be fine, but she's gone now and there's nothing I can do about it. Whether it was a smart decision or not, I don't know. All I do know is that I'm worried. What *exactly* did she tell you?" I asked.

"That her friends offered to take her to Italy and get her a job modeling. I told her that it all sounded a bit odd, but she was pretty pumped up. I also remember that she said she thought they might be going to Italy on a yacht that was docked in Croatia. Victor tried to tell her to be careful and said that people on yachts were a unique crowd, but she said he was being ridiculous. Then the conversation turned to another topic and we never talked about her plans again. So, you see, I really didn't think she would do it."

Though I was trying not to be accusatory, I could tell my questions were making them uncomfortable. I knew it wasn't their fault that Candi had left. I worked hard to end the conversation pleasantly and then headed down a remote hall to the travel office to look at the huge map of the world hanging outside the door. I wanted to look at the map of Croatia, a country that was about five hundred miles away from where I was standing. It's a small country, a little more than 10 percent the size of California, bounded on the west by the storied waters of the Adriatic, on the north by Slovenia, and on the south by Montenegro. Its topography too is a bit like California's with endless beaches, wine country, and mountains that rise up from the water's edge, but Croatia is also dotted with ancient cities, breathtaking waterfalls, and thousands of islands, many with picturesque harbors.

I had been to Croatia only once before and that was a trip to Dubrovnik, a charming historic walled city in the southern part of the country. At the time, I was new to eastern Europe and knew very little about the regional politics. The sad truth is that once the initial glow of European life wore off, it did not take long before I felt I had earned a PhD in the field of centuries-old simmering and overt hostilities. The one between the Croats (or Croatians, as I called them) and their next-door neighbors, the Serbs, is among the oldest and most complex.

I studied the map intently. I knew from the travel news that generally the cruise ships and charter boats left from Split on the north coast of Croatia, which was in an area that I had yet to visit.

Croatia, like any hot tourist spot, especially one so recently part of the jet-set scene, probably wasn't the safest place to travel for an unaccompanied young woman without international experience. Granted, I told myself, Candi wasn't alone—but then I wasn't sure any man who would encourage her to impulsively flee from her family was a man looking out for her best interests.

I was deep in those thoughts when I heard a familiar voice behind me.

"Planning a trip somewhere?" Matt said.

Ugh, of all people. Matt was the blue-eyed, blond-haired former marine who served as our RSO, as in regional security officer, at the embassy. He had the job of keeping us all safe, but he and I had never been on cozy terms.

"No, just looking."

Luckily, Matt just nodded his head and walked away.

Collin had stopped in the nearby gym to get a soccer ball, and upon exiting had seen the exchange. He walked toward me after Matt left.

"Why didn't you say anything about Candi?" he asked.

"Because he would do nothing and only succeed in making me feel bad about having an irresponsible niece."

"Probably, but you still might want to report it. I'm not sure about the rules."

"Well, right now she's just on vacation and I expect her back in a week or so with a really nice tan. If something changes, I'll report the matter to Matt. I am, after all, a rule follower."

He smiled. "I agree. Still, if there's anything I can do, let me know."

"Thanks."

That evening I talked to Zach, and for once he concurred with me. No information in our possession warranted talking to either Matt or any other police authority. If Candi were to stay away more than a few days, then we would tell Matt. In the meantime, I decided we just needed to go to church and pray that my sister Sue did not call before Candi did.

Chapter Sixteen

SUNDAY MORNING WAS sunny and mild, so Zach and I awoke early and walked to the downtown church a couple of miles from home. It was a real treat for Bucharest, when the morning air was crisp and the broad sidewalks were lined with flowers. Halfway there we stopped for a pastry and coffee at an outdoor *cofetaria.*

I was in a happy mood when we walked into the century-old redbrick building housing our little Anglican church, the Resurrection Church of Bucharest. We were a few minutes late, which meant we were right on time. The usual forty or so people were shifting in the antique wooden chairs. It took a second for my eyes to adjust from the bright sunlight to the dark interior and then for me to return the smiles of some of my closest Romanian friends and the English-speaking expats from around the world.

The sermon delivered from the simple wooden pulpit was about finding lost sheep. *Well,* I thought, *that is prophetic.* It was also problematic, because in the end, all it did was increase my desire to run randomly around the globe showing strangers pictures of my niece.

After church we had our usual small fellowship—very British. Tea bags and porcelain cups with dainty cookies were lined up on a white linen tablecloth. For those few Americans, there was Nescafé coffee, granules in small packets. Given that the hot water was typically only lukewarm, the coffee was always everyone's last choice.

"Where's Candi?" my friend Molly asked.

"I think she is in Croatia with some friends."

"For Yacht Week?" This seemed to perk Molly up more than her two cups of tea.

"I'm not sure. What's Yacht Week?"

"For one week in the summer, all the yachties and everyday boaters converge upon cool places on the water and party for seven straight days. They have celebrities and bands, and everyone drinks a ton. I hear it's crazy!"

"It does sounds like a wild scene," I said, but truthfully I knew nothing about it. I had no idea what I would later learn.

"Either this week or next it's Yacht Week in Croatia. That's why I asked."

"Well, she did tell people she was going on a yacht," I said no more, happier with this news than I'd been after seeing the price of Candi's new clothes.

"Some of my friends are going, but I've never been able to tag along with them. I can't go this year either since I am going to the States for August vacation." I loved how everyone took a whole month off in Europe.

"Seeing Patrick's family?" I asked. She had been dating a handsome young man, Patrick, from New Orleans, a city close to my home and my heart. It thrilled me that Molly might be living there one day, as it was the city where Zach and I intended to finally land. We would return to family and friends, and fishing in the Gulf. No matter how much we loved Europe, it wasn't home like New Orleans.

"Yes, and I'm hoping his parents like me!"

We discussed the latest news across Europe with the broad spectrum of people who attended this church, all connected solely by the fact that they were Christians of some type, spoke English, and appreciated the clarity of an English service.

Afterward, Zach and I enjoyed a leisurely walk home. I then took Scout, our orphaned ward, for a short walk, while Zach spent time putting the finishing touches on a weekly report that he'd been working on for submission to Washington. When I returned from the walk, I decided to use the quiet time to research Yacht Week on the internet.

In retrospect, it wasn't a great idea.

Basically, Yacht Week is a mass of high-end boats either scattered around the Croatian islands in marinas or moored in harbors. Many of the boats are chartered by young adults who chip in together to share the costs. The problem is that the partiers liked to be at a marina for the social activity and toilets, but there were not enough slips in the small country for the invasion.

The solution? They had pictures on the internet. Once an obliging boat actually paid in advance for a slip and was secure at the wharf, one boat after another tied up to it sideways, so they looked like a teetering and movable stack of cookies. In boating lingo, tying off to another boat is called "rafting up." And, though the idea of marina toilets and showers is an attractive one, the people on the last boat must climb or crawl over all the boats between them and the pier, plus walk up the long dock and wait in a line behind ten or twenty people at the bathroom. More often than not, people avoided the whole ordeal by just jumping in the water.

Croatia is not just known for the sleek and expensive sloops in the marinas, but also for the superyachts and megayachts. What, you may ask, is the difference? I did.

A mere yacht is up to 150 feet in length, but superyachts are the length of an entire football field. These boats do not raft up. They dock at the marbled entrances to the cities, they have sterns with names that are lit up in lights, and their stainless steel and teak gangplanks rise and fall at the push of a button. They have a crew of ten or more, and several matching tenders (little mini-me boats that go with them) that cost as much as a modest house. Some even have matching helicopters. I read that one was so large that it completely blocked the entrance to a famous harbor of one of Croatia's idyllic islands. In order to stay there without alienating the locals, the owner threw money at the people on the island who had been inconvenienced, and also bought free drinks for everyone. It sounded like Mardi Gras to me, but with real gold tokens.

I didn't get the sense that Candi would be on an actual yacht—more likely one of those chartered sailboats crowded with young people.

Social media was full of Yacht Week posts of young adults dancing on the tiny teak decks with wineglasses or cocktail glasses raised high above their heads, or floating in the water with long arms and legs wound around their shipmates—like the worst or best, depending upon your view, of an American spring break. Needless to say, no one wore more than an itty-bitty bikini, whether man or woman. But that was not what bothered me.

It was that partiers looked richer and more sophisticated than everyday beer-guzzling college students hanging out in the French Quarter. In fact, they were way more worldly than Candi. How, I wondered, would she navigate that world of excess? What if she fell from a boat and was injured or, worse yet, was served a spiked drink? She thought she had friends with her, but what did she know about them? I wanted to stand on the terrace and scream for her to come home. There was so much more that could go wrong on this trip than right.

This research had only made me more anxious about her safety. I wanted to turn my attention to other pressing matters, no matter how frivolous they were, but it was hard.

That evening I dreamed about Candi. Her pretty face with her big blue-green eyes was staring at me from the TV screen showing the evening news, while the perky anchorwoman asked the viewers if anyone could identify the young woman. I awoke in a sweat, clinging to Zach, grateful it was just a dream.

Chapter Seventeen

A MEETING WAS planned the next day at the Green Garlic for the embassy participants in the Diplomat Games. I decided to attend the meeting to make sure they knew about the two new additions to the games and that I would be playing tennis. Truthfully, I could have sent an email, but I wanted to get out of the lonely apartment.

The embassy committee was very laid back. To the seasoned State Department employees, the games were just that—games—and no big deal.

The Romanian restaurant with the rather oxymoronic name of Green Garlic was in a very old but stately renovated home known for its cozy interior in the winter and its outside terraces in the summer. It was painted green and presumably had something to do with garlic, although the connection was lost on me. I was told it was the favorite place for American expats to eat, with an easy menu to follow, good food, and not far from the US Embassy.

Eight people showed up. Both Collin and Matt were there. Collin took a chair as far from me as he could as if to avoid any further confrontation over Candi. I looked around and gathered that most of the people interested in the games were the ones who were also the most athletic—other than me, of course.

"I guess I need to explain why I'm here," I began, and proceeded to tell them the story about ILB and the two new sports that would be included in this year's games.

"Let me get this straight. You've gone off on your own and committed us to play golf *and* row, and you intend to play women's double tennis?" Matt said.

"Yes, but it wasn't like you make it sound. It was a process ..." I stopped when I saw the incredulous looks around me.

"Do you understand that we are a very small embassy and that we barely have enough people to field the sports we competed in last year?" he continued.

"Yes. But I have it under control. Zach will play golf with another person and they're sure to win."

"Who is the other person?" Collin asked, knowing full well there was no one else with Candi gone.

"I'm sure we have a golfer somewhere, and if not, I have my niece's clubs that someone can use. Surely someone here knows how to play golf."

Everyone was quiet as they thought for a moment and then shook their heads no.

"How about rowers?" another person asked. "Who here rows?"

With that, Collin smiled. "Victor. Victor rows. And he has his own boat, although it needs a bit of work. He showed it to me at the park one day."

"Do you think he'll participate?" Matt asked.

"Positive."

Smiles began to emerge from the previously sullen faces. Then things got ugly.

"Jeni, I didn't know you played tennis, at least not on the level of the players in these games," Matt said. Ooh, he was so condescending.

"I'm playing with Victor's mom, and she's good. We'll see what happens." I am pretty sure I sounded confident, but my game face exterior was beginning to crack.

I also didn't sense any confidence in my playing from the others, but since I was taking an open slot with no one else clamoring to play, there were no objections. Even worse, I think Matt was already fantasizing about the stories he would tell at the next embassy party about my tennis debacle. What if I fell? I almost groaned out loud. We quickly moved on to other sports.

We always had volunteers for men's solo or double tennis, volleyball, and Ping-Pong, but it was soccer that was the hardest to field. It required a lot of people who'd grown up playing and knew the rules—typically a more European experience than a US one, despite the game's rising popularity back home.

"I'm working on it, but I think we're going to have to use some of the embassy kids—as in teenagers—to play. Some are really good, but I doubt we'll score a goal, much less win a match," Collin said.

"It's a shame we can't play baseball or softball. We would win for sure," I said.

"You know, Jeni, the last thing we need are more games," Matt said. "This will be the first year that you actually play. You'll find out soon enough what I mean."

With that, we talked about T-shirts and who would do what. It was a pleasant enough meeting, even with Matt there.

I left the Green Garlic in a slightly better mood and drove on to the Diplomat Club to deal with Moira and the ILB committee. As much as I didn't want to go, I knew it would keep my mind off Candi for another few hours.

As soon as we sat down, it became the all-Moira show. She had planned the food, the budget, and even the aprons that the members would wear. I wanted to complain, but I had to admit that the aprons were really cute. Most Romanians were incredible seamstresses and designers, which meant that the aprons were far more chic than your run-of-the-mill kitchen garment. In fact, they hardly looked like an apron at all with their pink-checkered fabric, white lace borders, large hand-stitched ILB in a fancy green embroidery scroll in the middle, a fitted bodice, and a cinched waist. The designer had somehow made us look less like food servers and more like hot waitresses.

Our cost for the enormous amount of effort someone had put into the design of the apron? Almost nothing.

I wasn't interested in planning the food or figuring out the budget. I had other things to worry about, so if Moira wanted to handle it all, she could. But just as I decided I wasn't going to pick any fights, one erupted anyway.

"Who'll handle the money?" Anna asked.

"I will, of course," Moira responded.

All of a sudden I could sense tension in the room.

"How about our treasurer? Won't you run it all through the accounts like we do with everything else?" Anna asked.

"I hope not. What a waste of time. I'll just get the cash, buy everything, and then give you the receipts," Moira said. She was getting hot under the collar. Her cheeks began to deepen to a blood red.

"I don't think you should do that. It should be handled just like we always do. Does everyone agree?" Anna looked at the women for a response before Moira could say anything further.

Predictably, they all nodded yes. I found that most of the time ILB members were very agreeable.

"Well, that's it then. You just need to meet with the treasurer to confirm the budget. It's not that I don't trust you, but this is so much easier," Anna said with a sweet smile toward Moira. Despite the smile, everyone in the room got the message—she didn't trust Moira.

Moira did not return the smile. It was obvious that she didn't like Anna for spoiling her attempted coup d'état. In fact, her eyes narrowed, her red cheeks flushed even more, and she mumbled something incoherent under her breath. I knew it wasn't a compliment.

After the meeting adjourned, Anna pulled me aside.

"That should curtail her a bit. Now that there is no opportunity for 'lost' petty cash or sweetheart backdoor deals with vendors, she might stop trying to take over your role."

We had all heard rumors about her questionable money dealings from the past.

"I think that's why she is so excited about these games—it's an easy way to skim off some money. I know that you don't need that drama right now," Anna whispered, smiling sweetly to comfort me. I was so grateful to have a Romanian like Anna to tell me the backstory when I needed it.

Just then Moira came up to us.

"I hope you're not accusing me of anything, Anna. You do know that it's only a matter of time until you are off the board. If I were you, I'd remember that." So much for Moira backing off. I could hear the hissing in her voice.

At that moment in time, 2:54 p.m., I realized that the Diplomat Games were no longer going to be the semicivilized sporting event they were intended to be. It appeared that this year the games would include a bit of boxing, unofficially, of course.

Chapter Eighteen

WITH CANDI GONE, time seemed to crawl at a snail's pace. By Tuesday I found that I could barely eat. It had been almost four days since Candi left. The lack of news weighed upon me. Even my morning coffee was no longer the treat it once was. Why hadn't Candi called me?

There was no doubt in my mind that Sue was beginning to worry as well, probably thinking, *Why hasn't Jeni given me an update on Candi?*

It was summer and many of my friends were off on vacation or busy with children. Zach suggested that I plan a trip somewhere, but my heart just wasn't in it. While wandering aimlessly about the park to kill time and to walk the dog, I became convinced that Scout had made more friends than I had. He had not barked at another person. He was the right mutt for a diplomat to walk on a leash.

"What would I do without you?" I asked him, leaning down to his level to gaze into his eyes.

Herastrau Park has statues and monuments everywhere, ranging from one of Charles de Gaulle to some of more obscure Romanian politicians and educators. Even Joseph Stalin once had a place of honor. In the middle of Rose Park, there is a large circle of enormous heads in the likenesses of the founders of the European Union. Once I figured out whom the heads belonged to, it made me wonder what would happen to the British representative now that Brexit was a reality. It would be so odd to take a head out of a perfect circle. And how would they do it? Just take a saw and hack it off at the neck like Anne Boleyn, or topple it over like Saddam Hussein and let it roll down the hill?

Of all the monuments in the park, the only two I found acknowledging the contributions Americans had made to Romania were in the form of a large bust of Mark Twain on a stone pedestal and a marker that they designated as a tribute for Michael Jackson. It's a long story as to why these two are there, but the abbreviated versions go as follows: *Tom Sawyer* was an English book the dictator allowed the Romanian children to read in school. Perhaps it was because he felt it depicted Americans as cruel racists. His plan might have worked, but in a country with virtually no diversity and where even the disabled were shut away, his plan backfired, as children instead focused on the wonderful adventures of Tom Sawyer and Huck Finn. Just like us, children of that generation loved, and still love, Tom Sawyer. As a result Mr. Twain withstood the test of time and still stands in a prominent place in Herastrau Park.

Since Michael Jackson's death in 2009, his tribute has become a destination stop. He is a legend in Romania because only three years after Communism fell, Michael Jackson brought the phenomenal Dangerous tour to Bucharest. It was no ordinary concert. In fact, it was such a sensation that it was broadcast *live* in over sixty countries and at the time was reportedly the highest-watched show on HBO. One can only imagine the enthusiasm felt by the young people on that amazing day when their struggling country was the center of the world.

Unfortunately, the only notable thing I remember about that concert was that Michael Jackson stood on the balcony of the palace—where my husband now worked—and yelled to the adoring crowds, "Hello, Budapest!" instead of "Hello, Bucharest!" Budapest is in Hungary. It was a monumental faux pas for which he was roundly booed, although once his concert began, he was quickly forgiven.

I thought it was as good a day as any to photograph the Twain and Jackson monuments and send the photos to some friends in the States. So, with Scout on his leash, we proceeded on a scavenger hunt to locate them in the huge park. Before we found either destination, I was surprised to see Anna jogging around the lake's edge.

"Wow, I'm glad I ran into you," she said, huffing and stopping, only to jog in place. "I was going to call as soon as I finished my run."

"What is it?"

"I think that Tina woman is in the hospital."

"That's not possible—she's with Candi in Croatia."

"Well, the woman I told you about from my shelter went to the emergency room for a bad cut. She said she saw Tina, or whatever her real name is, taken into the hospital on a stretcher. She looked badly injured."

"When? When did you hear this?" I tried to act as if the information was irrelevant to me, but I couldn't help but react otherwise.

"I stopped by the shelter on my way here, so just a few minutes ago. I had to meet the other runners and was worried I wouldn't have enough time to talk to you before our run." I could see the backs of her group as they jogged out of our sight.

"Did she hear the woman's name or anything?"

"She heard a man say another name in French, but he had an accent and she couldn't tell what he was saying. That's all I know."

"It's probably not Tina, but if you hear anything else, let me know." I had to say that—that it probably wasn't Tina—because I knew that if I believed it was Tina, then every bit of my willpower not to fall to pieces over Candi would evaporate.

"Jeni, I know you're trying to be strong, but listen to me," Anna said, earnestly looking into my eyes. "I think this woman in the hospital is Tina. I'm not sure we can do anything about it, but it changes things. Let me finish up. We can talk more later." With that she ran off, adjusting her earplugs, while I stood with my mind now numbed, looking at her back as she ran.

I should do that, I told myself as I stood there, still in shock over her news. *I should jog instead of walk.* But I knew I wouldn't. Walking was my choice of exercise. I walked everywhere, sometimes out of necessity when Zach had our car, and sometimes because it was simply easier than driving in Bucharest and finding parking. Mostly it was because Bucharest had broad sidewalks, parks on every corner, and pleasant neighborhoods. And, frankly, I wasn't a runner.

Two young lovers were on the bench ahead of me, oblivious to my angst. Public displays of affection, or PDAs, weren't frowned upon in Romania, at least not yet.

When my thoughts went to the young lovers, the anxiousness over Candi that was always within me once again bubbled up, casting a pall over the beautiful scenery. I wanted to believe she was safe and madly in love with a perfect man, but the longer I heard nothing from her, the more concerned I became. Anna's news confirmed my belief that something was wrong, no matter how hard I searched for an innocent explanation for Candi's departure and current AWOL status.

Anna called me when I returned to the apartment, just as she had promised.

"I talked to the woman at the shelter again. I think it was definitely Tina in the hospital because she was wearing a dress with an African print."

"Are you sure?"

"Yes, and it's unusual for Bucharest. That's why the woman remembered it."

"Anything else?" I asked.

"No, but she swears it is the woman who approached her asking questions."

Later that afternoon, I sat outside on the steps to our apartment with an equally sad Scout and waited for Zach to come home. Zach had told me he would come home early. Once he arrived and pulled me up into his arms for a hug, I told him about Anna's news as we walked up the steps to our apartment.

"That's not good news," he said, rubbing my back to comfort me. "I'll try to find out if the agents know about her, but I'll be in and out of the office tomorrow. It may be later before I know anything."

"That's okay," I said. I had little optimism that anyone would know her.

"I did think of something on my way home from work, something you could do," he said lightly, attempting to brighten me up. "Maybe you should go to the store where Candi bought the clothes to see if they know anything."

I couldn't believe I hadn't thought of that. I would do it first thing the next morning.

The rest of the evening, we nibbled on food and watched a documentary on the Japanese TV channel. Every once in a while I would look at the computer screen for a message from Candi, but nothing came.

"Tomorrow I'll have to tell Sue that we haven't heard from Candi," I told Zach.

"Yes, and I'm sure it will upset her."

With that we clicked off the TV and went to bed without further talk.

Bus no. 32 was the fastest route from our apartment to the enormous modern mall in Pipera, right outside a fancy suburb north of the city and conveniently next to the US Embassy. The bus was almost empty when I got on, and it arrived at the mall in no time at all. Like malls all over the world, this one opened at 10:00 a.m. and not a second earlier.

When mall security finally opened the doors to the main entrance, I walked past the Starbucks, the tempting local chocolate shops, and Cinnabon (yes, it is there and smelling delectable) and ignored dozens of the best food shops from across the world. The restaurants were anchored around the bustling McDonalds, which sometimes whispered to me a warm welcome in a sea of unfamiliarity. The truth is that the food court was about the only thing I could ever easily find in this sprawling mall, and only because of the mixture of international smells. Once I escaped the pastry aromas, I got lost in the three-story semicircular building with two parallel sets of shops on each floor and random escalators. The floor layout was as whimsical and unpredictable as the park paths.

The expensive stores were generally scattered about, but I finally spotted the shop I was looking for. Thinking ahead, I stopped outside for a second or two and observed it from afar. I needed to concentrate on my game plan.

I wasn't sure there were more than a hundred items in the store. It was more focused on décor than on shirts and pants. Its walls were decorated with shards of purple and yellow glass suspended on almost invisible wires, as images of international runway models flashed from flat-screen TVs placed above each of the clothes racks. Most of the clothes were arranged along the walls, partitioned by little half walls that made them appear more select.

In order to mentally prepare for what would be an awkward conversation, I took a quick look at my reflection in a nearby mirrored wall and pushed a stray hair out of my eyes. *Ugh,* I thought. *Why didn't I wear heels?* But it was too late to turn back now, so I stood tall and charged in like I was a regular customer and knew exactly what I was doing. After making a beeline for a rack of lace skirts, I held one up to inspect it more closely. This was an unwritten signal that I was a real shopper and worthy of engagement.

As I hoped, the smartly dressed store clerk in strappy high sandals took the bait, clicking her heels across the wooden and then Plexiglas floor as she came over to help me. First she spoke to me in Romanian. I started to respond in kind, but she easily and quickly transitioned to English in order to facilitate the potential sale.

"This looks like a good gift for my niece," I said, holding up a tiny black lace skirt. The movement of the skirt allowed the fancy price tag to fall free. I held back a gasp. Over $300, if my conversion calculations were correct. I tried to appear as if I hadn't seen it or, if I had, that the price didn't matter. I needed a much longer conversation with the clerk about Candi and wanted to keep the clerk hopeful for a sale.

"It's so beautiful. I'm sure she will love it. It's our best seller," she said, smiling with all her gleaming white teeth exposed.

"I'm not sure what size I should get. How does it fit?"

"Well, it fits a bit small." Of course, I knew that they always fit small in these shops. It was clearly a badge of honor for an upscale European chain.

"Hmm," I said as I inspected the lining of the skirt.

"Do you have any idea of her size?" she said, trying to keep me interested. She knew that as long as the skirt remained in my hand, a sale was possible.

"No, but I have her picture, and perhaps you can tell from looking at her. I think she shops here." With that, I pulled my embarrassingly cheap phone out of my ordinary purse and showed her Candi's picture. The clerk didn't seem to notice either the purse or the phone, which are both usually indicators of a patron's shopping wallet size.

"Yes, *I know her*!" The clerk's enthusiasm was immediate and heartfelt in a very commercial kind of way. "She bought some dresses here not too long ago. She would be a size 6, I think." Taking initiative, she began searching for a skirt in the correct size before even asking me if I wanted her to do so.

"I'm glad you remember her. I think she was with her friend Tina," I said.

"No, she wasn't with a woman when I saw her. She was with two men, and they paid for her purchases."

This stunned me. It took a second or two for me to respond.

"Oh. Do you know who they were?" I asked, trying to be casual.

"No, but I assumed one of them was her boyfriend. He was really nice to her and they seemed to like each other a lot. The older man seemed to be telling her what she should buy. He appeared to be the one with the money."

"Oh, her boyfriend. Was this the one from Moldova? You know, Candi has lots of boyfriends. I have a hard time keeping up with them." I tried to be light and breezy, but I'm sure I sounded like a nosy old woman.

"I don't think he was from Bucharest, but I didn't pay too much attention. I remember that they paid in cash, or I would check for more information. Do you like the skirt?"

"I do, but I'm reluctant to get it without her approval. She's so picky."

"Really? I didn't see that when she was here last time. In fact, the older man chose the clothes, she tried them on, and then she modeled them for both men, you know, for their approval. She didn't seem to mind the modeling. Now, she did laugh at the clothes sometimes, but she never complained about the ones they picked out."

That sounded like Candi. She would think the whole clothes shopping lark was funny. Clothes had never been her highest priority, which was probably a rebellion against her fashionable sister.

"It depends on what she's buying. She'll probably call tonight. I'll come back."

"What about you? You two look a lot alike. I bet the skirt would be pretty on you as well." I had to give her credit for effort.

"Maybe I should consider it," I said. The thought took me aback. Wasn't that what I had been saying? I needed to get a skirt like that. I needed to loosen up. But although I tried hard to make myself buy the skirt, in the end I still couldn't do it. It cost too much.

"Not today. Thanks ever so much. Mulţumesc."

With that, we said our goodbyes, with her knowing that I would never return for the skimpy black lace skirt.

I went home from the mall without any purchases. My mind was full of both rational and irrational responses to the news from the dress store.

Maybe Tina really is in the hospital, I pondered with a sickening feeling. I didn't want to believe she was hurt or possibly dead. Although initially I had worried that Tina meant trouble for Candi, now I was forced to consider that I may have been wrong. *What if the slight French woman with her thick hair and odd clothes had been my niece's protector? What if something was now terribly wrong with her? What if Candi is in trouble too?* I had to find out more.

Chapter Nineteen

"ANNA, IT'S ME, Jeni. What hospital is that Tina woman in?" I said into the phone. I was alone on my seat in the bus and free to talk for a minute or two.

"Floreasca—right by you. Why?"

"I don't know. Maybe I can find something out if I go there in my role as the ILB president. Maybe they'll tell me if she is there."

"Sounds like a smart thing to do at this point. Let me know what you find out."

Floreasca Hospital was within walking distance from my apartment. Instead of just taking off right away, I stopped at home to grab a quick lunch and put on my best walking shoes.

I hoped that the long walk would give me time to figure out a plan. It didn't. Upon my arrival at the hospital, there was no great epiphany. I decided I would have to just wander around and look through open doors.

All hospitals are a bit alike with wards and operating rooms in different areas. That eliminated half of the hospital. Once I located the wards, I also eliminated those with children or with women having babies. This plan, I thought, no longer seemed so daunting, but I was quickly proved wrong.

For almost an hour I wandered through the halls and peered into various rooms. I walked the same halls so many times that ultimately my actions aroused suspicion. The attendant, who must have doubled as the designated hospital bouncer, stopped me by tapping me on my shoulder and speaking in Romanian. He let me know that he did not speak English, but he appeared to want to help me as opposed to arrest me. As a result of his kindness, I started to describe Tina.

"*Doamna* … French …" I began, but he abruptly interrupted me.

"Da, da," he said.

Yes, yes? I was confused, but before I could try to communicate further, the attendant's earlier patient disposition suddenly evaporated and I could tell he had other things to do.

He hurriedly pointed to the end of the hallway where a security guard sat. Soon he was back to his work and rushing to stop an elderly patient from straying too far from his room.

The lone guard was sitting outside a hospital room door with his chair tilted against the wall. I hoped he spoke some English and could point me in the right direction. Romanians had not yet learned about HIPAA, the US law that forbids hospitals and doctors from releasing private information about their patients.

"Er, excuse me," I tentatively said as the guard's eyes bored into me with a menacing stare. It was odd that he wasn't wearing a hospital uniform. *Is he private duty?* It was just as I started to ask about Tina that I heard someone come up behind me.

"Pardon, Jaynee." He pronounced my rather simple name with a smooth silky French accent. There was no doubt he was talking to me.

I turned around and looked into the blue eyes of the most handsome man in the world. He could have killed me right there and I would still be thinking about the fact that his eyes were the color of the Mediterranean Sea. He wore a light blue shirt under his European suit. It could only have been Armani. Even his fashionable tie had thin blue and white stripes, making the mysterious man look like he'd been picked out by central casting for a major motion picture.

At the sound of the man's voice, the guard's metal chair clanked back down to the tiled floor and he stood up.

"Nu problemo," the French man said to him, and the guard relaxed before sitting back down. Still, his eyes never left me and his trigger hand never left his right pocket.

"How do you know me?" I asked as boldly as I could.

"This is you, is it not?" he said. With that, he showed me a picture taken at the International Ladies of Bucharest meeting at the Hotel Intercontinental.

How unnerving! Plus, it was really awful. I was eating a chocolate croissant with my mouth wide open. I shook the image out of my head. The photograph could only mean that I had been under some sort of surveillance.

"You are Candi's aunt, no?" he asked, although he knew the answer was yes. He casually slipped the photo away in his inside front right suit pocket.

"Yes, do you know her?" My heart almost stopped. What *was* Candi involved in?

"Please, let me buy you an espresso and we can talk," he said smoothly as if he were inviting me to sip champagne.

I waited a second to ponder what other options I had. It was then that I remembered why I was there, and I pointed to the guard and the locked hospital room.

"Okay, but first, is Tina in there?"

"Oui."

So she was there and he knew this woman, whose real name was not Tina. I was too curious to walk away. If the only way to get answers to my niece's disappearance was to follow him to the coffee machines, then I would do so.

Once the vending machine had dispensed coffee into thin plastic cups that we now held, he put his free hand on the small of my back. The gentle pressure guided me to an open table, and then he deftly pulled out a bulky wooden chair and offered it to me. I lowered myself into it without comment. Once I was settled in my chair, he adjusted his slightly so that we looked directly into one another's eyes.

For several seconds he did not speak but rather leaned forward with his hands on his knees and gazed intently into my eyes as if he could determine my trustworthiness by telepathy. In the end, he must have decided that I was okay and it was safe to tell his story. He sat up tall and had a sip of the espresso.

"My name is Jean-Claude. I am an Interpol agent assigned to a human trafficking task force. Tina, whose real first name is Antoinette, is my colleague."

With that bombshell, I jumped back in my chair as if jolted by a small shock of electricity.

He appeared to take no notice of my reaction, but rather paused and took a sip of coffee. When he spoke again I was sitting on the edge of my seat so as not to misunderstand a word of what he was telling me.

"We have traced a ring of traffickers to Bucharest. Antoinette thought she knew the woman who died in the park. It was very sad, no?"

"Yes, it was." I responded.

"We think she was on her way to slavery, but we could prove nothing. The police checked and have confirmed she died of a drug overdose. She had bruises on her arms and neck, but they were from a few days before."

"Was she Romanian?" I asked.

"We think she might have come from a Moldovan village where other women have gone missing in recent days. We are checking on that," he said.

"Oh no."

"Oui, I am afraid it is true. Tina—*excuse moi,* Antoinette—is very brave, and she volunteered to go undercover as a person who helps people get jobs. She went to the Hotel Intercontinental, which is where some of our criminal suspects like to stay. It was the same day that you and Candi were there."

I listened intently as he told me what he knew, or perhaps only what he wanted me to know. Antoinette had been in the lobby when she saw Candi talking to a young man who was with an older guy they believed was involved with the traffickers. She pretended to be joining ILB in order to speak with Candi.

"It worked. Candi sat with Antoinette, and Candi told her about her encounter with the younger man," he said. Then he paused to think for a second. "From now on I shall call Antoinette by the name Tina, as that is the name you know. It is simpler."

"Thanks," I said. It was already confusing enough.

He said that Tina thought the younger man was overly interested in Candi and she became worried. That is why she went out clubbing with Candi one night. After that night she told Jean-Claude that she was even more concerned about Candi's safety.

She knew that both men thought that Candi was on her own in Bucharest. Candi kept saying that she was backpacking through Europe and staying with different friends and relatives. Tina hadn't told the men that she knew the truth, that Candi was with her aunt and diplomat uncle. Instead, she had played up Candi's story.

"Who are these men?" I asked, absorbing the shocking news as best I could.

"Tina said the younger man who liked Candi is from Moldova, and his first name is Dimitri. His last name is somewhere in my notes. He does not appear in any criminal database—not even a traffic ticket. With Dimitri, surveillance was difficult. A few minutes at a time at the club was all Tina could manage."

He told me that Tina had instead focused most of her surveillance efforts on the older man. A source told her she needed to watch him closely. Unfortunately, the hotel clerks did not have his real name. His room had been rented in the name of a defunct business, and another person's passport had been used for identification.

"She told me that he was Italian-looking and looked powerful in a *very bad way*," Jean-Claude said.

"Why would someone from Italy be involved in trafficking? Doesn't it make more sense that he was scouting for potential models?"

"Oui, that is one possibility. But do you know that Italy is the main gateway for incoming sex slaves to Europe due to its *grand* coastline? They also do not worry so much about prostitution. That is a possibility as well."

"*Sex slaves*? You've got to be kidding. You don't think that what's happening here, do you? Not Candi!"

He shrugged his shoulders. "Maybe not. Maybe she is just along for the ride," he said.

"That's also crazy. Candi is the most caring person in the world. That would never happen."

Again, he shrugged. I wasn't willing to let the matter go.

"Okay, let's think through this. You don't have any reason to believe Dimitri is involved in human smuggling, do you?"

"*Non*—right now it is his companion that worries us."

"So then you have no evidence that Candi is either," I said.

By then my mind was reeling with the information Jean-Claude had divulged—or, in the case of two men, the sparse nature of it. It was then that I remembered why I was there in the first place: to check on Tina.

"Did you know that Candi has left? I think she went to Italy with Dimitri." I told him about the note she left and the clothes she purchased.

"Non. That is not good news," he said. "I did not know. But there is a chance that I know where she might be. When Antoinette—*excuse moi,* Tina—was with Candi and Dimitri that night, the two of them talked about a trip to Croatia and Italy. Tina reflected that she couldn't hear all the details over the loud music, but she was concerned enough to document it in her report. Dimitri told Candi he had a small job on a yacht and offered to take her with him to Italy in order to get a job modeling in Milan. He told her he had friends there. Tina wrote in her report that she told Candi to wait and maybe go on a later trip.

"Sadly, that is the last report I received," Jean-Claude said. "Yesterday she was found on the top of a balcony canopy two floors below her apartment. She was badly injured and has not regained consciousness." He paused. "The police said it was because of drugs."

"Drugs? Did she use drugs?" I asked.

"*Non!* The police said they were in her apartment, but I doubt they found any in her blood. The results will be back soon. It would be easier for the police if it were about drugs. No one cares. One policeman told me she looked like just another French drug addict jumping out of a window."

With that Jean-Claude grumbled something in French that let me know the comment had angered him. He took a breath and leaned toward me even closer.

"Such an idea is preposterous!"

I had to agree. The Tina I met didn't appear to be a drug user. But then, in the back of my mind, I wondered if perhaps Jean-Claude protested too much. I found I was still unable to discern who was good and who wasn't in this sea of Italians, Moldavans, Frenchmen, and Romanians.

Jean-Claude continued, oblivious to my doubts.

"Someone wanted to force drugs into her and cause an overdose. I believe that she jumped out of the window to save her life. An undercover agent knows all the safe ways out of a place, and jumping onto a fixed canopy would have been one of the options. *And she is the best undercover agent I have worked with in my career.*"

"It doesn't make sense. Who would want to hurt her? It couldn't have been Dimitri if he was with Candi."

"The police said that witnesses have told them that two men entered the apartment at one point, but no one knew anything about them other than they looked like they were Romanian. They both wore sunglasses and caps."

As soon as he'd found out about her fall, Jean-Claude told me that he arranged for a guard to watch the hospital room and made sure Tina received good medical care at the hospital. He paid the attendants to give her the best doctor, paid for her bed to be changed, and paid for appropriate pain medication, which Romanian hospitals don't provide. Mostly, he paid for the guard to keep her safe while he tried to find the men who had done this to her.

"I'm so sorry about your colleague," I said.

"And I, mademoiselle, am sorry about Candi," he said.

That brought me back into the real world.

"Yes, Candi. What do you think I should do?" I asked him.

"I cannot go to Croatia until I have things in order here. When Tina awakens, she may need surgery. Then I can go find your niece."

That was terrible news. Anytime other than the present seemed too long to wait.

"But, but … do you even know where she is in Croatia?" I asked, my voice stammering over this news.

"Tina told me she heard them talking about a yacht. I can only assume it will eventually dock in Split, where all big boats go."

I knew all about Split from the articles about Yacht Week—it was yachts and partiers. Just like that, the light bulb went on in my mind and a plan began to formulate.

Before I could say more, Jean-Claude's phone rang and he signaled that he must leave. Before departing, he took a card from his front pocket and, with the subtle flair of a Frenchman, slid it into my hand as I sat still in my chair. He curled my fingers around the card and held them in place while he looked at me intently. Then he stood, and kissed my cheeks goodbye, first on the left and next on the right, a customary Romanian farewell. The smell of his aftershave lingered long after he had left the room.

For once I was speechless.

Chapter Twenty

THE OLD BLUE suitcase that had traveled the world sat ready to go at the front door, stuffed with a mixture of clothes for a trip that was not for vacation, education, family, or business. At first I was stumped as to what I would need to bring. What was the appropriate attire for spying?

I ultimately decided upon knit sundresses, light sweaters, and similar packable clothes that could pass for casual business dress if needed. I added one bathing suit for a day at the beach, in the hope that I might discover that Candi was fine.

At the last minute, I tossed in a go-to-court suit because realistically I needed to plan for the worst-case scenario. What if Candi was in jail? *What if I was arrested?* It could happen in a foreign country if I was without diplomatic privileges or had questionable privileges at best.

I was in a melancholy mood when Zach came home.

"Going somewhere?" Zach asked as he unloaded a stack of files on the table.

"Yes, we need to talk. But first, what are all those files?"

"It's all reading about some regional political issues that I've been putting aside until I had time to analyze them. Work has slowed down so much that I thought I'd take advantage of the summer lull and read them now. I was just thinking on the way home that it's a shame you didn't plan a summer trip. If you had, I could take them to read on the beach."

Suddenly he stopped moving for a second, looked at the suitcase once again, and turned to look me in the eyes. His manner changed.

"However, I have to say that now it appears you're going somewhere without me. You're not smiling and you're not happy. I'm not sure what this means, but it can't be good." He paused for a moment and then he spoke, but this time so softly I almost couldn't hear him.

"Part of me isn't so sure I want to know what *is* going on." I could see his shoulders droop at this comment.

"Zach, it's been a long day. Pour a glass of wine and I'll fill you in."

For the next half hour I told Zach the information I'd gathered from the store and the hospital. He was both mesmerized about Tina, or rather Antoinette, and genuinely relieved that I wasn't leaving him.

"Jean-Claude? Do you know more about him?" he asked when I was through.

I knew Zach would seize upon that one name, as it was my only real chance at corroborating evidence. Plus, Zach's agency worked with Interpol.

"Yes, here's his card." I put into Zach's hand the standard government-issued piece of identification that Jean-Claude had given me at the hospital.

With that, Zach took out his cell phone and called the number on the bottom left corner.

"Bonjour, Jean-Claude. Je suis Zach ..." Before I could hear more, Zach walked out to the terrace with his phone in one hand and a glass of red wine in the other. I had no idea whether he was moving away from where I stood in order to get better reception or to avoid me repeatedly asking "What is he saying?"

Too anxious to idly sit and wait for news about the call, I went into the tiny kitchen, put two dinner plates on a tray, and then filled them with fresh tomato and cucumber salad and cabbage rolls from the neighborhood restaurant. I liked to shop at the market and prepare dinner at night, but it was far too difficult for me to replicate the moist and flavorful Romanian cabbage rolls. Since Zach liked them so much, we had agreed that we would order out on busy days. This definitely counted as a busy day.

By the time I finished getting organized for the meal and had taken the tray to the terrace, his conversation was ending.

"Oui, oui, au revoir," Zach said. He hung up the phone.

"Did you really speak in French the whole call?" I asked incredulously. Zach was good but not that good.

"No, we spoke in English for the most part. I guess you want to know what he said?"

"I can't believe you'd even ask."

"How about if I just tell you that I also need a suitcase? I think I'll join you. It's as good a place as any to use up some vacation time."

At first, I smiled broadly. This was good news, but it unleashed a torrent of questions in my mind.

"So, did he confirm everything? Does he know if Candi is okay?"

"It's strange that I don't know him, but he says it is his first case in Romania. By the way, you did an amazing job today following your instincts. As for Candi, I think she's physically okay because she has no value to them if she isn't. I hate to speculate too much beyond that. We may find her in Croatia and discover that she's run off with the nicest guy in town, at which point we can go relax on the beach. So far, no one knows much. And until the woman you call Tina recovers or the blood tests are back, we don't even know why she jumped from or fell out of her window. I'm not sure we can do anything in Croatia beyond getting a tan, but I'll get tickets to leave tomorrow."

"Not leave tonight?" How would I ever sleep?

"I wish we could, but both you and I have had contact with a French Interpol agent and I should report it to Matt. It's the rule. In fact, it's a fairly important rule."

"What if he says we can't go?"

"He won't, primarily because it's our vacation and also because Candi isn't committing a crime or anything like that. I'm sure he'll be fine with a simple report about the contact, and then we can leave."

"I'll be crazy stressed all night." I was already visibly agitated and pacing the terrace.

"I'm going to write a quick report about my call to Jean-Claude. It might be a good time for you to write Sue."

I groaned, but I knew he was right. It had been over four days now. I went inside to the computer and forced my fingers to type.

Dearest Sue,

I know you are wondering about Candi. I have not heard from her but was told that she might be in Croatia on a yacht and then headed to Italy. Her phone must not be working. The good news is that Zach has some time off and we're going there tomorrow as well. I think it's Yacht Week. We are going to Split, which is where all the yachts pick up their charters.

I want to check on her and get more details about her trip to Italy. Is it possible for you to check her credit cards to see if they have been used? That might give me information about where she has been. Then I can track her down and get her a new phone.

I know her new friend's name is Dimitri and he's from Moldova. He should be easy enough to spot in Croatia.

I hope you are still having fun on your trip. Don't let any of this bother you. Europeans do this all the time.

Love and kisses,
Jeni

I read it several times before I hit Send. What signals would she pick up on?

Thirty minutes later my phone rang.

"Jeni, it's Sue."

"What a surprise! Are you okay?" I said.

"Jeni, no, of course not. Oh my gosh, what is going on?" I could tell Sue's tight control was slipping. "What has happened to Candi? What do you mean, you don't know who she is with or where they are going? Look, I've borrowed a satellite phone and don't have much time, but this is awful. *No,* I don't have a record of any charges made by her. *No,* I haven't heard anything from her. Neither has Kate. You know yourself that she hasn't posted anything on social media either ..." At that moment I could sense a pause in her voice, giving me enough time to interrupt her.

"I didn't mean to worry you. This guy she is with, Dimitri, might really care for her. Candi said he is a gentleman. She fell for him before I knew it. I just want to find out her plans and make sure they aren't going somewhere with Dimitri's older Italian friend."

"What older Italian friend?" Sue's voice became elevated with a sharpness I had never heard from her. She was clearly becoming more upset.

"Well, I don't really know much about him. Don't jump to conclusions, but I've been told that he might not be a good guy," I said, knowing that was not going to help the situation with Sue at all.

"This is insane. Who said she was in Croatia?" I could almost see her shaking her head in disbelief.

I took a breath. I had hoped she wouldn't ask that question.

"Some embassy friends and an Interpol agent from France."

"An Interpol agent from France? Is Candi in trouble? Should I fly there? Why an Interpol agent? Oh, Jeni, are you telling me everything? Why aren't the police looking for her?"

"It's a long story—probably too long for this call—but please, please trust me: it is not Candi that Interpol thinks is bad."

I told her what I knew, that Candi had been with Dimitri and the Italian guy when the Interpol agent first saw her. Nothing else was clear other than the fact that Candi went willingly with Dimitri to Italy. That is why the police couldn't do anything. I emphasized that Candi didn't seem in fear for her life; she'd packed a suitcase and left a happy note.

"Sue, I promise—you don't need to come right now. I'll go to Croatia and find Candi and send you pictures. If I don't find her or if I get worried that she is in trouble, I'll let you know so you can fly here right away. But for now, assume she is okay. Please?"

"I can't help but worry. I don't know a thing about Croatia or Yacht Week."

I wanted to tell her not to look up Yacht Week, but she was too smart. It would be the first thing she would do.

"I'm learning all about it. Let me handle this for now. I know I have said it already, but please trust me." To my dismay, I could hear Sue's rapid breathing on the other end of the line. She wasn't ready to trust anyone yet.

"I should have let her go to India. Instead I sent her to stay with you—and *we may never see her again*. Bob is beside himself with worry. I thought you told me eastern Europe was *so* safe," she said, her anger now mixed with her anguish.

"It *is* safe. I don't know what Candi was thinking by leaving like that, but she's smart and we'll find her."

"I don't know … I don't know if you can take care of this. We're her parents after all. Bob wants to leave the cruise and fly there immediately," she said.

"*No, please don't.* You wouldn't even know where to go. I promise I'll call as soon as I know more, and then you can fly here."

"Jeni, I want to trust you and Zach, but look what's happened. If I don't come right now, can I trust you to tell me everything when you know it? Do you promise you won't hide anything from me?"

"I won't keep anything from you," I said, knowing just how hard that promise would be to keep. "And I intend to find her. Nothing will stop me."

After a few more minutes of talk, I could hear Sue's voice finally return to a semblance of normal. She reluctantly gave me more time to find Candi and said they would wait to hear from me before taking any action. Then she said a teary goodbye from the other side of the globe. I didn't tell her, but I wanted to cry as well.

Chapter Twenty-One

"WE FLY OUT at two o'clock this afternoon," Zach told me the next morning after he had talked to Matt. I had waited over two hours for those words, and what a relief they were. It turned out that Matt hadn't objected to the trip, but he did tell Zach that if we found Candi in trouble, *we were not* to take the matter into our own hands. Zach said Matt was even sympathetic, knowing that young visitors are always making crazy choices. He said the good news is that they usually turned out to be okay. Matt was of the mind that Candi was just a pretty girl with a rich boyfriend and that the worst thing that could happen was a broken heart.

"Come on, Zach, really. Who would kidnap a diplomat's niece?" Matt had done his best to assuage Zach's fears.

Matt was right, but what Matt didn't know was that Candi hadn't told them about us.

Zach used the embassy travel office to help with the trip details, but that never helped on the price for a vacation. This time it was an eleventh-hour decision, which meant using our own credit card and getting hit with lots of added costs for the last-minute flights in the middle of the high season. Plus we got terrible seats. The good news was that it was a short flight with only one connection between Bucharest and Split.

I was energized about the trip. We were finally doing something to find Candi. Suddenly, I felt like Matt might be right. Maybe Candi was okay. Because Zach was going along, I went back to the suitcase and threw in a dress for a romantic evening out. One never knew.

Zach got cash from the embassy bank and some dog food from the commissary. He left the key to our apartment with Collin, who had volunteered to watch Scout. Finally, he picked up a short guidebook on Split, Croatia, from the lending library for me to read. Things were falling into place.

It was a good thing Zach had brought me the book on Split so I could have a more enlightened understanding of the region other than its pet population. I devoured snippets of its incredible history while on the plane ride.

Although it's a busy port city, Split is best known for Diocletian's Palace, built for the Roman emperor Diocletian's retirement on May 1, 305. What happened within a mere decade of time almost two thousand years ago still defines Split today in the twenty-first century.

Emperor Diocletian was born in a place that looked a lot like Split. As legend has it, when he decided to leave Rome in a voluntary abdication, he was drawn to the climate and terrain of what is modern-day Split. Others say it was not such a romantic plan, that Split was chosen because it was a safe location; it had a peninsula, was easy to defend, and was far away from Rome.

The "palace" is not so much a palace as it is an enormous square fortress in the middle of Split's city center, with four major entrances called the Golden Gate, the Brass Gate, the Silver Gate, and the Iron Gate. The grand and elaborate Golden Gate is the main entrance and is the one through which Diocletian first entered his retirement home. Historians point out that the palace had been built so large because it housed not only the emperor and his entourage but also an entire Roman military garrison. It was built out of the unique white stone found only on the tiny Croatian island of Brac. So, too, is our White House built of Brac stone—a source of pride for Croatians.

The structure is in wonderful condition—a rare feat for old fortresses. That is primarily due to the fact that as cultures changed throughout the centuries, residents simply built upon the old ruins rather than destroyed them. They kept the walls for protection. Sometimes they cleverly repurposed old artifacts for their "newer" homes, giving historians a window into architecture and embellishment across the ages. Extensive restoration efforts by the government have revealed many rooms once buried underground in the rubbish of generations past. Much has been uncovered and examined from a historical perspective, but it is very much a work in progress. On a really hot day, the refuse that still remains within the palace emits its original aroma.

The best tour of the palace is that of the underground basement, but only if given by a good local guide. It is an exact footprint of what the main floor of the building would have been if left completely intact. In fact, the palace is so authentic that a whole season of *Game of Thrones* was filmed there.

In the almost two millennia after Diocletian's death, the people of Split have lived within the walls of the palace, each generation building upon the foundations of the others. Zach said our apartment for the evening was in one of those dwellings within the palace walls.

I have been to many airports in the world and can say with confidence that when I walked out of the front doors of Split Airport and gazed upon the blue-green surface of the Adriatic Sea, it was the most stunning view from any airport I'd ever seen. With only a slight ripple of waves flickering in the sun and a smattering of sailboats on the horizon, it beckoned tourists to its shores.

I couldn't wait to join them. In no time at all we were in a cab and headed to the apartment we had rented for the night.

Quickly we discovered a problem. The cab could not go inside the palace walls.

The driver chided us for having been so foolish.

"Why did you stay inside the walls? Why did you not stay outside the palace where there is parking?"

He ended with "Why don't you stay at my friend's apartment?"

We had no satisfactory answers for him, but we kindly assured him that he didn't have to help us any further once we were safely at the Golden Gate of the palace. With that, we gamely began to walk through the rambling streets—or, more accurately, alleys. We rolled our own luggage because the only other option was to hire a small scooter with an open boxlike trailer on the back. When I first saw one of the homemade contraptions zooming down a narrow passageway in my direction, I plastered myself into a doorway to avoid being hit. It was overkill. It was clear that the drivers were not in the habit of running over tourists. And even if hit, I was unlikely to die in Diocletian's Palace by way of a moped or Vespa.

Zach and I roamed aimlessly, searching for our apartment, until the owner kindly sent us a text suggesting we stay in one spot and he would meet us. Per the reservation, an earnest young man met us with the key, directed us to the apartment, took our payment, showed us how to operate the hot water and the appliances, and gave us suggestions for the evening. Then he left us on our own.

"What next, fearless leader?" Zach said while he opened a window to welcome the fresh sea breezes. He had picked the apartment because of its view and location, and we weren't disappointed in either.

"I beg your pardon. I thought you were the leader now."

"I'm not sure that would work for long," he responded. "How about we pretend to be happy tourists and make decisions as we go? For now, I think the owner's idea of a glass of wine on the wharf is perfect. It's a likely place for someone like Candi to hang out."

"As usual, a perfect suggestion," I said. I realized that once we'd entered Split I had mellowed a bit. *Surely,* I thought, *nothing in this tranquil place could harm Candi.*

Chapter Twenty-Two

THE SEASIDE GATE of the palace opened up to an expansive stone walkway on the edge of the Adriatic Sea. The panoramic scene around us—a deep harbor, dazzling in the late afternoon—rendered us speechless. The lowering sun caused diamond reflections on the tops of small waves, while empty wooden fishing boats bobbed gently at their moorings, each one worthy to be in a great master painting.

The café table was the perfect spot both to watch people and observe the activity on the wharf and in the water. The harbor was a very ample horseshoe-shaped body of water with large ferries and cruise ships to the left, laid up against wide piers. Reaching them was a long walk but doable. On the right side, almost equidistant away, were the marinas and boatyards for private owners and chartered boats. In the middle or bottom of the horseshoe, where we sat, were ancient buildings, restaurants, outdoor cafés, shops, vendors, and row after row of park benches. Behind the restaurants were the palace and the Old City, and beyond that lay the mountains.

"What do you think now? This seemed like an obvious place to find her, but I haven't even seen anyone who closely resembles Candi," I said.

We had finished our meal, and it was time to leave. Zach once again stood and surveyed the area as best he could, before sitting back down and shaking his head.

"I know. It doesn't seem like she's here. In fact, there aren't many boats here—just lots of people. I thought it was Yacht Week."

Our waiter returned with our check—about a third of the price of a similar meal back in the States or in western Europe.

"Excuse me," I said. "Is this where all the yachts are?"

"Well, not right now. They should be here tomorrow morning. Most are chartered. They bring their guests back on Saturday, get cleaned up and restocked, and then leave again in the late afternoon. Although tomorrow might be different, as a *bura* is coming our way."

"Bura?" I asked. It sounded to me like he said "boar-ah."

"Yes. It is a strong storm that comes over the mountains and makes it hard for the mariners. It can flip boats over." He pointed to the mountains in the distance behind the palace. "Some of the boats may board new passengers and leave earlier than usual for safer harbor."

"Oh." That was not welcome news.

After we paid, Zach and I walked to the water's edge and strolled along the wharf because that is what Europeans do—stroll in the evening, not walk. We discovered a marina filled with charter vessels. The charter company had a fleet of Lagoon multihull boats (catamarans) and a smaller fleet of monohull boats. The catamarans were mostly built for sailors who wanted a houseboat-type experience with all the trimmings. A forty-foot-long Lagoon with four staterooms and four heads is twice as large as our first home and probably cost five times as much. Though catamarans are capable of tremendous speed, these were designed for safety and comfort.

"I think, given a choice, I would take this Benetau," Zach said, coveting the expensive high-gloss hull with an enticing charter sign on its mast. Male deckhands in matching shirts were scampering around the boat, shining the stainless winches and hardware, while a female housekeeping crew in the same matching shirts were changing the linens down below decks—presumably getting it ready for the guests tomorrow. I had to agree. It was beautiful with its blue-and-white-striped outdoor pillows and teak cockpit table, and I was sure it was fast.

I looked around and saw that the same sleek French sailboats in varying sizes were everywhere. It made sense. They were built for European waters.

It was then that I remembered that a couple of years back I had been told by someone that the EU gave money to people wanting to buy Benetaus for charter in order to prop up the marine business. It seemed like a much cooler program than our "cash for clunkers" stimulus bill.

By the time we were finished with our dinner and the walk, we were tired and it was dark. It was a beautiful starry night, which we might have enjoyed but for the fact that we had seen no sign of Candi. There was not much to say to each other. We simply resolved to do the same thing the next day, hoping she would eventually appear.

Zach's phone rang just as we entered the door to the apartment, startling us and breaking the quiet. It was late at night and we weren't expecting any calls, especially one with a US number.

He hit the speaker button before answering so I could hear the caller.

"Hello," he said tentatively. A call so late at night usually meant bad news. I began to prepare myself for whatever it was.

"Hello. I'm trying to reach Jeni. Is this, by any chance, her number?" I could hear the person speaking on the other end of the call. It was a deep southern voice with a slight drawl, and it sounded like an older gentleman.

"Well, before I say more, who's this?" Zach was always cautious, but he was even more so now.

"I apologize. My name is Robert Harrison. I'm trying to reach a woman named Jeni whose nieces were students of mine at Tulane University in New Orleans. I was given her number from Kate." Zach and I looked at each other. Indeed, this did not sound like it would be good news.

"You have the right number, and Jeni is listening in as well. My name is Zach. I'm her husband."

"Yes, I remember your name. Do you have a few minutes for me to tell you a rather odd story?"

When we answered affirmatively, he began to talk.

"I'm an English professor at Tulane, and Candi was one of my favorite students. She's bright, funny, and an excellent writer. In fact, she was a teaching assistant for me last summer."

I remembered her telling me about that summer job. He went on to say that the last thing he'd heard from her was that she was applying to graduate school for a degree related to sports and spending the summer in New Orleans playing golf.

"That's why I was shocked to see a young lady who looked like her in Hvar yesterday. I was walking past the yachts to an ice cream parlor when I saw her."

"Candi?" Zach and I said at the same time.

"Well, at first I wasn't certain. It was confusing because she wasn't dressed like the Candi I knew. I'm not sure how to describe it other than to say she was dressed up," he said. He went on to tell us that Candi was with several foreign men and that she wore very high heels, a short tight dress, hair piled up on her head, and lots of makeup.

"What did you do when you saw her?" I asked.

"At first I didn't think it was her—just a look-alike from another place. But then ..." He paused while we were on the other end of the line with bated breath.

When he got closer, he realized it was definitely Candi. She has a long scar on her right hand from a biking injury when she was a freshman. It couldn't be missed if you knew to look for it.

"That's true," I said.

"It was apparent to me by then that the young lady was pretending not to see me. It was very unusual, so I called her name out to see if she would answer me. It worked. Sort of. Both she and the men she was with turned to look at me, confirming that it was Candi—but she still said nothing. In fact, she seemed somewhat flustered."

"Nothing?" Zach asked.

"Nothing. So I introduced myself to the men. And still thinking it would be welcomed, I went to hug Candi."

He said she allowed it, but she was stiff and not friendly.

"I asked what she was doing in Hvar," he said.

Despite the easy question, the professor said that Candi searched for the right words to say, while her companions stared at her as if they wanted to know the answer as well. The silence was awkward, yet still she never spoke. Eventually the man who appeared in charge interrupted and said he was sorry, adding that they were expected for dinner and had to leave.

"That's when it became even more peculiar. I went to kiss Candi goodbye on each cheek—European style, of course—and I could have sworn I heard her whisper into my ear to call someone, but I couldn't understand the name," he said.

"Can you guess at it?" I asked.

"No. Not at all. I didn't press the matter because it was clear she didn't want them to hear whatever she was trying to tell me. Afterward, I decided that it only made sense to call Kate, who told me to call you. But the whole encounter was very strange."

"Was she hurt or in pain?" I asked.

"No. She wobbled a bit in her high heels, but she didn't look drunk or on drugs when she boarded an expensive blue yacht."

"That's great information. Do you have the yacht name?"

"I wrote it down on a receipt, but I'm truly embarrassed. I'm afraid that I seem to have left the paper in my hotel room, and I just left Hvar for Zagreb. I remember that it's a short name that begins with a *T.* It's docked on the main wharf," he said. Then he added with a bit of dismay that he was hoping we would know the yacht name. "I'm sure you can easily find it."

"Did you see the yacht leave?" Zach asked.

"Not while I was standing there, but I left shortly after I saw Candi. They are probably there for a night or two," he said. Then he asked what we knew about Hvar.

"Just a little. I read that it's popular with the young, rich, and famous, and that when the bars close down the partiers are ferried to another island to continue the nightly drinking," I replied. "It has the reputation as the premier partying destination in Europe. I don't know whether or not that reputation is deserved."

"That sums up the recent trend, I guess," he said. "I know it as an ancient port city with marvelous architecture. In fact, I was there for a conference on medieval literature. Unfortunately, it was accidentally scheduled the same time as Yacht Week."

He sounded not at all pleased by the onslaught of drunken young people. By then, I had a picture of him in my mind—scholarly, probably with glasses and a small gray beard.

"I may be wrong, but I'm concerned she is in over her head, or worse, in bad trouble," the professor concluded. "I hate to tell you because I know you'll worry, but I believe she asked me to let someone know that I saw her, so that is what I'm doing."

"Thanks. One more question if you don't mind: what did the man who spoke to you sound like?" I asked.

"He was from eastern Europe, but I don't know exactly where. He had dark hair and dark eyes and an average build. Most women would think he was handsome. I'm sorry, but I didn't pay much attention to the other men. They didn't speak."

By then we knew he had no more information to convey, so we thanked him profusely and offered to have dinner the next time we were in New Orleans. Once the call ended, Zach turned to me and smiled to keep me from crying.

"How about we go to the marina in the morning and hitch a ride on someone's boat to Hvar? I guess you know it's an island. The only way we can get out there is by boat. I'm sure there are a lot of boats headed there. In the meantime, please don't cry. This is good news. She's alive and we know where she is—on a yacht with rich men. I'm sure it's all fine."

With those comforting words, he hugged me until I was able to relax into his arms.

"I promise, Jeni, it'll be okay." He was doing his best to reassure me, but I wondered what he really thought.

It was Wednesday night and Candi had been gone for five days.

Chapter Twenty-Three

THE NEXT MORNING the blue skies were beginning to fill with wispy clouds and a strong breeze. I guessed the bura had already begun to blow from across the mountains. By the time we had finished our cups of Nescafé, the wind was really gusting. We had found the granules of coffee in small plastic wrappers on our dresser and had dissolved them in hot water from a kettle in the room. It was barely passable as coffee, but it gave us enough kick before we headed to the harbor early that morning to find a boat to Hvar.

Overnight the marina had filled with vessels ready to discharge their cargo, mostly consisting of sunburned and exhausted sailors. Now the charter boats were being readied to take on the fresh new crews and passengers. It was easy to tell the difference between the two groups. Zach went to the charter company and asked if there were any boats available for a trip to Hvar. The young man at the desk smirked and said something like, "Are you crazy?" We quickly learned that boats are chartered a year in advance for this time of the year.

"So, what do we do?" I asked Zach. "Perhaps we should take a tour boat or ferry. Maybe we aren't too late to get a ticket for today."

To contemplate our options, we went to enjoy a real cup of coffee and pastry in the restaurant next to the marina, an open-air bar and café with tables filled with expectant boaters who were watching their reserved slip for a chance to jump aboard their vessel of choice for a dream vacation.

"Say, you're Americans," a voice next to us said. We turned to see the smiling face of a gray-haired and very fit man at the next table. He had overheard us speaking. He waved his arm around the room to emphasize his words. "I think we're the only Americans here today."

"You're probably right. I'm Zach, and this is Jeni. We're sitting here and trying to figure out a way to Hvar."

"My name is Edwin. I'm headed there to meet up with friends. Right now I'm waiting for my partner, who is taking the boat over with me. I hope he hurries and gets here before the weather turns even worse. In any event, I think we may just go to Trogir for tonight, and then to Hvar the next day."

I couldn't help looking up. The clouds were becoming much more ominous, and the wind occasionally was gusting so hard that the canvas over the café shuddered with loud popping sounds.

"If all you're doing is looking for a ride, I don't mind you joining us. You'll be able to stay on the boat one night, and then when we get to Hvar you can jump ship. Once you are in Hvar, you'll have to get home on your own, but you can probably find a way without too much trouble."

"Really? If you don't mind, we'll take you up on your offer. We'll pay our fair share, and more. Zach, is that what you want to do?" I asked. I was desperate to get to Hvar. This was the perfect opportunity.

I looked at Zach, who nodded his approval. At the same time, he subtly put a finger to his lips and mouthed the name Candi. Knowing what he meant, I agreed: they didn't need to know the reason for our trip.

"It'd be a dream come true for me! What kind of boat did you reserve?"

"A 45 Benetau. And no worries about paying anything. I paid long in advance, and I'm not worried about that now. You do know how to sail, right?" I saw the man momentarily concerned that perhaps he had acted too rashly. He looked at Zach for a response.

"Yeah, I sailed at home. I haven't had the opportunity in Europe, but I should do fine," Zach responded. It was an understatement. Zach was a racer and a great helmsman. *And,* I thought testily, *I'm a good sailor as well, but nobody asked me.*

"Well, this will be fun because we're going to have some wind!" Edwin stood to shake our hands and told us to meet him in an hour at slip no. 10.

We went back to the apartment and threw some clothes in a duffel bag we'd bought at the market. It took less than an hour for us to get prepared and return to the marina. As we waited, the skies darkened and a light rain misted us—enough to make things slippery on the deck. The marina had become filled with foam as the choppy waves on the outside of the breakwater had doubled in size within just an hour's time.

It turned out that there were two more men, not one—Ted, the former business partner of the owner, and the Croatian captain. Edwin and Ted had owned a small bank and financial business, which they sold last year. It seemed to have been a very profitable sale.

The captain was young, tan, and dashingly handsome. I could tell he was also competent, but Edwin told us that he would make all the sailing decisions and take the helm. The captain was just there for translating and helping with the logistics. He gave us the basic information we needed to know about the boat, and remained on board in case we needed any kind of assistance.

"Okay, the weather is getting bad. We need to leave this harbor, or we may be stuck here for another day. We're going north to Trogir, where we'll spend the night in a nice slip. If the weather lets up, then we can easily head out to Hvar in the morning. To get to Trogir, we will have to be in the open water for a couple of hours. Just letting you know."

I whispered to Zach that this didn't sound like a good idea. It would be awfully rough outside of the protection of land. By then, the wind was blowing so hard that the mooring lines to the boat were taut. I saw other crews wrestling with their lines in order to keep from swinging into boats near them.

It also meant another night without Candi.

"Jeni, the tour boats aren't going out in this weather. The best thing we can do is go on a sailboat that can take the waves. Even tomorrow morning will probably be very rough. This is our only realistic shot to get there tomorrow."

It would have helped my argument if the other boats in the marina were staying put, but they weren't. One after the other they negotiated the narrow harbor exit in the awful weather and seemed to survive. The catamarans ahead of us bobbed up and down like yellow ducks in a bathtub as they headed to Trogir against the wind. I knew that their occupants were surely seasick as they slammed into wave after wave below the now-ominous skies.

By the time we pulled out, I was resigned to the fact that I would soon be joining them. Never would I have considered taking such risks with strangers before, but a feeling of desperation compelled me to find my niece. I had a palpable sense that she needed me, that it really was a matter of life or death.

The trip to Trogir was rough but worth the effort. Once we rounded the outcropping of land that protected the harbor, we entered into much calmer waters and a splendid harbor. If the marina in Split was for the rich, then this marina in Trogir was for the richer. It was filled to the brim with high-dollar boats, and only one slip remained unfilled—ours for the night. To get to it, we first passed by the part of the harbor that held the yachts too large for the marina. I estimated they were all more than a hundred feet long. Little did I know that I would soon discover that the vessels here, only one hundred feet in length, were the small yachts; the really large ones we would encounter in Hvar.

As usual, the docking in Split was stressful for me, finding mooring lines and carefully adjusting fenders to keep our sailboat off the adjacent boats' newly buffed hulls. This time it was even worse because I was paying attention to everything around us and found it hard to concentrate. We were smack-dab in the middle of a smorgasbord of the finest sailboats from virtually every place around the world, with many of them from countries that often served as tax havens—Malta, the United Arab Emirates, and Montenegro.

Nothing in my past life had prepared me for the opulence I would see on Croatian waters. Never mind the region's depressed economy, there were two rows of boats worth millions upon millions of dollars just on our single pier.

"It has to be hard for the residents," I told Zach. "We know how little they make."

I had to admit that it was also hard for me. It appeared that each sailboat was more impressive than the last, with the latest colors, gadgets, electronics, and styles out for show. The grandest boats were up against the marina's main bulkhead, and you could see their names in lights and watch as crew members adjusted tenders in large compartments under deck floors, with large doors that opened and slid them out to the sea.

That's right, they had hidden berths for their lifeboats. In the States Zach and I pulled our inflatable rubber tender behind the boat on a leash like a giant gray cork. Just the cost of the stainless steel winches on the sailboat next to us exceeded that of a new car. It was like the Miami Boat Show on steroids.

It bothered me greatly, but it was too hard to reconcile the inequality of wealth at the same time I was desperate to find Candi. I turned my attention back to the tasks at hand. Once we were satisfied that our rented catamaran was secure, Edwin instructed us to get ready, saying that we had reservations for dinner in the best restaurant in town. He wouldn't take no for an answer even though I pleaded "I'm too tired." Despite my protests, worries, and lack of appetite, I put on my only "going out" dress, added a red slicker for the rain, and pulled my hair into a respectable knot at the back. I hoped it would do for my first experience in *Lifestyles of the Rich and Famous*.

Chapter Twenty-Four

THE RESTAURANT WAS in the heart of the UNESCO-designated Old Town, on a small alley across from a centuries-old cathedral and a popular gelato shop. We slowly strolled to it past the crowded docks, stopping occasionally to comment on a particular boat or some specific gadget. It was worth the tortuous sail in order to be able to walk into the city from across the narrow old bridge that cinched the two sides of the harbor together at its narrowest point. The rain had finally ended and the city's lights offered a warm and welcoming glow. They were first mirrored in the harbor's rippling water, and next on the standing puddles in the cobblestone streets.

The clouds moved on toward Italy about halfway through the meal, revealing a crescent moon over the nearby tiny church's steeple. I was lulled into silence by the scene around me and the wine. I half listened to the men talk about the next day's sail and the marina in Hvar, but I spoke little as my mind kept drifting back to Candi and wondering what she was doing and whether she was safe. Each time I convinced myself I was being foolish by worrying, something within me would make the opposite case, arguing to me that she was in dreadful trouble.

When the check was paid, we all went our separate ways. Edwin returned to the boat to make some business calls, Ted went to find a pharmacy for allergy medicine, and the captain went to find his girl in this port. That meant Zach and I had an hour or so to wander around the city. For the first time ever, I understood how frustrating it must feel to be on a cruise ship. Although we weren't in the mood to sightsee, who can explore a city like Trogir in only one hour? I couldn't even do it if I had a full day.

It was when we were headed back to the boat that I saw a man walking in front of us, lugging two bags of clanking bottles from the local wine-and-spirits market. I absentmindedly watched his back as he ambled away from the city center. There was something about him that nagged me. I decided it was because he had a big bandage on his right hand between the thumb and middle finger, which had to be painful for him as he carried the heavy bags. After a minute or two, he darted in the opposite direction from us and then jumped aboard a sleek-looking motorboat that was waiting for him, its engine purring. As he boarded, he yelled to the driver in Romanian. Although it was at best only two or three words, his voice sent a chill through my spine.

"Did you see that guy?" I asked Zach. By then, the boat was throwing off its lines and the engines were roaring. In no time at all it was headed out to sea.

"The dark gray boat leaving now? I definitely saw the boat leaving in a hurry. I'm surprised he's allowed to throw a wake like that in a harbor and rock all the other boats."

"I know, they made quite a scene leaving, but there is something about him," I said as I watched the boat, now in the distance. Boat owners continued yelling their obvious anger toward the departing speedster.

Just as soon as I'd said it out loud, it dawned on me what it was that bothered me. It was the bandage on the hand carrying the bottles of liquor. It appeared to cover the very same finger that Scout had bitten belonging to the man in Bran. I tried not to jump to any wrong conclusions. Lots of men have mangled fingers, especially around marinas and in fishing communities. But the more I considered it, the more I began to panic. He was wearing a foul-weather gear jacket, but I just knew that if we checked under it, he would have a tattoo. And the voice—I'll never forget it. It was his voice.

"Zach." I turned to my husband and pulled him close so that he was looking me in the eye. "I know where I saw that man—in Bran. He's the one Scout bit—the one with the men and Candi. He has something to do with Candi being missing. He probably killed that woman in the park. We have to follow him!"

"Are you serious, Jeni? How do you all of a sudden know who he is?"

"I'm sure. I knew that the man looked familiar, but I thought it could be anyone until I thought about his hand. He also walks the same. I know it's him!"

At that exact moment, in my excitement, I tripped on a cobblestone and fell forward onto my knees.

"Ouch! Oh, how embarrassing!" Blood began seeping once again from my tennis court wound on my right knee. People were coming to help from all directions, only intensifying the awkwardness.

Zach pulled me up gently, and I walked gamely around to prove to the onlookers that I was in no obvious discomfort. It was all an act, but I was determined to show everyone I was quite okay despite the blood. A nearby waiter gave me a wet towel and some ice, which I was then forced to use if I didn't want to appear ungrateful. I cleaned myself up and kept the towel for the walk back to the boat. It seemed like the ordeal went on forever.

When the crowd finally dispersed, the boat with the mystery man was long gone.

"*Zach, I'm sure it was him.* What can we do?" I asked.

Zach stood there and looked around. I could tell he was considering our options.

"Okay, let's say you're right. We don't know where he has gone, and we aren't in a position to get another boat. I understand that we are leaving first thing tomorrow morning and will be in Hvar in no time at all. Let's stick with our plan. If he was restocking a boat with liquor, then most likely he is also headed to Hvar. In any event, I don't think we have another option. Did he see you?"

"No … at least I don't think so."

"That's good news. Let me think about this." Zach paused. "I wish I had seen him up close," he said. He shook his head back and forth. "Jeni, I'm afraid I don't have enough information to do anything here. If he assaulted you, it was in Romania, not Croatia. Plus, he'd say it wasn't him."

"What should we do?" I asked, nervously tugging on Zach's arm as I waited for his response.

"Wait," he said. "I know you don't want to hear it, but just wait for now and see if he reappears."

He was right. I knew I shouldn't jump the gun and call the police, but my gut instinct said it was too much of a coincidence. *It has to be him.*

I felt a little sick. Maybe it was just queasiness from the roily two-hour sail earlier in the evening, but my meal suddenly felt as if it was sitting on the top of my stomach. I hated myself. How could I have eaten dinner in Trogir while Candi was in the grips of men who would cavort with that thug with a missing index finger? Now I was filled with self-loathing.

Day six was ending.

Chapter Twenty-Five

BY THE TIME I rolled out of my berth the next morning and went topside, a fourth of the boats had already left the harbor. Laying over in Trogir because of the storm was an unexpected delay for many of the captains; they were anxious to get back on schedule.

I found Edwin and Zach studying the chart to Hvar, cups of freshly brewed coffee in hand. The captain said that we would be stopping at a marina across the bay about two and half miles from the town of Hvar. This time of year, when everyone who is anyone wants to be in Hvar, the city wharf could only be used for a few giant yachts and by small tenders ferrying people who had moored elsewhere. There was no room at the inn for the ordinary boat owner.

On our way to Hvar, the captain told me a lot about the world of yachting, which has transformed over the last twenty years. For the most part, our conversation kept my mind off of Candi.

Yachts are a lot like airplanes—toys for the very rich. What the rich really crave are new, custom-made superyachts or megayachts with the latest and most expensive electronics and marine equipment known to humankind. Up to a football field in length, many superyachts in the Adriatic have shadowy owners who charter them when they don't have time to enjoy the fruits of their labor, inheritance, or corruption.

I watched one on the horizon just ahead of us.

"It would be fun to have five couples get together and rent one," I told Zach.

"I bet it would. Have you ever checked the price?"

I pulled out my phone and discovered they don't hide the prices like high-end jewelry stores. The glossy yachting page that I had picked out let me know that chartering a yacht was not for the middle class. It turns out that the classic 150-foot yacht that I liked, with its wooden decks and perfect lines, shown lying seductively at anchor in a medieval harbor, was available in the high season for a one-week charter for the mere price of $145,000. That did not include provisions (food, liquor, and other expendables), pay and expenses for a crew of six, or the docking fees. The "guests" would also have to pull out their platinum American Express card with no limit in order to pump in enough fuel to cruise around for a few days in the Adriatic.

I rolled my eyes at the information.

"Not interested anymore?" Zach asked when I finished my search. He smiled sweetly at my forlorn expression.

I saw no need to respond to his question. Instead I turned toward the captain to express my dismay.

"Who are these people who can spend money like this?"

The knowledgeable captain had a ready answer.

"They are soccer stars and movie stars, and celebrities of all types. They are organized crime figures, oligarchs, and those who inherited a fortune from their parents. Occasionally, they are just ordinary people who've worked hard and feel they've earned a life of luxury," he said with a smile.

It made me very curious about the owners around us. I pointed to a sleek yacht with a deep silver hull, tinted windows, and all-black trim on the decks leaving the harbor like a masked robber at night. I asked if he knew who was chartering it.

"Of course, but I can't tell you." He smirked as he spoke, and then implied it was someone famous.

I turned red. Why couldn't he tell me?

"The idea that boat captains have some sort of confidentiality is absurd. Lawyers and psychotherapists have confidentiality. For sure, priests do. But boat captains?" I said.

He insisted it was true. Apparently the more money you have, the more silence you can buy, especially if you charter a superyacht.

But then he told me that the ordinary superyachts are actually becoming passé. Now, the really rich, the truly decadent, have even bigger yachts—someone even coined them as "gigayachts." They can be twice the length of a football field, with nine to eleven decks, multiple helipads, swimming pools, a slew of mini-me boats, and glittering bars with the world's most expensive wines. They are not always available for charter; they are the exclusive toys of their owners and their friends—Russian oligarchs, Arab sheiks, Western CEOs, Chinese developers, and other men (face it, they're all men) with dubious sources of income who absolutely love the idea of a brand-new yacht that flaunts their wealth to the rest of the world.

When the marina on Hvar was in sight, worry crept back deep into my mind and consumed me. I could almost feel my niece nearby, but where Candi was I didn't know.

Palmižana Marina was in one of the best-protected natural harbors I'd ever seen, a perfect *U* shape with the same tight fit as a paper clip. It looked as if it had been carved out by an overly ambitious developer rather than by God, with enough room for two docks down both its long sides and a wide one in the middle. Steep hills rose up around the edges. Tucked under a canopy of trees was situated a restaurant, showers, a shop, and even an outdoor masseuse.

It was also very welcoming—a full-service marina for the ordinary boater. In fact, the marina attendant was waiting for us as we arrived, and helped tuck Edwin's boat neatly between two similarly sized sloops. We were lucky. Again, we had snagged the last available slip.

I felt very sorry for the boaters who arrived after us, pleading for a slip. I'm sure that would have been us but for the forethought of our captain. I discovered that latecomers near the end of the day were able to raft up against those of us who were in slips, one after the other, snaking out into the water like bobbing tentacles. It was just like the pictures I had seen online before I left home. No one seemed to complain, no matter how much noise and aggravation was caused by the occupants on the last boat jumping across those between it and the dock.

Once secure, we decided to leave our bags on the boat. The captain watched them during the day, and someone would take them to the very basic bungalow we'd rented near the marina for the night. Like the boat slip, it was the last available room. We decided to accompany Edwin to Hvar by riding in the boat's small inflatable tender. After that point Zach and I would be on our own. Edwin had made that quite clear. He had plans for the evening, and we were definitely not part of them.

We took off on a direct line to Hvar, the most famous of the Croatian island destinations. From our vantage point on the water, Hvar's deep green harbor reminded me of a wide-rimmed cup, with the city attached on one side like an elaborate curving handle. Old churches, palaces, an arsenal, and other ancient stone buildings lined a large piazza. Small alleys led visitors up the hillside to an imposing fortress that looked down over the city from high above. There was a maze of five-star restaurants and high-end shops from the town square to the fortress, ready to satisfy the weary wanderer's hunger or thirst. For those people who preferred a simpler style, there were picturesque outdoor cafés serving pizza with glass pitchers filled to the brim with nice Croatian wine.

As expected, only superyachts were moored in Hvar, with their names in lights and their automated gangplanks lifted high to prevent a stray curiosity seeker like me from climbing aboard. In fact, when we arrived, all the yachts were so quiet that it appeared as if they were asleep. Although it was just late afternoon, we detected only an occasional crew member scurrying around with a tray of drinks. I assumed the occupants were resting up for the night.

I was looking ahead to the place on the wharf where we were about to land, so I saw them before I heard the cheery hellos.

They were maybe twenty-five years old, Croatian, and gorgeous. Now, Croatian women are among the most beautiful women in the world, but these specimens were even more stunning than most of their peers. It was clear that they were Edwin and Ted's "friends"—and were happy to see them. Well, what can I say? I shouldn't have been surprised.

It wasn't like Edwin and Ted were ugly or poor. They were just *old.*

Edwin jumped off the inflatable dinghy at the same time he threw the line to a boy with an outstretched hand standing on the edge of the wharf. Edwin leaped from the inflatable to the pier as if he were a college kid. I had to hand it to him—he was in shape. He then pulled the closest woman to him and landed a big kiss on her just as he groped her bottom—well, what little bottom she had.

I was dumbfounded. A glowing Edwin introduced her to us as Natasha, and her friend that she'd brought for Ted as Natalia.

"Nice to meet you."

They both smiled brightly at the greeting, and then turned their attention to the men.

"Well, it's been nice spending some time with you, but we're heading off," Edwin said to us with his hand outreached to shake goodbye, or rather to shake us off.

"That makes me *so mad*," I said when they were out of hearing range. "Rich old men with women so much younger … He wasn't even embarrassed!"

"Jeni, you know better. Of course, it works that way—sometimes. I feel for the regular guy in countries where women see money as the prime qualifier for selecting a mate."

"And old men who just want a young woman who looks good," I replied.

"Yeah, it's just not the basis on which you and I operate, but in lots of places throughout the world it's the accepted practice. Pretty girls are groomed to marry well. Think about Candi. Do you think she would be on a yacht in Hvar with rich men based upon her ACT score and golf game?"

Oh, I hated it when Zach made me think past the surface and confront the nuances in life. He was right. There have been whole civilizations that used pretty women to protect their sovereignty. I shook my head as if to clear the clutter within it. At the thought once again of Candi, I dismissed Edwin and whatever proclivities he had. I knew he would never again be in my social circle, and I was ready to move off the topic.

"For the record, Candi's ACT was 33. It's unbelievable. I can't figure out how someone like her all of a sudden is willing to be with men like Edwin."

Zach laughed at this. He said, "Let's get a bite to eat," and took my hand to guide me toward the café for a late lunch of pizza and wine.

We walked to an open table but had to navigate the crowd. It was a madhouse at the waterfront, packed with people anxious to take advantage of tours and cafés.

"I have to agree with the professor's assessment," Zach said after he was jostled by a group of young adults in a hurry to join a tour. "We'll come back one day—but not in the high season like this."

Chapter Twenty-Six

THE WAITER WAS in the process of delivering the tiny slip of paper with illegible lettering, yet very clear prices, to our table. We began to formulate a plan for the search. Until then, we had spent the downtime people-watching in hopes of catching a glimpse of Candi in the town center—the most obvious place for her to be.

"I'm going to stop in that internet café and send a quick note to Sue. I'm sure Kate will have told her about the professor's call, but I don't know how much she told her mother about what he had witnessed or even if he explained all the details to Kate. I think I should let her know we made it to Hvar and that it's great news—Candi has been seen here."

"I'll wait outside while you're doing that and try to get some idea where she might be."

I went into the café and sent Sue a quick note.

Dear Sue,

We are in Croatia. Late last night we got a call from one of Candi's professors at Tulane. He is here at a conference. The great news is that he saw Candi yesterday. He said she was well and was with some men on a yacht. I think one is Dimitri. He didn't know more. Zach and I are on Hvar right now. I'm sure we'll find her tonight or tomorrow and I'll tell her to call you!

He said that she asked him to call someone. It may have been you, but he had trouble understanding her. It made him worried, so he called Kate and she gave him our number.

I'll write more tomorrow!

Love,
Jeni

With that accomplished, we set out to see if we could find Candi. There were many times when we thought there was a possible Candi sighting, but we were disappointed to find out it wasn't her. Hvar was full of tourists from around the world, including bikers, vacationing families, and thousands of young people. To my dismay, a twenty-something blonde wasn't as unusual in Hvar as in Romania.

"We probably need to try going back to the waterfront and look at the yachts," Zach said.

"Oh, I forgot—it was a blue one, right? I was so mad when we got here about Edwin and the state of the whole world that I never specifically looked for a blue yacht."

"Me either, but many of them are just arriving for the night, so it's better to look around now. It may have been out for the day when we arrived. If we don't find the yacht, we'll check out the stores. Where does she shop?"

I rolled my eyes. Before now, Candi had never been a big shopper.

"At this point, I have no idea."

"What about food?"

"I don't know. She likes gelato, but that's too much of a shot in the dark. Maybe a museum or art gallery would be a good place to visit. She likes those."

"Okay, let's look at the yachts first, and then in the museums."

Just as Zach predicted, more yachts had arrived when we returned to the wharf later in the day. All the big boy toys were finally beginning to show signs of life. I surveyed the area for a blue yacht and saw yachts in varying shades of blue, but nothing a deep shade of blue like the Facebook logo. That made sense. Bright blue would be an awful color for a yacht.

On the other hand, there was every other variation of blue known to humankind. There were yachts painted turquoise, navy, sea foam, greenish blue, pale baby blue, and even a gunmetal gray blue. A few had touches of blue on the hull and the undersides, just enough to make you wonder if it qualified as blue. There were too many to narrow down our possibilities to one or two boats, so we resigned ourselves to sitting on a short stone wall at the end of the harbor. After a while, it became very uncomfortable.

"Let's just wander around the rest of the city until it gets closer to dusk. We'll have more luck then. People have to get on and off the yachts at some point," Zach said.

Wander we did—up and down every alley, peering into any establishment with open doors or inviting windows. It was demoralizing and frightening. I was convinced Candi was in the city, but how could I find her?

The sun was slowly sinking, along with my optimism. After a few hours we were tired and sunburnt. My sore knee was throbbing. Pessimism began to consume me.

I tried pulling up a picture of Candi on my phone and showing it around the marina, but no one recognized the American girl in a golf T-shirt. My desperation to find Candi was frightening to many of the people whom I approached, especially those who didn't speak English, and my voice became more plaintive and desperate as the evening wore on. I began to look and sound like a nut, and I knew it.

Zach was also feeling the pressure of time, but he believed that we just needed to sit in a good spot and watch for her. Surely if she was on the island, she would show up at the harbor's edge. Patience was not my virtue, but he had it in spades.

"How about a gelato? The best place is across from the yachts. We can watch them while we eat. I know you don't want to hear this and I don't want to say it, but our ticket for the ferry back to the marina will have to be used in less than an hour. The last ferry leaves then, and we have to be on it. After that we won't be able to leave Hvar and we will be stuck here all night."

I knew we didn't have a hotel room, and Zach didn't have enough time off from work to extend this trip much longer.

"I'm sorry, but I need to return to Split soon," he said.

He saw my stricken face and pulled me toward him in a gentle but genuine public display of affection. I buried my face in his chest to hide my tears and returned his embrace. I murmured to him that I didn't know what I would do without his love. He squeezed me tighter.

There was not much else either of us could say. I knew he was right. We couldn't stay in Hvar forever.

I'm convinced I was the only person that evening in Hvar trudging like a prisoner to a gelato shop. Everyone else was almost electrified with excitement for a night in the hottest town on the Adriatic. You could feel it in the air—the music, lights, and laughter. To them it was a magical evening with cool breezes off the sea and the stars up above. It just wasn't magical for me.

The beep on Zach's phone startled me in the midst of my self-pity. It was a text from Jean-Claude.

> I am free to leave Bucharest. Can we meet early tomorrow morning in Split? Where are you now?

Zach responded saying we were in Hvar and providing our bungalow information.

"How odd," I said. "He didn't say anything about Tina—I mean, Antoinette."

"I think it's implicit that she's better. And if he's coming here, that means he knows more. No need to tell the world."

"Why come tomorrow? Why not tonight?"

"Well, it's too far to drive over the mountains in a day, and he probably had to get a connecting flight from Bucharest to Split. Nothing is direct. I'm surprised he'll be here that soon."

I nodded yes; he was right. I sat with Zach at a small iron table as close to the edge as possible. In the midst of a chocolate gelato, I thought my eyes were once again deceiving me.

"Oh, Zach! I think that's Candi!"

It took a second for me to process the scene. Was it really her? No golf shirt, no flip-flops. The young woman dressed in a skintight blue-and-white-striped sundress wore four-inch-heeled silver sandals. Her hair was puffed up to make her look even taller, and her face was heavily made up with shimmering eye shadow and false eyelashes. Large silver earrings glittered in the light each time she took a step.

She was with three men, including the one I recalled from Bran—the one I'd seen her with at Dracula's castle. I presumed he was the Moldovan named Dimitri, but the two other men I didn't recognize. They could have also been the men in Bran, but I never saw them up close. If Candi was dressed to kill, the two men with Dimitri were as well. Nothing looked cheap about their clothes. And they walked like they knew it, occasionally tugging at a monogrammed cuff or brushing away an imaginary fleck on a silk sleeve. I saw one of them look at himself. He could see his reflection in the polished hull of a yacht. He smoothed his already slicked-back hair. They did not make eye contact with anyone as they passed. They were meant to be seen, and had no desire to engage with the common people.

By then, it was almost dark and all the yachts were readying for the nightly entertainment, each seeking a share of the limelight. I glanced at the navy-blue yacht and saw a young man with a tray of drinks in crystal glasses headed to the helm on the upper deck. Its name, Taku, in big bold letters, was backlit on the stern, while party lights were aglow around the main deck. There were even bright spotlights under the boat's hull directed into the water, enabling onlookers to see fish swimming below. The diffused light created an eerie halo effect around the hull, which was incongruous given the unlikely chance of an actual angel being aboard the 150 feet of floating fiberglass.

"Are you sure?" Zach said. "That girl doesn't look anything like our Candi."

"I know her walk. It's Candi. What should I do?" I almost whispered the question, fearing what might happen next. The men looked intimidating.

Zach thought for a second while I sat in anguish.

"Let me stay here and observe. You go talk to her. If you're wrong, you're just wrong. No harm done. If you're right and anything goes wrong, I can get help from the policeman right there." He pointed to a nearby table, where an officer was eating gelato in a waffle cone and trying to catch the drips off the bottom with his tongue. I wasn't so sure he could help, but he was better than nothing.

Once given the green light, I jumped up from my bistro chair, almost knocking it over, and ran to the group. I wanted to talk before they got any closer to the gangplank, and they were closing in on it.

"Candi!" I said excitedly as soon as I was close enough for them to hear me.

They all turned to me as the professor said they had done with him. That confirmed it. It really was my niece.

For a split second I thought she was happy to see me, but I quickly realized that wasn't the case.

"*Whaaat* are you doing here?" she said before I could get close enough to hug her. She spoke not like a child who was angry, but like an imperious queen who was ready to chop off the head of her no-longer-loved lady-in-waiting. The *whaaat* seemed to go on forever.

I was stunned, and stopped like I had been tased.

"Zach and I are taking a short vacation ... so we came here, and I saw you ... and ..." I started rambling in the hope that she would soften. Somehow I thought that if I was sweet enough, then we could make peace. But I floundered upon looking into her impassive eyes. She interrupted before I could finish.

"Look, you were nice enough to let me couch surf at your house for a couple of weeks, but I think this obsession you have with me is weird. I had no idea you would follow me." She was as cold as ice.

Couch surf? Obsession? I could say nothing.

She turned abruptly toward the Moldovan man to signify she was ready to leave.

"Let's board the yacht. I'm really tired of this woman following me," Candi said while pointing at me in disdain. "*Really*, I'm over it."

In accordance with her wishes Dimitri motioned to a waiting crew member to lower the gangplank. I watched in dismay, knowing I had little time to stop them from leaving me on the dock.

When I turned back to Candi to try to talk to her once again, she was lining her already red lips and checking out her reflection in a compact mirror.

What has happened to my niece? How had she changed into this vacuous vamp in only a week? She had never been deliberately hateful, especially not toward me. If anything, I always worried she might be too agreeable and compliant. Nothing made sense. *And why in the world would she refer to me as "this woman"?*

"Candi, can we *please* talk?" I knew she heard me, but there was no movement from her except to continue to fool with her lip liner.

No response. I kept on.

"Your mother is wondering about your plans. *She's worried about you since you haven't called her.*" The sounds of desperation were entering my voice.

At first I thought I saw a flicker of softness in Candi, but then she loudly scoffed at my words and said nothing.

The Moldovan man finally spoke. I took my eyes off of Candi. He seemed polite enough, but his words were like a knife in me.

"Madam, we have to go. The young lady does not want you around. As you can see, she is fine and happy. I am sorry, but if you continue to bother her, we will have to call the police."

"Wait, please—just a minute ..." I stopped once I realized that no one was listening. I took a deep breath and contemplated my options, turning to look for help from Zach, who had already begun to walk toward us. Before he could reach us, I heard Candi snap her compact shut and turn her back toward me.

Once again I begged Candi to wait, but the gang of beautiful people turned in unison and hastily walked up the wide gangplank with stainless steel railing connecting the *Taku* to Hvar. I was left standing dumbfounded with tears beginning to fall on my cheeks as I watched a younger crew member dressed in a navy-blue shirt and pristine white pants take Candi's slim hand and assist her aboard. Without even a single glance my way, he hit a large chrome button that caused the gangplank to rise high out of my reach and blocked any further view of her from my vantage point.

The crew member was no different from the king's guard lifting the wooden bridge above the moat surrounding a castle. Just like ancient royalty, Candi was gone from my sight. Worst of all, it was before I had gotten the chance to tell her that I loved her, or to tell the men she was with that I was her aunt and was very worried about her.

Surely they would understand, I told myself, *if only I'd had the chance to explain everything.* But deep down inside, I knew these men would never comprehend the extent of our bond; I was holding my sister's hand when Candi entered this world.

Chapter Twenty-Seven

I FELT ZACH'S arms encircle my waist from behind and pull me toward him while I was standing looking at the massive and seemingly impenetrable fiberglass jail my niece had entered. At least I felt like it was a jail.

I was numb. Zach knew it would be just minutes before I broke down into tears. He was making a stab at keeping me calm and in control. He whispered into my ear that he loved me.

"She's fine, Jeni. It's not over yet. We just have to find another approach. It's going to be okay. Anyway, trying to board the *Taku* like pirates will only land us in a Croatian jail. Matt wouldn't be happy with either of us if that's how we decided to handle the situation."

"How do you know she's fine?"

"Because she's smart. Remember—she got a 33 on her ACT," he said, eliciting a small smile from me.

"Oh, Zach," I said as I tried to stifle the tears. "I don't know what I would do if I were here alone and Candi left on that yacht."

"I don't even want to imagine it," Zach said, shaking his head to rid it of the thought.

"Should *we* call the police?" I asked, knowing full well what the answer was.

"No, I worry they'll arrest you. It's late at night. We neither speak the language nor have a lawyer."

Then he suggested we get on the ferry and find our bungalow for the night. We could talk more there.

Once again he smiled, but more ruefully this time. "Don't get too excited about the place. Trip Advisor only gave the place a one. I'm not sure we have ever stayed at a one-star, but now we can check it off our bucket list."

I tried as best I could to return his smile as we dashed hand in hand to the ferry for the ride back. It was scheduled to leave in a matter of minutes. The wind was really picking up. Spray from the waves crashed into the marble walls of the wharf, covering me in a light mist of cold water.

We dutifully boarded the small ferry built for ten passengers and tried to ignore the fact that they were loading twenty ticket holders. The ferry operators were making a good living off the boaters wanting to get to Hvar during the summer season. It was a rigid inflatable boat that had been retrofitted with a wooden box covering two rows of five seats. The remaining passengers sat around the side gunnels and a piece of wood across the stern of the boat. The extra weight caused the tiny ferry to sit dangerously low in the water.

The excess of passengers on this boat was the least of the many safety issues in play that night. The trip was made worse by the deep rolling seas and pitch-dark night with just a crescent of a moon high in the sky. The only real illumination was from the lights of the spooky edifice atop the city.

I found myself finally spiraling into that hole of self-pity that had opened up for me. But then just as I started to consider another bout of tears, I looked toward Zach, who was sitting outside so that women and children could take seats inside the tiny cabin and stay warm. Our eyes met as I watched him sit uncomfortably on a board out in the wet and cold, miserable from the wind and the waves that occasionally hit him. He smiled at me to let me know it was all okay.

I stopped my tears from falling, climbed away from the hole of self-pity, and smiled back.

The boat was also not designed for ease of disembarking. On this very busy night, passengers were required to step up, without a ladder, about three feet onto a slippery piece of fiberglass board that was installed to stabilize the bow in rough seas. It was never meant to be a platform for walking or standing, as evidenced by the fact that it sloped at a forty-five-degree angle back toward the boat stern.

The way the exit protocol worked was that a man on board helped the shorter passengers step up onto the board by cupping his hands for their foot. Once the passengers were standing on the board, another man waited on the wharf to grab them and help pull them ashore before they slid back into the boat. It probably worked well on a sunny day with bikini-clad women, but it didn't work well on this particular night.

Too tired to argue, I followed their directions. It should have surprised no one that when I stepped on the wet board, just as I had anticipated, I immediately slipped and landed hard on my rear end. My slip must not have been all that uncommon an occurrence, because before I could land in the water, two alert crew members adroitly grabbed me—one by my arm, and another my waist—and lifted me ashore.

Zach and I found our way to the bungalow in silence, ready to fall into bed. Despite our earlier intentions, we both knew that after the fall I was too upset to begin a conversation.

Unfortunately for both us, once in the bungalow we began one anyway.

"Jeni, I saw Candi drop this on the wall beside the gangplank, right as she left you. I grabbed it to give to you," he said, handing it to me when we entered the room.

"What do you mean, *grabbed* this?" I asked. Irritation showed on my face as I held the gold compact he had given to me. Why hadn't he said anything earlier?

"That's what I mean: I just grabbed it. I didn't want someone else to pick it up. In the rush to get to the ferry, I forgot to say anything," Zach said, bowing up in defense of his actions. "It's just a compact."

I sighed. It *was* just a compact, it was late, and he looked as tired as me. I let the matter drop.

Then, like most women would, I instinctively opened the compact.

Suddenly it was as if I'd accidentally opened a box of dynamite. My hands began shaking and my heart pounded like a drum. There on the glass of the small round mirror, written perfectly in thin red lip liner, was this: "Help not only 1."

My mind began reeling. What did it mean, "not only 1"? Was it the number 1 or the letter *I*? What was she trying to tell me, if it was even meant for me? Help her do what?

"Did you see this?" I asked Zach.

"No, I didn't look inside it."

"But this is awful. We have to go back right now. We have to get the police. We can't stay here."

"Jeni, you have to be reasonable. We can't do anything tonight."

"Reasonable? What do you mean, *reasonable*? Candi's in trouble!"

"I know that!" Zach said, becoming defensive. "I mean that even if the police believed you and were convinced that your niece, who voluntarily, in the presence of a thousand people, boarded the yacht, was in fact kidnapped, even in Croatia they would have to find a magistrate to give them a search warrant, and they aren't going to find one in Hvar tonight. Period. *That's how it works.*"

"You know you don't have to be so reasonable all the time." I almost stomped my foot in frustration, losing my patience with the situation.

"It's my job to be reasonable. I'm sorry you are so unhappy with me at this point, but I didn't cause this situation. If you want me to head back to Bucharest, I will."

We both glared at each other. All of a sudden, given my falls on the boat and on the cobblestones in Trogir, and with a sore bottom, scraped knees, and a wounded ego to match, the self-pity that had eluded me earlier now washed over me like the crashing waves we had navigated for the past two days. Tears streamed down my face in the dark of the night. That upset me even more. *I'm not a crier,* I told myself. *I'm a doer.* But suddenly I could do nothing.

We said nothing more to each other. I knew Zach was as tired as I and just as worried. Emotionally exhausted, we fell onto the small bed in the one-star bungalow that had almost no hot water and minimal upkeep. It suited me. I told myself that it had a bathroom and a bed and that was all I needed on a breezy night. Any other perk would have been an assault on my miserable mood.

By the time I awoke the next morning, the sun was high and streaming through our open windows, giving the bungalow a rather charming rustic feel. It was so pleasant that it took me a little while to realize why I was there. Even when I remembered, I stayed still in bed for a few minutes and listened to the sounds of birds chirping in a flowering tree outside my window. Eventually, I put my feet on the floor and took a deep breath.

"Hello, sleepyhead. Do you know that you were out for over eight hours? You have to feel better this morning," Zach said as he came through the bedroom door and handed me a cup of coffee.

"I do. *Much better.* Thanks. I'm sorry about last night. You were right. There was nothing we could do. Where did you get the coffee?"

"Back down at the marina. I'm afraid that it's not real hot. While I was there I got a text from Jean-Claude. He's arriving in Split in a few hours. We're going to meet at the place we went the first day. If we have enough evidence and the yacht is still there, we will come back to Hvar with Croatian customs and police. For now I've rented a private speedboat to take us back to Split. It'll be ready to go in about an hour. You need to charge your phone while we have some time."

"I'm glad Jean-Claude is coming. Do you know whether he thinks Candi is in trouble too?"

"Well, I doubt he's coming to Split based upon a hysterical aunt. He probably knows more than we do at this point. Let's just wait and hear his story."

"Can I use your phone to email Sue? I'll give her an update, but I really don't want to tell her about the compact and what it said."

"Jeni, you promised. You have to tell her the truth—no matter how bad it is."

"Ugh," I said. I put my head into my hands, resigned that he was right.

> Dear Sue,
>
> I talked to Candi last night in Hvar. She is fine. As the professor said, she is on a yacht with Dimitri and some other men.
>
> This is the bad news—she was not happy to see me and I don't know why. I told her you wanted her to call you and asked her to do that, but she didn't respond.
>
> Then, after she left us and got back on the boat, Zach found a compact that we think she left for us to see. It had the word *help* and something written on it that might mean more women are on the boat. I *know* this will upset you, but I promised not to keep anything from you. *Please don't panic!* We are meeting with Interpol this morning to see what it all means. I will let you know more after we talk with the Interpol agent.
>
> I know I told you not to come, but perhaps it is time for you to see how it would work if you and Bob left the cruise ship and flew here. But don't buy tickets yet! I'm not even sure where the yacht is going.

We can't talk right now—my phone is dead—so we'll talk to you later.

Love,
Jeni

Zach's choice of a private boat to rent was almost the same as the one used by the man with the missing finger in Trogir.

"We are in a hurry, and this guy gave us a great price because he's already going to Split to pick up some passengers. It should be a quick ride."

"I agree—totally." The powerful outboard engines combined with a bright sun, calmer seas, and a new day were just what I needed to recharge my batteries. With reinforcement and more evidence, we might be able to convince the local authorities to board the *Taku* and rescue Candi.

By the time we would meet with Jean-Claude, it would be almost a week since Candi had left. It was time to take her home.

Chapter Twenty-Eight

ZACH TRIED TO reassure me on the boat ride that it would all work out.

"Jeni, I know you don't think I believe you, but I do. I'm worried as well, especially after Hvar. I know Candi would never be that mean to you. She loves you. And remember," he said, grabbing my hand and looking into my eyes in order to convince me of what he was about to say, "she's very smart and her acting in Hvar was extremely effective. She certainly convinced you. But she also knew to write the message in the compact and leave it right next to where we were standing. She knew that even if you didn't find it, someone else would."

"But still …" I started to spiral out of control again. My eyes stung. I was on the verge of a torrent of tears, angry at myself over having seen and then lost Candi.

"Jeni, I don't think that they'll hurt her. It's just not in their best interests, especially if they found out about me. They'll just drop her off somewhere safe. I know how you're feeling—that things are more urgent now. And you're right. But we have resources. Soon we'll be able to find the yacht and get her off as safely as possible."

Zach told me that he thought the guys were a minor-league organized crime outfit and would be afraid of an international incident. If they were a sophisticated operation, they would have done their homework and never taken Candi in the first place.

At Zach's suggestion, we decided to wait until Jean-Claude arrived, instead of wasting more energy wondering what to do without his input.

It was a good move for us to stop conjecturing. Because if Zach was wrong, if the men didn't let Candi go, I knew what it meant. And I couldn't bear to think about it. Sex trafficking was for sex. My faint hope that Dimitri was in reality a good guy and protecting Candi from harm made little sense when spoken out loud. The odds were against it.

The good news was that Jean-Claude was early. He strode toward us through rows of outside tables like a *GQ* apparition with Ray-Ban sunglasses, tan skin, and an open-collared white shirt. He was walking eye candy, and I wasn't the only woman who took notice. I could sense jealousy around me when he stopped at our table and bent down to lightly kiss me on both cheeks before introducing himself to Zach.

I had forgotten that they had never met in person.

"Bonjour," he said, settling into a seat.

"Cabernet, s'il vous plait," he called to a nearby waiter. Even the waiter seemed mesmerized by his smooth moves.

I soon discovered that our companion's early arrival was not accompanied by good news about Candi.

"Is your colleague better?" I asked.

"Oui. She has many broken bones, but she is awake and she can speak. I now know that she jumped out of the window *just as I suspected*. She is *very* smart." With this, he pointed to his head. He smiled to himself, likely at the thought of his colleague's quick wit and tenacity—not to mention his own correct assumptions.

"Two young Romanians tried to force her to take drugs—drugs that may have killed her. She politely refused, but 'Non merci, monsieur' was not the correct answer. One man tried to make her change her mind. Au contraire, she jumped. She is lucky to be alive. Someone wanted to get her away from Candi. That is why I am here. She told me that I am to find Candi."

Those were welcome words.

"Have you discovered anything?" he asked us.

I listened quietly as Zach told Jean-Claude the tale of our trip to Hvar. He ended by handing the compact to the agent. The agent read the inscription several times before he put the compact back on the table, cursing under his breath. He was just as shocked as I had been. *Perhaps,* I thought, *up until now he had also convinced himself that Candi was really okay.*

"I believe that's why she wouldn't leave the boat. They must have other women. It makes sense—as pretty as she is. One pretty woman isn't enough of a prize to pay for this operation," Zach said. Then he sighed and looked back at me.

"Oui. It is as I thought," Jean-Claude said, pointing again to his head with his left hand as he paused to sip from the glass of red wine in his right. "May I have this for now?" He moved his pointed finger from his head to the compact.

"Of course," Zach said but then hesitated. "Let me take some pictures ... just in case anything happens and I need them later."

Afterward Jean-Claude neatly placed the compact into a ubiquitous ziplock bag, which some law enforcement men always seemed to have at their disposal.

"Please, tell me about the yacht that you saw," Jean-Claude said. Zach showed him a picture from his cell phone that he had taken from a distance. You could barely make out the people because the lighting was so bad, causing the image to be fuzzy. He forwarded it to Jean-Claude.

It turned out that Zach had taken a few other pictures while he sat at the gelato shop table, when I was speaking to Candi. It was in an earlier photo that I saw the go-fast boat from Trogir that the fingerless man had boarded. It was not a close-up shot, but the distinctive lines of the boat were clearly evident. I shuddered at its sight, and told Jean-Claude about my experience in Bran with a similar-looking man. He did not know about him or the boat.

In fact, only one of the two men in the picture with Dimitri at the yacht was known to Jean-Claude. It was the man I'd seen looking at his reflection in the boat hull and adjusting his hair. Tina had taken a picture of him. She told Jean-Claude that the man worked for the Italian businessman she was investigating—the Italian businessman in the Hotel Intercontinental with Dimitri the day Candi met him.

Jean-Claude said the Italian businessman, whom they believed was the leader of the operation, had a past criminal record for various crimes, including arrest for a murder-for-hire. For some unknown reason he served no jail time, so he obviously skated on that charge. Recently, the Italian government accused him of bank fraud, but he bought his way out with a large fine. Now, it appears he was dabbling in the lucrative trafficking business.

"He does not have a giant criminal ring, but he is very bad and more slippery than escargot," Jean-Claude said, confirming in part what Zach thought.

"Do you know why they have Candi?" I asked Jean-Claude, the same question I'd asked days ago.

"Non. I still do not know. It is possible that it is just a mistake."

His answer was no better than the last time.

"Shouldn't we be headed to Italy, or wherever they're going?" I said.

"Oui. Now that I know the name of the yacht, we can find out the itinerary and where to go in Italy. *Ce n'est pas un problème.*"

He was right, it was no problem. It turned out that all he had to do was go on the internet to the right website and type in something like "yacht charter" and the name *Taku*. The website would give us the complete past and intended itinerary. It wasn't like a yacht can simply go wherever it wants like a much smaller boat. Arrangements must be made in advance, docking fees paid, reservations made.

So much for secrecy, I thought. It's like Google Earth and your residence—it's pretty easy to check it out.

Within a few seconds, we had our answer. The yacht wasn't going to Italy. The *Taku* was headed for Montenegro, immediately south of Croatia, and it was due to arrive there tomorrow.

We were all momentarily dumbfounded. Even I knew that our search and rescue was going to become a great deal more problematic.

Chapter Twenty-Nine

IF CROATIA WAS the setting for *Game of Thrones*, then Montenegro was the perfect place for James Bond in *Casino Royale*. While Croatia has tourism, Montenegro has money laundering, and whereas Croatia is in the European Union, Montenegro is not.

Things are complicated in eastern Europe's smallest nation. As the newest member of NATO, it wants to be a part of the Westernized world, but despite its good intentions and incredible scenery, it still has little wealth.

Montenegro's struggling economy got a boost a few years ago when its government allowed billionaire Canadian gold tycoon Munk, along with his billionaire partners, like Lord Nathaniel Rothschild, to build a small marine empire to cater to the very rich on the otherwise pristine Kotor Bay. It is called, simply enough, Porto Montenegro, but the luxury it offers is anything other than plain. Mr. Munk's vision was for a place that catered to a clientele who unabashedly liked to spend piles of money, the kind that can't be earned on a modest salary or any salary at all. Their clientele liked high-priced possessions and to be seen with pretty women.

In the past few years Porto Montenegro has earned the nickname of Porto Moscow for all the Russian oligarchs who now descend upon the high-end penthouses, yachts, apartments, and hotels. Many go for the money laundering. I knew someone who once went to an anti-money-laundering conference with Montenegrins and reported back that he was matter-of-factly told by an attendee that "laundering money beats laundering clothes."

Porto Montenegro didn't sound like my cup of tea, but it made the most sense as the likely destination for the yacht. Despite my initial worries, Jean-Claude reassured us that it didn't matter that Candi was in Montenegro, because it was still an Interpol member country and he would be allowed to continue his search for human traffickers, especially if anyone on board had "red notices" and was already wanted for human trafficking charges. A red notice alerts member countries to persons wanted for arrest in another member country.

"I'm going, too," I said.

"Not so fast, Jeni," Zach said. "I can't go without a couple of approvals. Yes, this situation is clearly about criminals, and yes, I'm a diplomat authorized to go to another country for law enforcement purposes, but even though my job is related to what is occurring, I can't *just* go. It doesn't matter that I only want to help retrieve my niece—I have to get country clearance. Plus, I have to call Matt at the embassy and tell him what's happening. I have to follow protocol."

I groaned. Country clearance is something that all diplomats must get before they go to another country in an official capacity. It's similar to registering as a foreign agent. If you don't comply with protocol, you can get into trouble. Therefore, in order for Zach to go to Montenegro to find Candi, he had to make a formal request to the US Embassy for approval of the trip, and then they would presumably communicate with the embassy in Montenegro to approve it as well. If they both approved it, then his proper role and status would be known when he crossed the border. Additionally, the Montenegrin government, like the governments of other countries, could, if it wished, "monitor" Zach's actions to make sure he was doing what he said he was going to do and nothing else. In other words, there would be no spying by the United States.

If Zach didn't get country clearance, he would be considered an ordinary tourist, but that would be untrue. And if anything went wrong, it would be a mess.

"The approval might go fast, Jeni," Zach said, but we both knew it was almost four in the afternoon. Other than employees of the United States, everyone in Europe was enjoying their monthlong summer vacation. I knew that nothing would happen late in the day.

"But I can go now. I don't need approval, just you," I said. "I'll travel on my personal passport like I do on all vacations. I don't have to get permission."

"No, Jeni, that isn't a good idea. We don't want to split up. I don't want you to get hurt. I don't want to do anything other than leave it to the experts already on the case. Please don't pursue this path."

Jean-Claude was silent as we talked.

"Zach, I can't just sit here. You can work on the case from Split and get information to Jean-Claude from your phone, but I can identify Candi and be there for her when she's rescued. I can ride with Jean-Claude to Montenegro, and then you can join us as soon as the clearance comes through, that is, if you can even go. Do you think Matt will let you?"

"I'm sure he will, so for now please just stay here until I get approval."

We argued back and forth for a while, discussing the merits of our respective plans. His plan was seriously flawed, and mine was potentially disastrous. Eventually we made a decision—more to my liking than Zach's. I would go, and if anything happened he would probably kill Jean-Claude, in addition to anyone else involved. In the meantime, Zach would change our flights home to a later date and report in to his office to request clearance to travel to Montenegro. He said he would also contact the Trafficking in Persons representative from work, an expert on human trafficking. Maybe he would know something that could help our situation.

While Zach and I talked through the situation, Jean-Claude pulled out a thin cigar from a silver case in his shirt pocket and lit up. He took a long drag and then leaned back in his chair, tilting his head slightly to the side in order to expel the smoke away from our table, his movie star actions almost eliciting moans from the women watching him from nearby tables. I wasn't so excited. All I thought about when I saw the puff of smoke was that it was going to be a long car ride to Montenegro if he couldn't make it through lunch without a tiny cigar.

When Zach and I finished talking, the sun was still up high. The drive from Split to Porto Montenegro was only about six hours due south. We quickly decided to leave right then. I refilled my duffel bag in the apartment and ran back to the table, where Zach and Jean-Claude were in a heated debate about something.

"Jeni, I'm still not sure about this," Zach said. I could tell he was seriously exasperated with me.

"Excuse us while Jeni and I step aside and talk alone?" he told Jean-Claude, who nodded his acquiescence.

"Look, he's new to Interpol and I don't have much information about him. There's something about his confidence combined with his lack of experience that worries me. He's the kind of new guy who might make a bad decision and get you in a lot of trouble. Don't do this," Zach said, concern written all over his face.

"I know. He's pretty full of himself, but I have to go. Candi's in trouble, and I owe it to my sister to do what I can to help find her."

"Okay then. I give up trying to talk reason to you. Just promise you will call me all the time. *Don't* let your phone die. *Don't* lose it. I can track you as long as you have your phone. And *don't* do anything crazy. Promise?"

"I promise," I assured him with full sincerity. I had no desire to get in over my head this time.

Zach just sighed. He knew better.

"Will you please email Sue and tell her we are headed to Montenegro, so she won't worry?" I asked.

"Sure. I can only imagine how much more that's going to make her worry, but she has to know," he said.

We hugged a quick goodbye, and I ran to meet Jean-Claude in his rental car. It was a Peugeot, of course. The rooftop was opened, the windows were down, and the engine was fired up.

"Where to?" I asked.

"We are going to Porto Montenegro. The capital is Podgorica—*it is so beautiful*—but it is not close enough to the marina, so we will stay in a hotel closer to the marina but not in it. I do not wish to use my passport at the marina. Plus, it is too ..." At this point he rubbed his thumb and forefinger together to signify money.

The car had a navigation screen, so we plugged in the beginning and end points and began our drive. I relaxed in my leather seat with its back perfectly tilted, and we talked amiably about banal things for the first hour. At some point I mentioned the marina, and he encouraged me to look up more information about it on my phone to keep my mind off of Candi.

It didn't help. Apparently the marina had been sold to a Dubai investment group, and the marina had added to its inventory of boat slips the largest superyacht berth in the world. Now that was a claim of monumental proportions, and one fit for billionaires. The berth was an unbelievable 250 meters in length, which in American terms is 820 feet or, to be more illustrative, almost three football fields long. The even more amazing thing to me was that there were enough yachts in the world of that size to warrant the investment. I decided that it probably was the rich man's Field of Dreams—build it and they will come.

But the news wasn't just about the marina. The Montenegrin government recently accused the Russian government of trying to assassinate their pro-Western prime minister. Holy cow!

Suddenly, I felt like naive Candi. Everything I thought was benign suddenly had sinister undertones. And here I was, speeding to the unknown with a novice French agent.

I tried to mention my concerns about the marina's shady clients to Jean-Claude, but he laughed them off before I could get very far. "No worries," he told me. He turned up the radio and ended the conversation.

I wanted to believe him, but I saw worries everywhere. My mind darted from one to the other.

Jean-Claude drove the first half of the trip, but as I'd predicted, we stopped often for him to smoke. After the third time, I offered to drive the remainder and he readily agreed. I soon discovered that he talked on the phone as much as he smoked.

For the next two hours he called various people, including several women, and had lengthy conversations in French. I could understand some words but not much. Whether they were about love, lust, or work, I had no idea. By then, I had noticed that everything he said seemed steeped in sexual innuendoes, even when he asked the attendant to put diesel in the car.

After running out of women to call and flirt with, he dozed off until we reached the hotel. I called Zach to confirm that we'd safely arrived and to say that I was fine. Emotionally and physically exhausted, I crashed for the night.

The next morning I was up before Jean-Claude. I tried to wait for him, but I was hungry and needed caffeine, so I walked to the adjacent restaurant for breakfast. It was a typical eastern European setup with lots of tables filled with a busload of seniors, a bike-riding tour group, and some other random tourists. It took a second, but I found a table for two and ordered a hearty breakfast of hard-boiled eggs, cheese, toast, and homemade yogurt. I found that the small amount of time alone was nice. I loved to people-watch, and this was a particularly interesting assortment to observe and consider.

My attention was drawn to someone looking rather incongruous among all the patrons, a man about my age wearing glasses and sitting at a small table with his back to the wall. He was alone and without food. He toyed with an empty cup of coffee, turning the handle this way and that. Each time the waiter came and offered a refill, he politely declined. I decided that he wasn't a tourist since he was dressed in a regular shirt and pants and he spoke the local language. I couldn't tell if he was waiting for someone or not, but he was very definitely watching the room.

I eventually decided to apply everything I had learned from foreign service training. He had his back to the wall, he was not ordering anything, etc. Was he a bad guy watching the room for some nefarious reason? It occupied my mind for a while as I wondered who he was and what he was doing at breakfast.

Chapter Thirty

AFTER FINISHING MY boiled egg and cheese assortment, I grew bored watching the man and decided to go to the toilet. I wanted to freshen up before I had more coffee to drink and Jean-Claude arrived. I took my purse into the rather ordinary small room in the back of the building that served both guests and staff. It had a small sink and counter to the right as you entered, and a single walled stall to the left. I locked the door and entered the stall. When I exited, I looked in the mirror and began to comb my hair.

I thought I was imaging it at first, but I wasn't. There, just a few feet behind me, I saw the face of the man from the restaurant reflected in the mirror. He was so close to me that I could hear him breathing. *How had he gotten in the locked door? What does he intend to do to me? Is he going to choke me from behind? Oh my gosh, am I going to die here in a lousy bathroom in Montenegro?* I was frozen, waiting for something to happen.

Neither of us spoke for a second or two as we stared at each other in the mirror. It was like he was waiting for me to go first, but he hesitated. *What is going to happen? Is he going to kill me? If something happens to me, who will push to find Candi?*

Suddenly, his failure to act fast emboldened me.

There was no way anyone was going to stop me from finding Candi. I'd had enough! He wasn't much taller than I, and I had been trained for an assault just like this by an off-duty marine who taught classes for extra money.

Before I could change my mind, I turned toward the man and, with all my might, grabbed his head into the crook of my left arm in order to pull it downward. I mustered my strength and then hit his chin with an upper cut from my right hand. Next I kicked up my right knee as fast as I could, landing it in its intended spot, the groin. It took a second for him to react, but it was exactly as I had intended. He bent over and let out a slight groan.

It worked. I had surprised and hurt him, and now I had the advantage.

Strangely, he didn't yell at me, but started jumping around in pain, cursing under his breath in some foreign language while he looked at me as if he was ready to kill me right then and there. I hastily looked around and discovered that during the fight we had traded places. He was now blocking my exit to the door. I had to think quickly. The only thought I had was to lock myself into the single tight stall.

There were no other boxing moves to pull out—that was the extent of what I had learned in class. I ran inside the stall, slid the locking bolt across the metal door, and stood with my feet on the toilet seat so they could not be grabbed. I tried to control my breathing and shook my right hand to relieve the pain I was beginning to feel. I knew I had to call Zach, but then I groaned.

How could I be so stupid?

I slumped my head against the stall wall. My purse was still sitting on the sink! I wanted to bang my head against the metal door in frustration. The only thing Zach made me promise was not to lose my phone, and I'd done it the first day. In fact, he'd asked me three times to always have it charged and ready. I even promised him I would keep it by my side each time. He was going to be so mad, whether I lived or died.

The thought of dying made me desperate, and the fact that my assailant wasn't leaving didn't help.

I tried an even bolder approach.

"I want you to know I have a gun! I'll shoot you if you don't leave! I'll shoot you dead right now! I'm only going to give you one chance!"

There wasn't a sound from outside my stall. No footsteps. He wasn't leaving. I even could hear his breathing settle. Maybe he didn't know English.

My confidence was eroding, and it appeared to me that his was increasing. Still, it was a shock when I finally heard him speak.

"Jeni, I know you don't have a gun."

Just like that, matter-of-factly, that's what he said—and he said it way too calmly.

I, on the other hand, was no longer calm.

"Yes, I do. It's big and loaded and in my hand right now! And how do you know my name? Have you been in my purse?"

"I know you because Zach asked me to watch you, but to tell you the truth I am not so sure I want the job."

"I don't believe you," I said.

He let out a long sigh while I watched his feet move back and forth in the space under the door. He walked around for a moment. Finally, his hand slowly slid an identification card on the floor into the stall and quickly jerked away. He probably thought I might stomp on it, which I was in fact considering.

The ID said his name was Davor and he was with the Montenegrin police.

"How do you know Zach? How do I know you aren't lying?" I asked. I needed details.

"Okay, Jeni, I'm going to slide your phone to you. *Don't* try to hurt me again. Call your husband and let him tell you."

He slid the phone across the tile floor toward me. I opened it, only to immediately see the notification of a text that I had missed from Zach. It said that he had a friend named Davor who was going to meet me at breakfast.

Oops.

I put my feet on the ground delicately so as not to accidentally fall into the toilet and then slowly opened the stall door. Davor was standing against the sink with his arms crossed. He was not in a happy mood. My purse was beside him, just as I'd left it.

"Sorry," I said.

"Okay, first things first. Don't try that again! I could have broken you into pieces but for the fact that you were under my protection. In fact, I had to restrain myself because you *really* know how to aggravate someone. In a way, I still do. Want to break you in pieces, that is. If you find yourself in trouble, *get your cell phone,* not your boxing gloves. You aren't strong enough to win by might, but you certainly have the wits to think yourself out of a situation. Try using *only your brain* next time. And for future reference, the gun idea only works if you actually have one or if there's an idiot on the other side."

I listened to my dressing down without interruption. I just prayed he wouldn't tell Zach anything about the incident.

"Any questions?" he asked.

"Why didn't you just come up to me in the restaurant?"

"Because I didn't know who might be watching and I'm local police. Someone might recognize me and wonder why I'm talking to you. Anything else?"

I shook my head no, even though I had many questions.

"Okay. Now, I'm going to leave, and you're going to pretend we've never met. Got that?"

I nodded yes.

With that understood, he smiled, put on his sunglasses, and left the restroom with me never knowing how he'd gotten through the locked door or whether it was okay for me to tell Jean-Claude about my bathroom encounter.

Chapter Thirty-One

AS I ADJUSTED my hair in the mirror before leaving the restroom, I thought about what Davor had said, that Zach had sent him to look out for me. The prideful part of me resented it, but the practical side was grateful. Candi was in real trouble and I needed all the help I could get.

Jean-Claude was outside the restaurant, smoking and on his cell phone. He saw me and waved through the window, miming that once he'd finished both the call and cigar, he would join me at the table for an espresso.

I took the brief opportunity to check my phone for other emails or texts that I had missed.

Here is the gist of the string of fourteen emails that I'd received in less than a day: Anna wrote that Moira had sent a tweet (yes, she tweets) to all ILB that read, "Where is our president Jeni? MIA?" Anna knew I probably didn't see it, so she responded that I was on a short vacation in Croatia with Zach. That was obviously a mistake. She should have said I was in the hospital with some rare disease or something like that. The image that I was out having fun in Croatia but hadn't bothered to tell anyone before I left was awful, especially to those back in Bucharest working on the Diplomat Games. Moira knew when she saw blood in the water and had elected to go for the kill. She responded with outrage.

"What kind of president is Jeni? Who is so selfish?"

When I didn't answer, she only became bolder.

"Jeni insisted she lead us. She has let ILB down!"

and

"Maybe she has done something bad. Who would know?"

and

"I agree to take over so things are done right."

and

"Jeni should have her head chopped off."

Actually, she didn't compose the last tweet, but the cumulative effect of her flurry of activity including texts and emails was about that bad.

Since my friends were puzzled and probably miffed that I had not told them about my travel plans, they said nothing in response to Moira. What could they say anyway? I had told Anna about my search for Candi when I left Bucharest, but I had not told her anything since then. The problem was that I didn't feel telling anyone that I was actually in Porto Montenegro would help my cause. No one would believe I was in the new Monte Carlo for any reason other than pleasure.

For once, I decided to do nothing. It was better just to let Moira spin herself into a whirling dervish and then pick up the pieces when I returned with Candi. Frankly, the momentary lack of control over the ILB situation was the least of my worries, although it did remind me to send Victor's mom an email about canceling our tennis game that week.

When I finished, Jean-Claude came inside, sat down, and ordered an espresso, all before turning to say *allor.* Almost immediately he got a strange look on his face.

"Jeni, you look *so different,*" he said, staring straight into my eyes.

"Your cheeks, they are *rose*. And your eyes—I have never seen them so alive. You look … you look … so *beau*—" at which point he touched my face with his cupped his right hand as if to emphasize what a thing of beauty I had suddenly become. I realized that it was because my face was flushed from my morning bathroom bout with Davor. His uninvited touch and comments caught me off guard and left me unbalanced.

I wasn't a great liar in the best of situations, so coming up with a lie for why the skin on my face was suddenly shiny would only serve to make my cheeks and neck blush. The whole situation was way too awkward.

"Maybe it's because I finally got a good night's sleep," I mumbled, but I could tell it sounded like a lie and he knew it.

And just like that, our easy banter vanished. When we spoke again it was all business.

As we exited the restaurant, Jean-Claude, as he had done in the past, put his hand on the small of my back to guide me toward my car door. I saw Davor in the background watching me. Our eyes connected. I knew what he was thinking: *What is she doing? Why is she not admonishing the agent for such a personal gesture?* I had to agree. What was it about the French anyway that made every little thing Jean-Claude did seem outrageous, yet still perfectly normal?

In order to avoid any further conversation in the car, I researched more about the marina in the short time we had left on the road. If I thought for a second that I had been mistaken about the dishonorable intent of the developers, my research confirmed there was no question that this marina existed first and foremost as a sanctuary for the tax-averse multimillionaire or billionaire. I was very relieved to hear that in addition to simply secreting money, jet-setters would not have to spend one dime more on their champagne than what the vineyard charged, and could go much further on a dollar of diesel than the local fishermen could.

But even more disturbing to me than the tax havens for the greedy was the second part that I'd read. Because it was non-EU, Porto Montenegro offered the following "Flexible Cruising Regulations":

- no restrictions on pickup and drop-off
- the ability to make multiple changes to guest and crew manifests
- the ability for foreign vessels to remain in Montenegro waters with no restriction on time

Multiple changes to guest and crew manifests? It made my head swim. Did that mean that the supposedly strict crew registration with fingerprints could be changed without going through customs again? How did they keep track of crew and guests on yachts when changes were made? And no restrictions on pickup and drop-off? Did that mean the yacht could leave the country and go back and forth into the marina without declaring anything? The implications for these lax customs practices were staggering.

This could do nothing other than but make me worry all the more about Candi and what had happened to her.

Chapter Thirty-Two

BEFORE WE KNEW it, Jean-Claude and I were at Porto Montenegro. The gates were under maintenance, so we entered into a parking lot without paying, and pulled into a remote parking space under the shade of a tree. Once there, I began to unbuckle my seat belt and search for my purse. Jean-Claude reached over and touched my arm to get my attention.

"Non, you will stay for now. I will see if the yacht is here, and then I will be back," he said.

"I want to go. I don't want to sit here in a parking lot." I really wanted to say *You're not the boss of me,* but I was trying to act like a grown-up woman.

"Just for a second. *S'il vous plait?"*

It was that French thing again. I reluctantly nodded that it was okay, at which point he said "super," pulled his sunglasses down from his head, adjusted the collar of the pale pink shirt he had chosen for this day, and then almost jumped out of the car.

My cell phone rang just about then. It was Zach. He was pleased that I was following through with my promises and sitting in the parking lot as opposed to roaming around the marina. He asked if I had met Davor. It was clear that they had not yet spoken.

"Yes, we had an interesting meeting. How do you two know each other?" I asked.

"He was an exchange student with a friend of mine from college. We aren't exactly the same age, but I was around him a lot. Then I saw him at a conference recently. He's a nice guy."

"Did you get a chance to email Sue?" I asked, eager to change the subject.

"Yes, and she wrote back immediately. Of course, she was panicked and said if we don't find Candi in the next twenty-four hours, she and Bob will have no option but to fly over here to help. They feel too far away. I wrote her back, but I couldn't talk her out of it."

"That doesn't give us much time, does it?"

"No. Our only hope it that it all ends in Montenegro today," Zach said.

Zach told me he had learned from the harbormaster in Croatia that the *Taku* was owned by a wannabee oil tycoon from South America who rented it out all summer to offset his costs. Zach was told that the yacht had become too much for the owner to handle, and it was listed on the market for $24,500,000—if we were interested, that is. We both laughed at that prospect.

Zach had spoken to the owner's agent and told him that he had met the men on the boat and was interested in a charter for himself. According to the owner's administrative assistant, they didn't know anything about the men who chartered it for the week other than the fact that they spoke to each other in Italian. The really interesting information was that the men had paid in cash and didn't quibble on the price. Unfortunately, nothing new was revealed about Candi.

Zach told me he had spoken to Matt. Zach thought he would be cleared to join me by the end of the day. Matt was sorry that his instincts had been wrong about Candi's disappearance. He wanted to help. I smiled at that news. Matt was finally on my side.

Also, Zach had received a text that said Scout was doing great and that Collin would go to our apartment and check on the plants. Anna's repeated emails to Zach asking him to relay to me that I needed to call her were undeniable proof that Moira was still on an ILB rampage and that things were deteriorating rapidly.

In general, my conversation with Zach was happy and upbeat. He told me that he was sitting at a table on the waterfront and reading files from work while waiting for calls about the clearance and embassy approval.

"I think this is going to be a great day," he said. "Stay positive."

As we said our goodbyes, I saw Jean-Claude walking to the car with shopping bags under his arm. *Really, he went shopping while I sat in a hot car?*

He glided back into the front seat of the car and handed me the bags.

"Allor. These are for you," he said.

I looked at him in surprise.

"Oui, you must change. *Just as I suspected,* the yacht *Taku* is here, but it is on the third dock, which is not for the public. You must change so we can go and see if Candi is on the yacht."

I opened the first bag. Versace. It was probably the cheapest dress in the shop—simple with a yellow-and-orange flower print—but it was Versace. The second bag held a pair of Jimmy Choo sandals—simple again, but very pricey. Finally, there was a pair of fake designer sunglasses.

"Huh?"

"You must change. You must look *magnifique* … uh … *riche*. But first we must cut off the tags and put the receipts and bags in the trunk. The sunglasses are a gift."

"What? Are you planning on returning these clothes after I wear them? How awful! I'll feel like a thief. And how do you know my size anyway?"

"Madam, all men know the sizes of their ladies," he said with his silky-smooth French accent. I knew that wasn't true of American men. Zach couldn't guess my correct size on a multiple choice test. "And," Jean-Claude added, "I must keep the tags and everything to account for them because I used my office credit card. I had to get special approval because the only stores here are very expensive. I must return the dress and shoes to the office."

With that, he placed the tags and receipt in another plastic ziplock bag for their added protection.

He told me his plan.

Because the *Taku* was on one of the three docks not open to the public, he insisted I would have to get access to it in order to find Candi. The only plausible plan he had concocted was for me to dress up like I belonged there—that is, like a Barbie doll—and for me to approach a guard and use what feminine charms I possessed to gain entrance. It meant he had to make me look the part.

"You must change here."

"In the car?"

"Oui. Do not be silly. No one is here, and no one can see you. I will leave you alone and have a smoke. I will make it look as if we are having a lovers' quarrel."

With that he abruptly left the car, said something rude to me in French, slammed the door, walked away, and pulled out a cigar. He performed well, as if we were in a classic French movie. I could almost hear a sultry soundtrack playing as I resigned myself to make a daring rescue, or attempt one.

I changed, wriggling around like a caged snake. The dress fit fine, but I couldn't seem to correctly buckle the sandals around my ankles. I had no choice but to ask Jean-Claude to return to the car to help me. He lifted my feet up into his hands to grasp the buckle and clasped it tightly. I prayed Davor was not watching.

"Super," he said when I was dressed. "Now you must give me all your jewelry," he said, pointing to my hand.

"My wedding ring?"

"Oui, it is too, um, *petite*. It is better to have no jewelry. They will know you are not *riche* if you wear it."

I knew he was right, but it just suddenly seemed so wrong in every sense of the word. Billionaires know when you aren't a billionaire. No matter how much you dress up, they can tell by some cuff or sheen or mannerism that you aren't one of them and you never will be.

As I twisted the rings off my fingers, I knew I was crossing a line that should never be crossed. I had just gone too far to stop.

Chapter Thirty-Three

JEAN-CLAUDE PUT MY wedding rings and earrings into a ziplock bag and carefully wrote all my information on it with indelible black marker. He put the bag in the glove box and then locked it. I pulled my hair back in a sleek knot, applied shiny lip gloss, and slid the sunglasses onto my face. When I pushed up the car's mirror signifying I was through, Jean-Claude seemed more than pleased with the final product. Without comment, he reached across me to open my door from the inside. This time when his forearm grazed my thigh, I forced myself to think nothing of it.

It was showtime.

When I exited the car, I saw my reflection in the side of a metal shipping container on the edge of the lot. I almost didn't recognize the woman behind the sunglasses. The perfectly fitted dress that hit just below my bruised knees, combined with high-heeled sandals, made me look much taller and thinner. The large, dark sunglasses made me mysterious.

The slight sunburn made my skin glow. *Ah,* I wondered, *is this how it feels to look well bred?*

The answer did not matter. Now it was time to act the part. I pushed back my shoulders and looked straight ahead. Then I strode in perfect step with my handsome costar toward the concrete marina with all the confidence I could muster.

I didn't know exactly what to expect, but I found that the comments I had read online were fairly accurate in describing my surroundings. Palm trees that almost looked fake were planted in nondescript planters around square buildings housing hotels, restaurants, bars, and high-end shops. *Everything* catered purely to the wealthy. Poor Jean-Claude was right: he had no choice as to where to buy my clothes. I hoped that they would believe him at the home office.

We went straight to the promenade, which was like all modern concrete boardwalks. They look incredible under the lights at night but appear hard and stark during the daytime. I was not impressed, but then again I had just arrived with a very bad attitude.

On the other hand, the view of the Bay of Kotor from the marina was worth the price of admission. The dark blue waters were surrounded by hills and mountains composed of brush, wildflowers, and rock—much like the terrain of Southern California. It was different from the coastal land, in large part because of its beginnings as part of a river system. It was deeper, colder, more ancient, and ominous—on any given day it could be one sailor's sanctuary and another's trap.

It wasn't just yachts at the marina that were competing with the bay for views. Beautiful women were roaming everywhere, with big diamonds on their fingers and carrying tiny purses on gold chains. Most were dressed in designer clothes like me, the only difference being that the younger the woman, the shorter the skirt. Mine was a bit long for my age, but given its tight fit and strapless top, I could be forgiven.

We walked past the lunch crowds and headed toward the piers, never looking anyone in the eye, as that was strictly forbidden for the ultrarich. I had observed that the wealthy didn't randomly look around and smile. They never, ever chatted up a stranger unless it was to point out the size of their boat. Whether it was out of fear, disdain, or breeding, I didn't know. But I copied it.

The *Taku*'s pier was easy to find. Although the marina was large, it was walkable in about fifteen minutes. The lone security guard near the dock's entrance watched as we approached, unsure as to my mission.

"Hello! Do you speak English?" I asked.

"Little." He was a typical bodyguard for a place that harbored those with secret lives. It was impossible to miss his huge biceps, huge neck, and unfriendly face. I felt sure that he could break Jean-Claude in half.

"My sister is on one of these boats. She didn't tell me which one, just the pier number. May I see if she's here?" I pointed to the yachts on the dock.

He stared at me, unsure of what I was asking or what his next move should be. I had strung too much English together for his skills.

"My sister? *Mia sorella*?" I didn't know if he spoke any Italian, but it was worth a try given the region. I pointed to the pier. Still no response.

I realized I would have to work harder. I walked up within two feet of him and then slowly bent down to adjust the strap on my shoe. I tried to imitate the seductive women I had seen in movies, lifting my skirt up a bit and turning my hips in his direction. When I stood up, I could tell I had been a fast learner. He seemed more receptive to figuring out what I wanted. I decided to try a combination of languages.

"Please? *Per favore*? I can't wait to see her. Mia sorella? You seem really smart, and I'm so glad someone like you is protecting her. Have you seen *signora americana*?"

When I stared into his eyes intently, I was close enough to smell his bad breath. "She told me that there was a really *strong man* as her guard," I said while deliberately looking at his muscles. "I'm sure it has to be you."

He may not have been bilingual, but he wasn't stupid. In the universal language of seduction, I was making a play for him and he was willing to go along with it. Signora americana must have gotten through to him.

"Taku?" he said before he could stop himself.

"*Possibile! E grandioso!* May I walk down and see?" I moved my fingers like a person walking.

"Pretty please? Per favore?" As I spoke, I adjusted the top of my dress one last time just for him. I pointed to the *Taku* and then put my hands together as if to plead, hoping he would understand.

I thought he would refuse, but he didn't.

"Un minuto." He lifted one finger to emphasize that I had one minute.

"Grazie! Un minuto!"

I started to walk away. Jean-Claude made a move to join me. The guard blocked his path.

"No." That two-letter word did not need any translation. I froze for a second, but recovered and dismissed Jean-Claude with a wave of my hand as if he were a nuisance. Then I proceeded down the dock.

Leaving Jean-Claude behind me, I proceeded alone toward the boat and tried to see if there were any signs of life. I didn't call out Candi's name for fear of being discovered. Instead, I waved back at the guard and shrugged my shoulders as if I were a coy teenager, signaling that perhaps it was the wrong boat. He smiled back at me and let me continue to wander.

I could feel perspiration begin to moisten my dress. Was it the heat or a sign of stress from this ill-researched strategy?

Just when I was about to leave for fear of being unmasked, I heard the distinct whistle of a cardinal from the bow of the *Taku*. I smiled. *It has to be Candi.* My father had taught his daughters and granddaughters to bird whistle, and I knew there were no cardinals in this marina.

It took me a few seconds to find her because she was sitting in a chaise lounge on an upper deck and was partially hidden behind a box that held an emergency life raft. She probably had seen me on the pier from her higher vantage point. When our eyes met, she said nothing, but she lifted up her elbow and crooked her finger like she was holding an invisible coffee cup. It was an unmistakable signal, one that I instinctively understood.

Immediately thereafter, she quickly stood up from her chaise and disappeared.

Chapter Thirty-Four

I WALKED THE pier once more, pretending to look for my long-lost sister, before returning to the guard. Then I made a sad face that signaled I'd had no luck finding her. He was obviously feeling pretty good about our exchange, and it showed in the friendly nod of his head and sympathetic smile. For once a pretty rich woman had paid him attention. He tried to tell me in English that he was sorry I hadn't found my sister, but the only word he knew was *sorry*. Still, it sounded kind of sweet coming from such a burly man.

Jean-Claude and I didn't speak until we were a hundred feet away from the guard. I told him about seeing Candi and the unmistakable crooked finger. I told him that it was our family signal for "It's coffee time."

"I think she was signaling for us to find a table in the nearest coffee shop, and fast."

Our host at the closest café was a tall Montenegrin. He was determined that we should sit at an outside table by the front entrance and didn't seem in the least inclined to change his mind. We needed privacy, so predictably Jean-Claude started to argue with him. It was interesting to watch—a fancy Frenchman against a poised, tall, and handsome Montenegrin.

We were making no headway, just a scene, until Davor appeared from out of nowhere. I watched in curiosity as he warmly shook hands with the host and then engaged him in a friendly conversation in their native language. It was not long before Davor pointed to a secluded table in the back, and the host nodded in agreement. I thought I saw Davor slip the man a folded bill of some denomination, but that was fine with me. I was ready to do anything to secure that private table away from prying eyes and ears.

Although I figured they probably knew each other's identity by that time, I felt the need to introduce Jean-Claude to Davor. Each agent gave the other a cool reception. Just like law enforcement in the United States, neither man particularly wanted someone from a different law enforcement agency in his territory or his investigation, especially something this large. The two men sat warily on opposite sides of the table, leaving a large roomy gap between them for when, and if, Candi appeared.

I could feel Davor's eyes studying me while I considered the ridiculous prices of the cappuccinos that he ordered and wondered who would pay, seeing as I had no money. He seemed fascinated by my transformation.

"Okay, what gives?" he finally said. "Pretty fancy clothes, Jeni. Did Zach get a raise?"

That made me furious. We were the only ones doing anything to get my niece, and he had the audacity to mock us. *How dare he?* I had no intention of telling him a thing. However, before I could convey my plan of silence to my partner, Jean-Claude was off to the races, spelling out in detail everything from beginning to end. It was only then that he turned to look at me.

"Remember—do not spill anything on the dress," Jean-Claude said as he watched me sip from the delicate coffee cup with the initials "PM" embossed in gold.

"I know, I know." I carefully put down the cup and slunk back into my chair. How demoralizing.

"So, what's the dream team's plan now?" Davor asked.

"How about me asking where *you* went to school to learn how to be so snide and nasty?" I'd had enough of his attitude.

Jean-Claude chose once again to ignore me and simply responded to Davor.

"We will get Candi, and then I shall have the boat seized."

Davor responded, "Okay, well, that really isn't a plan and it won't work." "First, Montenegro would never go along with that. Seizing a yacht here would be big news in the South of France. It would undermine Montenegro's plan of enticing yacht owners to this marina. Second, they have fueled up and are leaving in an hour, according to the harbormaster. He thinks their destination must be somewhere close because he said they'll return tomorrow."

Before Davor could say anything more, I saw Candi walking toward the coffee shop. Relief poured over me. Finally, I was close to having her home again.

She was with the Moldovan man named Dimitri. I hadn't planned on that. I began to think again that they might be in love. Candi seemed strong and confident as she strode toward the table with Dimitri in tow. But was it love? I couldn't tell. Something for sure had changed in her. Even from a distance I could tell there was a maturity and seriousness in the way she held her head high and her back straight, something that I had never seen in her before.

Once again my thoughts went back to the obvious. Although I had successfully avoided talking about the possibility that Candi was being sexually abused, it had never left my mind. Still, I clung to the hope that Dimitri was different from the other traffickers, when all the signals said he wasn't.

Davor apparently had instructed the host to lead them to our table. I could sense Dimitri's confusion when Candi and the host passed two or three empty tables and headed straight to the back where we sat. Even when Dimitri saw me, it took a second for him to realize what that meant. Once it sunk into his mind that I wasn't good news, his face became contorted and his eyes began to frantically search for a way out.

You could see his mind whirling. Really, who gets captured in a coffee shop? He turned and made a quick move toward the exit, but before he could bolt, Davor stood up in his path and then deftly flipped out his badge.

"Have a seat," Davor said as he calmly pointed to an empty chair.

Dimitri looked around and saw the host, Jean-Claude, and me blocking his other exit.

It was only then that he reluctantly followed the directions. He agreed that he was surrounded and any thought of escape was futile. There was nowhere to run.

Once Dimitri was contained, Candi fell into my arms, whispering, "Thank you, thank you," before she finally released me and collapsed in a chair at the table.

"Dimitri wouldn't let me out of his sight, and someone took my phone," she said, almost gulping for air before she took a deep breath. "Aunt Jeni, I'm so sorry I left you and Uncle Zach. I really believed Dimitri when he'd said that I could be a model. It sounded so exciting."

While Davor made a few phone calls, Candi hurriedly told me that by the time they were getting ready to leave Split, she became suspicious that things weren't what they seemed. The travel plans were vague and the crew was unprofessional in every way. She kept asking about her modeling job in Italy and was told it was "in the works," but there were no details, no names or contracts. She decided that they were all incompetent and it would be best to cut her losses and leave. Her plan was to jump ship when they got to Hvar and call us to come get her.

But then things got worse.

"I had no idea that other women were on board until we had already left Split," she said.

It was then that she overheard conversations about women who were locked in crew's quarters, and she knew that meant they were destined for trafficking. She felt strongly that she couldn't leave the yacht until they were free as well. It only made sense to her that if she ran for help in Hvar, the men would get rid of the women before the police could arrive.

"It was so hard to wait to be rescued. You have no idea. *I was so glad to see you in Hvar!* I couldn't figure out how you found me. It was the hardest thing I've ever done—being mean and getting back on the yacht for another night—but I had no choice. I knew it was only a matter of time before you'd read the compact and we'd be saved. But that night the police never came. We weren't rescued. It was so awful when I heard the engines turned on … I didn't know where we were going … I was so scared."

She paused and gave a slight smile.

"But I never doubted you would find me, no matter what I said or where we went. I waited on the top deck all morning, praying I was right."

I gave her a hug as tears fell down her face. "I'm so sorry for what I've put you and Uncle Zach through—and especially Mom and Dad."

"No need for apologies. They'll be so relieved to know that you were found and that you're okay," I said. It was the understatement of the century.

Chapter Thirty-Five

IN THE SMALL amount of time we had been in the coffee shop, Davor had arranged for the tables around us to be vacant. It gave us privacy while we considered the predicament we were in with Dimitri at our table and the *Taku* getting ready to depart. Davor finished his call to the office, took charge, and began with preliminary questions for Dimitri.

"So, are there other women on the *Taku*?" he asked.

Dimitri suddenly regained his composure. He smoothly tried to spin the narrative to his liking.

"Yes, but they are going to Italy for work and better lives."

"Prostitution?" Davor asked.

"No, it isn't prostitution. Most of them have jobs in housekeeping or factory work. They will be compensated. Maybe not immediately, but once they have paid off their costs to get to their final destination, they will have better lives. They all volunteered to go. They should thank the captain. It is almost like charity."

And that is when he went too far.

"That's not true, you dirtbag!" Candi seethed. She was no longer tearful; she was furious. She popped up from her chair, accidentally knocking a glass of water over, and leaned across the table toward Dimitri, glaring into his face. It was a good thing that she didn't have a gun, or else he might have taken a bullet between the eyes.

"Some of them might just be workers, but most will be slaves, and you know it. And I know for a fact that some of the girls are going to Italian men to be prostitutes—no, not prostitutes, sex slaves. They won't even get paid like prostitutes. I heard the men talking. They plan to sell them on the 'dark web' ..."

I interrupted in shock. "Dark web?"

"Oh yeah. The internet makes it easy for them. They lure them in just like they did me—with texts and emails and promises—and then they use sites similar to Backpage to coordinate with each other. It was just a matter of time before they sold them or worse," Candi said. Then she turned her attention back to Dimitri. "You idiot. I know enough Italian to understand you're part of organized crime. You're all so evil. I hate you!"

At first, her words seemed to rattle Dimitri. But then he recovered quickly.

"No, Candi. Not me. I am not like them. I protected you. I told you that I love you. I would not let them hurt you. You know that." Incredibly, despite his predicament, Dimitri managed to keep his voice low and soft and his eyes on Candi.

Candi was quiet, but I could tell she was breathing heavily as if in distress. The rest of us at the table waited in anticipation of how she would ultimately respond. All the while Dimitri gained more confidence.

"I would never let that happen to you. I do love you. I had a plan to keep you separate from the other women. You aren't like them. You really are going to be a model." His voice was smooth and calm as if he were the only reasonable person in the room. "We must go to Italy. It's your dream to model. You shouldn't hate me. Just trust me."

With that, he held out his perfectly manicured hand to her to leave, imploring her to do so with his dark eyes.

"I don't understand," I suddenly interjected. I couldn't help but stop whatever he was trying to do. "How is Candi different? How were you going to keep her separate? Why? Why would you even participate in locking up innocent women? Nothing you say makes any sense at all." I knew that even if he was being truthful, any plan he had was ill-conceived and dangerous.

While I spoke, Candi began to glare at Dimitri with all the intensity of a boxer inside the ropes right before a match.

"You don't want me to hate you? Is that what you want? Then you better figure out a plan to save all those girls right now, or I'll be the person who throws away the key to your cell. I'll be the star witness. If they had the death penalty for the cruelty that those men want to inflict on those poor defenseless women, I would happily throw the switch! You better believe that I won't rest until we rescue every person you have imprisoned on that boat. They are scared to death, they're seasick, and they need to go home to their families. You have about five minutes to do the right thing, and if you don't, they're going to lock you up on my testimony."

By the end of her stinging comments, Dimitri was in shock—the pathetic minor-league organized criminal really must have fallen in love with my American niece and thought she loved him back. She could be quite the little actress when she wanted to be.

It gave Davor his opportunity.

"Look, Dimitri, you are not getting out of this situation without going to jail. Your only hope is to help us and get some consideration from the prosecutor. Why don't you tell us the plan your people have for the girls and who you work for? I know you just got in over your head. You probably didn't mean to do it."

Without communicating a word, Davor had chosen the role of the good cop, which could only mean that Jean-Claude was the bad one.

"Non! Interpol is most certainly *not* agreeable to any deal. Interpol would like to lock him up in the Montenegrin jail. *Immediat*!" With that Jean-Claude stood up from his chair and threw his napkin onto the table to announce the end of the discussion, as if it were the proverbial gauntlet. He looked eerily like a French king ordering his betrayer to be beheaded.

It worked on the table's occupants. Even I jumped back in my seat.

"No, no," began Dimitri. He had lost all his swagger. "I will help. Don't do anything. I see … I see what I have to do. But do not put me into jail, okay? Until we go to court? Right? Deal?"

Davor looked to Jean-Claude for his agreement, but the Interpol agent shook his head in firm disagreement and said something in a variety of languages like "Never. I would like to kill this scum myself." It was effective. Dimitri was visibly frightened.

We were all quiet for a few moments until Jean-Claude theatrically pulled out his cell as if to make a call to headquarters. Dimitri said once again that he would tell everything. It was only then that Jean Claude nodded his reluctant approval.

"Okay, but first you must give me your passport and cell phone," Davor said, his hand extended.

Dimitri sighed and pulled out his Moldovan passport and mobile.

"Clever," Davor said, rifling through the passport's pages. Then he stood up and leaned toward Dimitri's face. "Do you want a deal or not? How about giving me the real passport with your real name? And your other cell phone."

The man we all knew as Dimitri smiled weakly and shrugged as if to say *I tried.* He then reached into a hidden pocket in his pants and handed Davor a second cell phone, plus his proper Moldovan passport with his legal name, something incomprehensibly long and totally unpronounceable to me.

"Now tell us the truth or you'll sleep in jail tonight." Davor was ready to get the show on the road. Time was against us.

Dimitri began, "The yacht is due to leave in a few minutes for Albania, only a hundred and twenty miles south of where we are. The Italians who run this operation will meet us there after dark, and they will transfer the cargo."

I gasped when I heard him refer to the women as cargo, and when I realized that they were going to Albania, not Italy. I had spent time in Albania a few years back and knew a lot more about it than the everyday tourist. Albania is known to most of the world for its criminal underbelly. It was not surprising to any of us that they trafficked in humans. Basically, they had no preference as to which criminal activity they engaged in, so long as it provided the most expedient profit. It could be drugs, humans, cigarettes, banned cargo, internet scams, or just everyday money laundering. The gangs were made up of equal-opportunity thugs, forming a web of criminal networks in large cities across the world.

The upside for our operation was that Albania, like Montenegro, wanted to join the EU and the Western world, even though it had less of a chance of securing membership in the EU than Montenegro. Its entry into NATO was a sign of progress. I knew that Albania had no desire to be known as the criminal capital of the world. It wanted to be perceived as the opposite. It also helped that Albania was a member of the regional law enforcement organization where Zach worked.

"The *Taku* is supposed to arrive in Albania at night and be met by a boat just off the beach near the city of Durres. The passengers will be ferried by a smaller boat or boats to various locations. You will have to intercept them before they leave the *Taku* if you want to save the women and arrest their captors. The problem is that you don't have enough time to stop the boat from leaving here. And if they get wind of the police following them, they will dispose of the cargo overboard as fast as possible."

I knew what "dispose of the cargo" meant. I immediately felt sick.

Once Dimitri finished, he gamely suggested that he and Candi return to the *Taku* so no one would become suspicious about her departure. They could travel with the group to Albania, whereupon Interpol and the Albanian police could arrest everyone in Durres. No one was biting on that plan, especially me.

"No way," I said. "Candi's through with all this."

Davor and Jean-Claude nodded their heads in agreement.

"I'll go in her place," I said, eliciting surprised looks. "I look enough like her, a little older perhaps, but we can change clothes and maybe no one will notice if they don't look at me too closely. Anyway, I owe it to my sister. I think she hates me right now and blames me, more than anyone, for Candi's disappearance."

"No, Aunt Jeni, you don't know ..." Candi said before I held up my hand to stop her.

"You're finished with these men. It's my turn to take care of you."

"I'm not sure," Davor said. "Let's think about what can go wrong, which is everything. Tina has already almost been killed, and she's law enforcement. You have no training or skills and it would be too dangerous."

"I know that I'm not a policewoman or an agent," I said, "but I'd be nothing but a decoy—not anything else. I'd act like a wooden duck. I'll just sit in her room waiting for the police and not say a word. It would work, I'm sure of it."

Davor thought for a moment. "Dimitri, who on the boat would know if Candi was exchanged?"

"The man who works with me—we call him Sam, as in Samson. His main job is to watch Candi and make sure she is safe, and also to help with the boat. There is the captain and his first mate—they will be busy at the helm. There is a cook, but he likes to stay in his cabin when he is not cooking the meals or cleaning up afterward. The maid and cabin mate might notice she isn't Candi, but they don't talk."

"Who is watching the women?" I asked.

"No one needs to do anything with them. The women are locked in berths below the deck, and other than to feed them, no one opens the doors," Candi said.

"Do you know who is paying for this operation?" Davor asked.

"Some rich guy named Rocco from Italy," Dimitri said. "I only met him once in Bucharest. I have met the other men who work for him. They are going to pick up the women."

Davor nodded his head. "Okay then, Dimitri, I think I have a plan. First, right now in front of me, call Sam and have him meet us at the fuel dock. In the meantime, Jeni, you and Candi go to the toilet and exchange clothes. Fast. I'm going to try to take Sam's place. And Jeni, you will take the place of Candi."

"Won't they be able to tell you aren't a real crew member?" I asked.

"Given that I spent every summer in college crewing on yachts, I'm sure I'll be far more competent than Sam. I know the life—too well. I have no desire to be one of them," he said, glancing toward the faraway yachts.

"Oh, and Jeni?" Davor turned to look at me. "Call Zach and tell him so I can make sure he is okay with this plan."

"Sure, I'll call him," I said.

My answer must not have been convincing, as Davor stood looking at me as if to read my face for a few seconds. He must have decided to believe me because he returned to the job at hand.

"If Sam comes and we can take him into custody, then, Jean-Claude, I'll get you the names of my Albanian contacts. I'd like for you take over my work with them. Once Sam is in custody, you can drive with Candi to Durres as fast as you can. It's only about a hundred and twenty miles, but drive fast so you get there in time in case we need your help or Candi's testimony."

I smiled. Driving fast was something Jean-Claude excelled at.

Chapter Thirty-Six

A FEW SECONDS alone with Candi was all I needed in order to confirm that we were back on the same team. We hugged tightly and then, as instructed, starting peeling off dresses over our heads.

"Versace? Did Uncle Zach get a raise?" Candi asked as she took the handful of fabric that cost more than his monthly income.

This time I laughed and told her no, suggesting she not get a spot on it for fear of Jean-Claude. If anything, I was happy to be rid of the expensive liability. The problem was that Candi's dress was way, way shorter, and tighter on me than on her. It barely fit.

"Ugh, my knees," I said, which were still red from my falls. Candi whipped out a cover-up stick from her purse and painted over them like a pro.

"I've learned a lot," she said with a smile. Then she became serious, grabbing my hand and squeezing it. "Aunt Jeni, please don't do this. Let them handle it. You have no idea what these men are like ..."

"The decision is made. We'll talk more later," I said as I pried myself away from her grasp. "We have to hurry!"

It upset me too much to think about what could have happened to her, but it wasn't the time or the place to discuss it. I retained the Jimmy Choo shoes since they kept me Candi's height. Plus, deep down inside I knew I would never buy them in real life. *Why not wear them one more day?*

The men had paid the bill and were waiting for us outside the café. The plan was that Davor, Dimitri, and I would walk together to the fuel dock and try to appear as normal as possible. Candi was told to wait for Jean-Claude in the parking lot, which she initially didn't want to do. She was still trying to convince me to abandon the plan, while I wondered if I ought to warn her to be careful around Jean-Claude.

It was only after she realized that her objections were useless that she gave in, pulled me close to her, and urgently whispered, "Aunt Jeni, if you go, I need to tell you: trust no one. And *don't* go near the helm. Be careful. I love you!" Then she hurriedly turned to catch up with Jean-Claude, who was already leaving.

Her comments sent shivers up my spine when I looked at my new companions. Candi didn't know it, but the truth was that I didn't trust anyone already. Now I was forced to wonder, *What is wrong at the helm?*

The man they called Sam was completely oblivious to what was going on when we arrived at the fuel dock. He just stood there looking at Dimitri as if he would issue instructions, and then in an instant Davor snapped handcuffs on his hands, one of which had a right index finger bundled in bandages. Sam, the man whom Scout had bit in Bran and the one I had seen getting on to the gray motorboat in Trogir, was finally in police custody.

Once Sam knew that he couldn't run, he began to stare at me rather than at Dimitri.

Sam clearly realized I was not Candi, but he seemed to be having trouble putting the puzzle pieces together and recalling how he knew me. I felt it was my duty to eliminate any doubt in his little mind, so I raised my right hand to wriggle my fingers and pointed to the one he had bandaged. I couldn't help but give him a big smile. He was no longer uncertain as to who I was and where we had met.

Despite the restraints, he couldn't control himself and lunged at me like a football lineman at the snap of the ball, attempting to push me off the pier and into the water. It took both men to restrain him. Despite my precarious position on the edge, I stood my ground, totally.

"Jeni!" Davor said under his breath, trying to keep his composure. He looked around to see if anyone was watching. "Is this how you intend to act on the boat?" He almost hissed the words.

I just sighed and walked away from the men, allowing them to quietly finish the transfer of Sam to a waiting Montenegrin officer behind a nearby building. I had accomplished what I wanted, which was to give Sam just a taste of the torment that he had given me. On the other hand, Davor was not finished with me.

"Jeni, are you going to continue pulling these stunts, or will you follow my instructions?" Davor was rattled. I could see him reassessing our plan. "By the way, did you tell Zach what we are doing? What did he say?"

"You don't need to worry. Everything is fine. Once on board I'll control myself. I promise. Zach always tells me to be careful." I didn't directly respond to the question about what Zach knew, but what I did say was enough. Davor took that response as "Yes, I called him," and said nothing more. The sad reality was that I had forgotten about Zach in all the excitement, so I tried to remedy the situation as fast as I could. I pulled out the cell phone only to discover that the battery was dead.

There was nothing else I could do now other than charge the phone on the boat and then try later to contact Zach. In a way, it was the best solution. Deep down inside, I knew he'd never agree to my participation in this crazy plan—and he'd be right.

Dimitri led us to the yacht, chatting about nothing important as if he had no cares in the world. That only made me more nervous. Was he a great actor, or did he have another plan up his sleeve? I worried that once on board he would turn on us, but Davor acted as if he were in control. He told Dimitri that he couldn't leave his side—not for a minute—or else he would be in jail before he knew it, if not shot dead.

I considered backing out for fear of both men and the unknown occupants aboard the *Taku,* and I panicked when Davor discreetly passed Dimitri a handgun. *That can't be a good idea,* I thought.

"Don't get excited. It has no ammo. My gun, of course, is fully loaded," Davor said, looking at me. "And by the way, Dimitri, my office has all the details about where your home and assets are located, and they expect me to come back unharmed—just in case you are having second thoughts about cooperating."

Dimitri nodded his understanding.

"Okay, then let's go," Davor said as we approached the *Taku.* With that, I regained my confidence and put on my game face. It was too late to back out no matter how scared I was.

The first mate and cabin boy were waiting for us when we arrived at the pier. The engines were humming loudly. The *Taku* was ready to leave. Dimitri yelled over the noise of the engines that Davor was taking over for Sam. He told the first mate that Sam's hand had gotten infected and Davor knew the waters at night better than Sam. The first mate nodded and did not appear disturbed in the least by a last-minute crew change. As they talked, I took the opportunity to scamper up the gangplank on the side opposite the first mate and Dimitri. I wanted to avoid eye contact with anyone. At the last second, I held out my hand to the cabin boy for assistance on board, just as I'd seen Candi do.

Strangely, the extremely shy cabin boy never even looked me in the face. The first mate was the opposite—very confident and observant. The good news was that he was busy with our departure and obviously assumed that I was Candi because of my clothing and my resemblance to her. He never looked my way long enough to see the change.

The men dropped the mooring line and threw the stern lines off the boat to the pier before the gangplank was totally secured. They were in a hurry.

The vessel's sudden movement away from the safety of the berth unnerved me for a minute. My unease was only compounded when I realized that I had forgotten to ask Candi where her stateroom was or about the layout of the yacht. I stood in place for a second or two, not knowing which direction to take, until deciding to bend down to my shoe and pretend to shake out a tiny pebble. Dimitri came to steady my arm, and when he was close enough I asked in a whisper where my room was. He smiled. It was stateroom no. 4, down the hall and on the right.

Already, Dimitri was proving useful. Or was he?

I worried for a second that my room was the same as his, but when I arrived in stateroom no. 4, I saw it was only for me, the new Candi. The cabin was full of high-end marine furnishings and had lots of clothes and makeup strewn everywhere. There was a single berth, a matching chair, an ottoman, and a desk, all in new light wood veneer, highly varnished and decorated with blue-and-white-striped linens. The desk had all the comforts of home, including lots of phone chargers.

My phone rang as soon as it was charged up enough to do so. Of course, it was Zach.

"Where are you?" he asked. No niceties.

"It's going to make you mad if I tell you," I whispered.

"So, it's true. You're on a yacht to Albania. Davor called and left a message to confirm I'm okay with this crazy plan. I'm *not*!" As quiet as

I was being, Zach was being loud on the other end. "Why, Jeni? You *promised!*"

"I know I said I wouldn't do anything foolish, but Zach, this isn't foolish. It's very serious. What they have done is a terrible thing, and for once in my life I can do something to change the situation." I worked hard to keep my voice as calm as possible despite Zach's anger.

I told him that if I didn't go and didn't pretend to be Candi, they would've been suspicious, and every woman on board would be in grave danger.

"All I'm doing is providing the police, or whoever, enough time to get to Albania and be ready for our arrival there. They'll make the arrests. Remember Davor is here to protect me and Dimitri is on our side. And that guy who was bitten by Scout—he's been arrested. I think the boat is pretty safe at this moment. I know it isn't the best idea, but I really feel that I didn't have any choice. We have to save these women."

Despite my argument, I knew Zach was still upset.

"I'm not going to argue with you right now. I understand your passion to help, but anything can go wrong and I won't be there to help." He paused and took a deep breath. "I'm trying to get to Albania as fast as I can. I already called the embassy. They're working on it from their end. Until I get to you, I want you to stay in your stateroom, lock your door, and don't do a thing. I'm more than halfway to Albania. I'll call Jean-Claude back to see where he is. Until then, anything can go wrong. So, again, just stay in your room and keep your phone charged."

"I will. I love you. Please don't be angry."

"Oh, I'm angry at everyone in your group right now. I love you, too, but I can't believe you did this. *Please* stay safe."

After our call, I sat on the edge of the bed watching the late-day sun floating on the surface of the water outside my oblong porthole—a porthole rimmed all around in polished chrome with bronze trim and anchor etching. As I watched the sun set, the tiny waves and gentle whitecaps of Kotor Bay began to reflect the lights from the distant shores. The rhythmic dance pattern the light made as it swung back and forth in the small swells almost lulled me into believing that all was right on the *Taku*.

I'd never been on a fine yacht at sea. There was no discomfort—no rocking or rolling. It was only as I peered through the porthole that I began to sense how fast the *Taku* was moving through the waters toward its destination. It was the speed that brought me back to my senses and caused me to remember the danger that lurked around me.

Please, God, let us continue to have calm seas tonight, I silently prayed before I turned away from the porthole.

Zach was right. No matter how beautiful the scenery, I knew I was in a terrible predicament. Of the seven people on board—Dimitri, Davor, the captain, the first mate, the cook, the maid, and me—I only trusted Davor. How could he protect me while he was required to constantly be with Dimitri in case Dimitri had second thoughts about which side he was on? I knew it wouldn't take much for him to reevaluate his allegiances and act accordingly.

Chapter Thirty-Seven

MY DREADFUL MUSINGS were abruptly ended by a knock on my door.

"Candi, dinner is ready. Come join us," Davor said. It took me a second to realize that he meant me.

"Who is *us*?" I asked.

"Dimitri and me."

"No thanks. I don't feel well enough to eat."

"What's the matter? Do you need something?" Dimitri asked.

"No, I'm tired and I just don't feel well."

"Okay … I guess," Dimitri said. I could tell he was thinking about what to do. "Would you like it if I sent the maid, Maria, to bring a plate of food for you?"

"Fine," I responded, "but Davor, do me a favor and make Dimitri taste-test my food to be sure it's not poisoned."

"By all means," Davor said. They retreated down the passageway. I wasn't sure he didn't laugh.

Maria, a slight young woman of Southeast Asian descent, was at my door in less than five minutes. She was wearing a white-and-gold uniform—short, of course—and pushed a silver cart filled with fancy-looking food, along with a bottle of French wine and a single crystal wineglass rimmed in gold. Each piece of the white porcelain china had an elaborate anchor logo in gold, intertwined with a *T* for *Taku,* as did the vase holding a spray of roses.

"Come in," I told her.

She entered but said nothing. In an almost military-like precision, she kept her head down and methodically staged my elaborate in-room meal. Once the food was arranged to her satisfaction, she adjusted the cart so it was perfectly situated for the optimum view from the porthole. Only then did she raise her head to see if I approved.

Her look of shock when she saw my face made it clear that she knew I was not Candi. She was visibly shaken. She momentarily covered her eyes with her hands.

"It's okay. I'm Candi's sister," I told her. I thought that the word *aunt* would seem way too complicated and distant.

"I'm also a policewoman," I said, ready to lie about anything.

She was still confused. At first, she looked me over as if to memorize my appearance, and then she resumed hanging her head and avoiding my eyes.

"Why are you scared? I want to help you," I said softly as I approached her. She began to shake in fear the closer I got, and then she shrunk back, as if at any moment I might strike her. Worried that she would scream, I realized that I had to convince her that I wasn't the enemy—and I had to do it fast.

I gently pried her hand off the tray, and held it in mine as a nurse might do to console a patient. She didn't pull back.

I led her to the empty chair and asked her to sit while I faced her from a perch on the edge of the bed. She sat erect in the chair and looked at me with an impassive face.

"You have to trust me."

She said nothing.

"Do you know English?"

"A little." I could barely hear her soft voice.

"Okay. I'm here to help you and the women below. I want to get you to safety. That's why we had Sam taken off the boat. Sam is gone, so you'll be safe."

"Sam gone?" Now she was really distraught.

"Yes, he's off the boat."

"Oh no! Sam not bad. Captain very, very bad." She spilled out the words, almost gasping at the end. Then she gathered her breath and wailed, "Sam save Tom."

"Who's Tom?"

"Cabin boy. Captain get mad at Tom. He drop drink bottles. Captain tell Tom he throw Tom overboard. Tom no can swim. Sam stop Captain and Sam buy more bottles, so no more problem. Sam save Tom."

I shook my head in disbelief. No wonder she was upset.

"Why didn't you and Tom try to get off the yacht in Montenegro?" I used my fingers to execute an acrobatic jumping maneuver.

"Captain has passports and money. Captain keep my clothes. No can leave. Captain say we get money and passports in Albania. But I no want to go to Albania." With this she began to cry silently, big tears welling in her eyes and rolling down the cheeks of her tiny porcelain face.

"I will help you, but you must trust me and do as I ask. Can you do that?"

She nodded her assent.

I moved over to her, hugged her, and rocked back and forth to assure her it would all be okay, saying that she just needed to do her job and pretend I was Candi. She assured me she would keep our secret.

Maria regained her composure as best she could and stood to leave, but suddenly she hesitated and turned around.

"Captain want to take Candi for him … He no good."

Candi's last words once again came to me: *Trust no one.* Why had Dimitri said nothing about the captain's lustful interest in Candi? *What if he comes in the night for me, thinking I am Candi?*

As soon as Maria left, I began to feel claustrophobic, stuck in a fiberglass box with nothing but dark seas and deception around me. I inspected the stateroom door with my hands. It was with relief that I found the builders had spared no expense in the quality and thickness of the doors or its heavy locks.

Zach called about the time I finished my safety inspection. I told him about Maria, and he said he would check out what she'd revealed and call me back in ten minutes. He wanted to get more background on the captain, the one man heretofore no one had considered to be a problem.

The background check was fast.

"Captain Arra is not just a problem, he's a huge one," Zach said when he called back with his findings. "Although he was raised in Kosovo, he's ethnic Albanian by birth."

Zach told me that maritime records confirmed that he has a captain's license, but had been cited repeatedly over the past ten years for marine violations, in particular the discharge of oil and refuse off the yachts he has captained.

"More worrisome is the fact that he was accused of smuggling goods and possibly people on two occasions, but they never found anything once the yacht was in port. It was assumed he threw everything overboard or passed his potentially illegal human cargo to another vessel," Zach said. He waited for this news to sink in before he continued.

"According to past news reports, Captain Arra has repeatedly denied his involvement in smuggling. He said he's targeted because he's Albanian and many Croats and Serbians don't like the Albanians, especially when they're successful. But the question dogs him about how a simple boat captain can make so much money, even if he's a very good one. He reportedly has three villas, one in Italy, one in Cyprus, and one in Albania, none in his name, just nebulous LLC's. The locals claim he's involved in organized crime."

As Zach spoke, I thought about the *Taku* and the absent and marginally rich yacht owner. Despite evidence to the contrary, Zach told me that he found it hard to believe the boat owner was a human trafficker. His agent was open and friendly and seemed to have nothing to hide. If anything, he thought the owner might be too naive to be in organized crime. He was probably just in debt and the captain exploited the perfect situation to charter a vessel that law enforcement had no reason to suspect was involved in smuggling activities.

We talked a few minutes more before Zach approached the border crossing to Albania and needed to end our call.

Before we said goodbye, Zach insisted I wasn't to open my door no matter what. Davor had arranged for a police go-fast boat to catch up with us before our arrival in Durres. Once the yacht was anchored, the police would board it. Until then, I was to sit and wait. We figured it would be about two hours by sea.

"And Jeni?"

"Yes?"

"Please don't drink any wine if they left it with your dinner—it'll cloud your judgment and it could be laced with something," he said. "Drink bottled water."

"I absolutely agree. I wouldn't think about touching it," I said.

"Thanks. Stay safe. Love you," he said. Then he hung up.

The truth was that I had thought about a glass of wine to calm my nerves and wasn't too happy about the prospect of sitting in the fancy stateroom and forgoing a taste of the French cabernet. I hadn't thought about it being poisoned because the wine was still corked, but he was right. I needed to be clearheaded for what was going to unfold.

Well, I'm not about to leave it on the boat. It's expensive wine, and I'm not wasting it, I told myself. In the end I decided to put it in Candi's suitcase to drink when we made it home. I saw it as an outward manifestation of my optimism that I would survive this ordeal. Or so was my hope.

Chapter Thirty-Eight

MY DINNER HAD great presentation, but it tasted dreadful—definitely not worth the calories. I pushed the cart aside after only a bite or two.

With nothing else to do, I reclined on the perfectly made bed and put my feet up in order to relax. The tiny shoes were beginning to lose their comfort. The sheets were made of silk.

Despite my determination to stay awake, the bed was simply too comfortable and I fell asleep. I was disoriented when I awoke to the unmistakable sound of a chain grinding as it was released from the bow of the yacht. That could only mean that the anchor was being dropped. Sure enough, the water outside the porthole was not speeding past us. We were still. *Finally, we will be saved.*

I thought that, for a moment anyway. When I glanced at the clock, I saw that I had only been asleep for an hour. Even worse, the scene outside my window did not look like Durres. It was a dark shoreline devoid of the city lights I was expecting.

What was happening? As soon as I went to grab my phone and call Zach, I heard a knocking at my door.

Oh my God, I thought. *It's the captain coming for me!* My heart pounded and I looked to see if the porthole would allow for an escape. What would the man do when he found I was not Candi?

It was just as I started to frantically call Zach that I reassessed the knocking. After listening closer, I could tell it wasn't the captain, since it was the small, fast knock that a woman might make. Maria's voice confirmed it.

"Candi's sister, Candi's sister, it's me, Maria. Please open up. Need help!"

"What's happening?" I asked through the wood and metal door.

"Captain say we finished! He say we go over. Tom no can swim! You police! Please, you help! He say spy on *Taku*! I no understand." She started sobbing.

I gave up trying to call Zach after not getting a signal and opened the door to the room.

"Where are they?" I asked when we were both inside with the door locked again.

She put up three fingers and pointed to the upper deck above us—what we called the third level.

"Who is there?"

"Tom, cook, captain, mate, Dimitri, other man."

"The man who came with me is with them?" I wanted to clarify and not assume anything.

She nodded her head yes.

"Are there women below in cabins?"

Again, she nodded her head yes, but this time she lowered it and began sobbing again.

"How many?"

She held up ten fingers, then added one.

"Eleven?"

She nodded yes once again.

"Are their rooms locked?"

"Yes."

"Do you have a key?"

"Yes. I … I feed them." She showed me the key on her ring. I held my hand out for her to give it to me, but she came apart once more, her shoulders heaving with her sobs. "Cook make me do it. I so … so …"

"Okay, okay, don't worry about that for now." I had no time to comfort her. It occurred to me that despite my promise to stay in the stateroom that I'd made to Zach and Davor, the women below had to be released from their locked cabins. That's all I would do, I told myself. I would release them and then hide.

"Just give me the key, and you stay in here. *Lock the door.* Don't let anyone other than me into the room. *Understand*?"

She nodded to indicate that she understood and then lay on the floor in a fetal position behind the bed.

With that I left the room as silently as I could, suddenly cursing the shoes and dress that I'd worn. I should have tried to unbuckle the straps while I was in the room. The heels on the fancy sandals made light taps unless I walked on my toes, almost an impossibility in a hurry. It caused me to scamper down the fancy carpeted circular interior stairs that led from the upper lounges and floors all the way down to the rooms below, where the crew usually stayed. The crew's quarters were smaller rooms in the belly of the boat with bunks that held several persons to a room. I wanted to release the women as soon as I could. I needed them.

The first room that I found was the captain's. I panicked for a second, although I knew he had to be at the helm. His room had a berth and a desk, and was larger and fancier than the ones for the ordinary crew members. I shut the door without entering. Ordinarily I would have made a fishing expedition out of an open desk, but it was not necessary. I knew enough about Captain Arra to stay away.

The next room I approached was a different story. I heard some rustling and a faint noise when I knocked on the door. I knocked again, but no one responded. It was only then that I slipped in the key and turned it, holding my breath until I heard the click. I turned the handle and opened the door, jumping back from the entrance to make sure no one attacked me.

I didn't need to be afraid.

The dark eyes of six terrorized eastern European women were fixed on me. They looked so much alike that at first it was unnerving. It was not unusual that all six had Romania's predominant Latin looks with dark hair and eyes, and it was not unusual that they were pretty. What was unusual was that they had almost identical bodies in size, dimensions, and height, like they were a matched set.

They sat three in a row on the outer sides of the two berths in the tiny stateroom, unmoving.

I attempted a few words in English and in Romanian, trying a rudimentary combination of languages, until I could tell a few women understood and they began nodding. It was then that I told them we had to get to a safe place. They were to quietly leave this room when they got a signal from me that it was time to go.

The final five women were in a smaller, adjoining stateroom. It took no convincing for them to leave. Little did they know that I had no weapons or protection, only my wits—and my wits were in disarray.

As I gathered them up to leave the crew's quarters—holding my finger to my lips to indicate silence—I noticed that all eleven were in a terrible state of hygiene and health. Their hair was matted to their heads and their faces shone with days of sweat and uncleanliness. The clothes they wore were dirty and wrinkled, and the white sheets on the beds were dingy. Most of all the tiny spaces were claustrophobic with stifling bad odors, caused in large part by a lack of accessible water. Two of the women appeared to be ill, barely able to sit up straight.

How long they had been in state, wearing the same clothes, I didn't know, much less the conditions that they endured before boarding the yacht. It made me sick and angry, and reinforced even more my commitment to help them. They were no different from the victims I had seen on TV crammed into trailer-trucks with metal doors locked from the outside, without clothes, food, money, or identification. And, to my dismay, I finally understood why this operation didn't require many men to keep them under control.

They made no sound as they followed me in a single line down the corridor and up the stairs to the only hiding place where I felt no one would look—the elaborate chef's galley. Once Maria had communicated to me that the cook was with the captain on the upper deck, I knew that it was a safe haven. No more meals would be served that night.

We snaked toward the galley, stopping occasionally so I could peek ahead and listen for noises. When we arrived in the yacht's kitchen, I looked to the oldest of the young women, who appeared to be their unofficial leader. I could tell she understood every word I said. She was pretty like the rest, but much more worldly.

"Do you speak English?"

"Yes," she said.

"Will you help me get us off this yacht?" I asked.

"Of course," she readily answered.

"Okay, this is the plan. Arm them all with knives—the bigger, the better—and then have them hide wherever they can in here." I pointed to the pantries and under counters. "Tell them if anyone comes after them to fight like banshees. Don't be afraid to stab them. There are more of us than there are bad guys. Do you understand what I am telling you? *They have to all fight, or they all might die.* Women have power in numbers."

"I understand." Then she translated my instructions to the women, and they silently began to arm themselves. It sounded as if she conversed in Russian—a language taught in both Ukrainian and Moldovan schools. Perhaps the women were from that region. Moldova used to be a part of Romania.

The women neither objected nor seemed reluctant to do as they were told. Their past lives and current reality had numbed them.

Once each woman had armed herself with a knife and identified her hiding spot, the woman leading the group looked at me.

"Guns?" she asked.

"I'm sorry, I have no guns."

"No, not you—guns below." She pointed toward the crew's quarters.

Oh. My stomach took a major turn. So, it was not just women; it was also weapons that they were smuggling. It made sense. Candi and these few women were not worth the cost of this yacht. I began to sweat. I hated guns. This intense elevation of the danger level was not in my original tactical plan.

"Can you lead me to them?"

She nodded yes and then turned to another woman to tell her to watch over the other women.

We crept back down the stairs to the crew's quarters. It turned out that some of the guns were under the very berths where the women in the second room slept. My guide told me she had looked into one of the rooms after they'd been told it was off-limits. She had been worried it was drugs or dynamite, and then she saw the guns.

I didn't know what to do. I knew how to shoot a pistol at a range with someone helping me, but these weren't pistols.

"Can you shoot one of these?" I asked her, lifting a rifle out of its case.

She smiled and nodded her head yes.

We quickly looked around for ammo but found none.

"The other room?" she suggested. So we searched the other women's room. No luck. It made sense the ammunition wasn't with the guns, but I felt that it had to be somewhere on this level, so we kept looking. It wasn't until the last crew's room, the one for the cook, that we had success. We found the stash in a suitcase in his storage locker.

The woman then deftly loaded one rifle, and then another and another. With that done, she sat on the berth and put one rifle in her lap. She put another one next to her as a backup. Then, she handed me the final rifle, checked the safety, and showed me how to fire it. She barely moved during the shooting lesson, sitting on the berth with her back straight and her face looking at the door, all the while instructing me on what to do. Finally she was through and ready for what was to come. She took a deep breath and looked me hard in my eyes.

"The captain—he raped my sister. I will stay here. He will come for guns. Then I will kill him."

I stood there with my rifle awkwardly held in both hands and didn't know what to say. I should have replied *No, don't kill him,* but I couldn't say that to this woman who had suffered so much. I could see her bruised arms and neck, and wondered what they had done to her as well—this competent and determined woman who could have been a doctor at home in the United States. My mind became clouded with the moral ambiguity that enters the equation when determining the appropriate punishment for a criminal who has committed serious crimes. I rationalized. Maybe he wouldn't go to the guns, I thought. Maybe she would miss. Maybe we would be saved before any of that happened. Maybe ...

But deep down inside I knew that life is often as predictable as it is unpredictable and that she was probably right: he would come to arm himself and she would be waiting.

Before I could change my mind and rip the rifle from her hands, I left the room and hightailed it back up the steps to the deck above us as fast as my high heels would allow. From there I took a side door off the main salon and, once outside, climbed the port side aft ladder to get a glimpse of the upper deck. I wanted to make sure all the men were there. They were all there—the cook, the first mate, the captain, Dimitri, Davor, and Tom, the cabin boy—illuminated in the moonlight and low-voltage deck lighting. They were speaking in raised but unintelligible voices and appeared too occupied to worry about me.

With all accounted for, I scooted back down the ladder and moved to the stern of the boat, where I got a signal on my phone. I quickly texted Zach: "Bad news. Captain mad. Boat stopped b/f Durres. Get location from cell. 11 w/m. Guns! I'm OK, but pls hurry!"

I prayed that someone with him could determine the yacht's location from the satellites and my text. I then turned the sound and light off on my phone.

Once that was done, I began to creep up the outside aft ladder again in order to get a better view of the men. I had to figure out whether they would all go along with the captain's plan, whatever it turned out to be. It was tough to climb with a rifle in hand. About halfway up, my right shoe heel got caught in between two teak treads, lodging in such a way that the heel could not be easily released. I gritted my teeth and pulled hard, hoping to extricate myself from the space. It didn't work.

I tried harder, flailing my body around like a fish trying to escape from a hook, only to sense that my movements caused the heel to dig deeper into the void between the threads. I became more frantic. It would only be a matter of a few minutes before something happened—I didn't know what. When this thing finally went down, I didn't want to be ensnared on a ladder.

Chapter Thirty-Nine

FORTUNATELY, I WAS close enough to listen and see a bit of the drama above me. It wasn't good. Things had changed quickly while I was texting Zach.

Now Davor was sitting in a chair with his back to me. He was tied with some dock line, and Dimitri was holding a small handgun to his head. I prayed it had no ammunition.

"Pistolas!" I heard the captain instruct the first mate in Italian, the word for "gun." "Fretta!"

"Si, Capitan, fretta," the first mate said, and as instructed, he hurriedly ran toward the ladder upon which I now stood in order to get to the berths below.

Gritting my teeth, I yanked as hard as I could on the errant shoe, pulling the heel from the sole and effectively destroying it. I left the heel in the treads and then jumped to the ground from the upper steps, plastering myself against the hull in the darkness behind the ladder. I knew he would not look for me unless he noticed the shoeless heel. Still, I held my breath when he ran past my hiding spot toward the cache of weapons.

All the while, I was aware of the unpleasant surprise that awaited him.

I stayed in my hiding place and kept listening until I felt safe enough to begin a slow creep back up the ladder's steps to where I could see what was going on.

The *Taku* was quiet. I could tell Davor was in trouble and was not at all surprised that Dimitri was holding a gun to his head. But the fact that I was still able to move about gave me a small glimmer of hope that the captain didn't know I was on board in place of Candi.

The men appeared to be waiting for the first mate to return with the guns, something that I felt wouldn't happen without a fight. I used the time to try to get the remaining shoe off, but the buckle was too tight for my nervous fingers, and the action only served to make me more anxious. Frustrated, I decided to simply rip it apart. I pulled as hard as I could, praying the tiny strap would break its hold. Still it held fast.

I stopped moving and jerked my head up to listen more carefully when the captain finally spoke in Italian to Dimitri. The best I could tell was that a boat for the women was on its way and that he was leaving with it. He also said the name Candi, which I assumed meant that he intended for her to leave with him. But then again, maybe he intended to kill her, or rather me.

By then the failure of the first mate to return with the guns became a source of anxiety for the men above. Their feet were at my eye level, and I could see the captain tapping his right foot. Dimitri began to rock from one foot to the other.

When the tension could not rise much higher, I saw the glow of a lighter and the smelled smoke as the captain lit a cigarette and took a few drags. It made my mind wander and worry where my niece and her cigar-smoking French Interpol agent were. *Why has help not arrived? I thought someone had arranged for a police boat. What has gone wrong?*

"Enough!" I heard the captain say in English. He ground out his cigarette on the expensive teak deck. He motioned for Dimitri to stand his ground and keep his eye on Davor. Then he turned toward the cook and the cabin boy and said something that made the cabin boy try to run.

The cook understood the captain's demand. He grabbed hold of Tom by both arms so tightly, pulling them behind his back, that I faintly heard a cracking noise. The thought that he might have broken the small man's arms sickened me, but I was not prepared for what happened next.

The cook pulled out a pistol and placed it against the boy's head. The frightened young man began to whimper.

"*No, no*" was all he could say, over and over again.

I desperately wanted to help him, but I couldn't figure out how to do it safely. Any move I made would get too many people shot. Just when I decided to act on my impulses by making a loud noise to distract the captain, regardless of the consequences, he yelled to the cook, "Adesso!"

I don't know if Tom knew the Italian word for "now," but he screamed in agony. I shut my eyes and covered my ears to try to shut out the sound of gunfire.

It all happened so fast—too fast for even Davor or Dimitri to do anything to stop it.

I only understood Tom's fate when some drops from the splash of water hit my ankles and I opened my eyes. The chef had thrown him off the boat from above, and he landed directly beneath the spot where I was hiding. I knew he couldn't swim and that it would be a matter of minutes before he drowned. I looked around and dropped the closest line down the side of the boat, but Tom was thrashing around, too panicked and stunned by the fall to move toward the boat and reach for it. Even worse, as I had feared, the cook must have literally broken Tom's right arm because he was having trouble treading water.

For what seemed like an eternity Tom continued to scream for help.

Then he began to gurgle water, his voice and cries for help became fainter, and he was underwater for longer periods of time. It was like a slow-motion horror film. I couldn't take it another minute.

When I could tell that the cook had walked away from railing from which Tom was thrown and before I could reason with myself, I put the gun behind the stairs. I started once again to fumble with my shoe but quickly gave up; the buckle wouldn't release. I stood at the edge and dove as quietly as I could, having perfected that art in the endless summers I'd spent in the neighborhood lake as a child.

Despite the tight dress and one shoe, it was as perfect an entry as I could muster. I grabbed Tom's foot to pull him over to the line dangling off the side of the boat and into the shadows of the hull, looping the end under and around his good shoulder.

"Capitan!" the cook yelled. I could hear his feet as he ran back to the railing above me.

As quiet as I tried to be, something attracted the attention of the cook because he came to look over the side and then turned on the underwater lights, the ones we had seen on other yachts in the marinas. Silly me. I thought the lights were to attract fish. Now I knew they also served as some defense mechanism.

"Tom!" the cook called in his thick accent. I knew it was a cruel ploy to get the desperate man to respond and ask once again for help.

I had moved too far under the curved hull of the boat for those on board to see us, even with the lights, but that did not stop the cook from ensuring that Tom did not survive. He shot his pistol a few times in the location where he assumed Tom fell and then went around the boat randomly shooting as far under the hull as his aim would reach until I heard the magazine emptied. I sighed in relief as he turned the lights off again, allowing me more freedom to maneuver.

By then Tom was almost listless, and his arm was loose in a weird way. It was definitely broken, but in more places than one. The water was very cold. I couldn't be sure he would survive another ten minutes. My fingers were already turning blue and becoming numb, but unlike Tom, at least I was moving with oxygen coursing through my veins. I was desperate for a plan, but I knew the only way out was with the rope. And it was impossible for me to both climb up the rope and save Tom.

About that time, I heard a boat arriving, one with loud engines but almost no lights. I groaned. The large engines rumbled as they closed in on us. I could already feel the wake. A few moments later, I could make out the boat outline.

It wasn't the police.

It was the same steel-gray metal boat I had seen in Trogir when Sam boarded it with the bags of liquor and then again in the pictures from Hvar. Its multiple four-stroke engines made almost no sound as it approached us in the dark—as if it was always meant for a stealth operation. Up close I could tell its windowless cabin had enough room for all the women and more.

"Arrivo della barca," the cook proudly relayed to the captain, although I was sure the captain already knew about the arrival of the boat. The cook was nothing more than a sycophant seeking the captain's approval.

"Si," the captain almost barked back to the cook. Then he yelled at him in frustration. "Dove sono le armi?"

This was not good news. *Armi* was "weapons." He wanted the guns, immediately.

But I had other pressing issues. I took a deep gulp of air and looked at Tom. We urgently needed to move from our safe spot, as the speedboat appeared to be headed to our location in order to tie up next to the *Taku*. Tom was unable to follow any directions. Taking matters into my own hands, I covered his mouth with my hand to keep him from swallowing more water, and turned over onto my back. Then I used all the strength left in my legs to swim to the stern of the boat where there was more cover. It was safer—provided the engines didn't start. If anyone turned on the propellers, we were dead.

I found a handhold on a piece of metal attached below the swim platform, which had been lifted out of the water while the boat was under way. If I had any hope of reboarding the vessel, that was dashed. In its upright position, the platform gave me no foothold from which to climb aboard from below.

We were barely hidden before someone on the speedboat threw a line to the cook-turned-assassin.

I heard the captain tell Dimitri that he was going below to get the guns and the women, but something must have made him angry because he suddenly yelled, "Sparagli!"

My heart stopped. *Does he mean for someone to shoot Davor?* Is that what *sparagli* meant? I couldn't be sure. I had no idea what was happening. It was awful.

Dimitri did not speak Italian, but he got the gist of the command.

Unlike the captain, Dimitri was as cool as a cucumber. He began speaking in English, perhaps to frustrate the cook. He raised his voice to be heard over the sound of the speedboat knocking up against the hull of the yacht.

"Captain, take the cook with you. We need Davor as a hostage. We can kill him after we get off this boat and then throw him in the water. Otherwise, his blood will be on the deck. I am not sure the Italians will be happy if you kill a police officer while they are here."

I held my breath until I heard the captain curtly reply, "Bene."

He then yelled to the cook, who was securing the speedboat's lines to the *Taku*.

"Vieni con me!" Relief poured over me when I heard the words that translated as "Come with me."

I wasn't absolutely sure, but I thought the captain and the cook were headed in the same direction as the first mate. The cook's wasteful shooting of his bullets into the water would not help their situation.

There was not much time to worry about them. In what seemed like a split second, two men from the speedboat began to board the yacht. I knew immediately who they were; they'd been with Dimitri and Candi in Hvar. They probably met in Bran and again in Hvar to finalize arrangements and, perhaps, for Dimitri to introduce them to Candi. Bran was far from any suspicious eyes in Bucharest. I remembered that Jean-Claude said one of them worked for the mysterious Italian businessman Rocco, which meant that the other must have worked for Rocco as well. Predictably, they didn't sound surprised to see Dimitri.

"Il capitano?" they asked. I could envision them looking around the almost empty deck.

"E sotto," Dimitri said. I felt sure *sotto* was the word for "below."

Davor began talking to the men in Italian in a threatening voice, presumably to keep them occupied. I couldn't understand the words, but the men laughed in that arrogant way that bullies have. Whatever he'd said, they thought he was funny. I didn't sense fear, but why would they be scared? There wasn't a sign of help anywhere in sight. So much for Jean-Claude.

I could hear the muffled sound of gunfire even with the noise of the water hitting the boat. Then the laughter above me suddenly stopped, replaced by an eerie silence. Time stood still for a moment. The only thing I didn't know was if the captain and cook were dead or alive. If they were alive, they would be a whole lot angrier.

I could tell there was confusion among the men as to their next move.

"Pistole? Donne?" one of the men from the speedboat yelled to Dimitri. He was ready for the guns and the women. It was clear that the operation was taking too long. I couldn't hear the response, but Dimitri didn't leave Davor. I imagined he had a smooth answer.

At that point another man from the boat came on board to help the two men.

"Problema?" I heard him ask.

My desperation was reaching a breaking point. With three men, they could easily move eleven women off the boat—if they didn't shoot them in the galley. I felt sure the smugglers had enough weapons on the speedboat to outgun kitchen knives. I wanted to let loose and cry. *What had I done moving the women from the safety of their rooms?* There were too many men against them, and help would come too late. They might survive if they just followed the men compliantly. *What if I had made a big mistake? What if I had cost them their lives?*

Chapter Forty

AT THE SAME time as I was anxious about my decisions related to the women, I could tell Tom was losing consciousness. I had to at least save Tom, and do so immediately, before I was unable to move as well.

It was just as I decided that I had to scream for help and suffer the consequences that I heard the sounds of a helicopter. I had seen helicopters on every megayacht in the harbor. A helicopter meant even more menacing problems. I cowered under the boat, praying not to be seen.

The pilot came perilously close to the decks and, as I knew it would, the helicopter started shining its spotlight upon us. It flashed over Tom and me hanging under the boat and came back once more to do it again. I tried desperately to dunk under the water to avoid the light, but I was too tired and Tom too cumbersome to go very deep.

It was after the second pass that I realized I wasn't alone in my fear of the helicopter. Strangely, its presence was not welcomed by the men on board either. I could hardly hear myself think between the sound of the rotors and the metallic *rata-ping* of rapid gunfire hitting the metal bottom of the helicopter.

Ricocheting bullets bounced off the helicopter's exterior and peppered the ocean's surface. I peeked around the hull and saw that one of the Italian men who had arrived on the speedboat had retreated back to it, leaving only the two point men from Hvar on board. I thought nothing could surprise me at this point, but when I focused on the Italian clothes of the retreating man in the helicopter's light, I saw the face of the man who'd been with the dead woman in the park right before her death, his neck still bedecked with gold chains.

So, I thought, *the Italian men with Candi and the Romanian men in the restaurant back in Romania are all connected.* But at that moment I had no time to figure out why.

I finally heard the sound of wailing sirens on a speeding police boat in the distance. My heart sunk when I calculated how far away it was. Tom and I were already suffering from the effects of hypothermia, Tom far more than me.

They may be too late, I thought. *We need help right now.*

I hoped that if I yelled for Davor, he would find a way to save us. It was a calculated risk. If I was wrong, it probably would mean a more instantaneous death by gunfire. *But,* I thought, *all I need is a little help until the police come.* If they started shooting, I would swim back under the yacht. Or maybe they wouldn't shoot me. I would tell them I'm a diplomat's wife. Perhaps they would keep me alive to use as a hostage or bargaining chip …

But I couldn't yell for help. The words wouldn't come.

The cold had silenced me—a fate almost as bad as death. I opened my mouth and nothing came out. I was shivering with hypothermia and was worried that I would soon act irrationally. To make matters worse, I had waited too late and had no energy to swim back to the line I'd dropped earlier. My fingers clutching the bolt under the boat had lost all feeling. It was like they were frozen in place. Panic completely took over.

I knew it would be only minutes before I shut my eyes, as Tom had done, and give into the cold, surrendering both of us to the depths below.

For the first time ever, I almost gave up hope.

It was at that low moment that a large orange Styrofoam safety ring plummeted from the sky and landed so close to me that it almost hit me in the head.

I grabbed it before it floated away and managed to pull Tom over the thick round edge so that his stomach was on the top of one side of the life ring and his face was out of the water. Then I slipped his arms into the ropes to secure him. I did the same with my body.

It was just in time. Almost instantly bullets began spraying the water around us. Someone was shooting at us from the yacht! A bullet slightly grazed my upper arm, and one hit Tom in the foot, but he was so gone that he never reacted. I desperately tried to dog-paddle with my one free hand, seeking cover for us under the boat, all the while wondering what demented soul would waste bullets on our pitiful bodies.

The helicopter reacted to the new gunfire, quickly shifting its spotlight to the upper deck so we were in total darkness. I could hear the helicopter's occupants return fire at the now well-lit criminals on the speedboat and upper deck.

"You are surrounded! You must surrender!" Whoever it was in the helicopter then said the same in Italian and two other languages.

At the sound of those words, the speedboat driver turned off all its lights and took off into the dark, leaving the *Taku* crew members and two of its men stranded on the yacht. I wondered where Dimitri and Davor were, but I heard nothing.

I didn't have time to think as I saw the two armed Italian men left on the *Taku* run to the back of the yacht under the protection of the eaves overhanging the side decks, darting away from the helicopter's fire. It frightened me even more.

I knew that they intended to open the hidden door under the swim platform and release the yacht's fancy go-fast boat for an escape.

There was no way to remain hidden from the men in my current position. Once the doors opened, the boat would slide out beside us, if not on top of us. There was no place left to hide.

When I saw the helicopter turn away from us and follow the speedboat, it sealed my fate.

"Tom, I'm sorry, but I can't hold on to the boat any longer. We have to float away into the dark," I said to my silent partner.

With that I gave up and let go of the swim platform, just minutes before the men dropped the expensive tender into the ocean for their getaway. I was right—it would have hit us or, at the least, revealed our position to the gunmen.

Tom and I were quickly swept away from the yacht in the evening breezes. Waves buffeted us back and forth like flotsam destined to be thrown on a far shore. I grew drowsier. It was not long before my view of the yacht was blurred, its lights as benign as those in an impressionist painting. And then my eyes closed to sleep.

When the police boat—as sleek and quiet as the Italians' gray speedboat—pulled up next to us and plucked us out of the water, I thought it was a dream. The officers had turned on no sirens or lights—it was a stealth operation. How they had found us so quickly in a sea of nothingness was beyond me.

Once we were on board, the officers went into action. It was obvious that Tom had serious hypothermia and without medical help would die. Several men dropped their guns and began emergency aid, mostly trying to keep him warm. I was wrapped in blankets and was given a cup of hot tea to drink.

Despite my hoarse throat, I was able to recover enough to give a quick short report on the number of women, the guns, and who else was still on the yacht.

The police captain made sure to tell me that Zach had received my text message and was on the helicopter with Jean-Claude. They had been too late to join the police boats. I knew then that it had to be Zach who'd dropped me the life ring. I smiled and patted my wet dress's tiny pocket with the now-soaked cell phone inside it. Zach would be proud that I had kept my promise. It was charged, turned on, and with me. It just no longer worked.

Our boat sped toward the *Taku*, the police ready to engage with the criminals, but by the time we arrived, the gunfire from the helicopter and yacht had stopped. Who was alive and who was dead? I was feeling anxious and cold once more when I heard someone on the *Taku* yell down to us: "Get medical help quick!"

Chapter Forty-One

DAVOR WAS SITTING in the police boat across from me while the jagged seven-inch cut on his arm was being crudely stitched up by an officer. It was going to be one ugly scar unless redone by a licensed medical professional at a local hospital. He was drinking a glass of scotch that some quick-thinking person had retrieved from the *Taku*. Other patients were being treated on the *Taku*, its teak decks now riddled with holes, and its white carpets and tiles stained in blood.

Davor took a long swig and glared at me. Then he took another. I thought he would never speak. When he did, it was with the same tone he'd used after our bathroom brawl.

"Can you explain why you never thought to tell us that when you took the women to the galley, you armed them for war? We went to help them, and it was like a bunch of knife-wielding ninjas came after us. I've never been so scared in all my career. They came out from under counters and the pantry and everywhere all at one time, shrieking at the top of their lungs in some language I've never heard. I thought they were going to kill me! I didn't even have my gun drawn. I ran like hell out of the galley, but one of them still got me."

His face was red from anger. I didn't say anything but played the scene over in my mind.

I couldn't help it. I wished I'd been there to see it all. I tried hard to stop it, but I was so tired and relieved that I started laughing until I was bent over in my chair.

"I'm sorry. I shouldn't laugh," I said when I partially regained my composure. "I feel terrible, and I know you'll hate me forever for your scar. But you have to admit, your description was ... so ... so ..." I hated to use the word *funny*.

At first I could tell he thought I was crazy, but then slowly he saw the humor as well. He began to laugh too, a nice laugh I had never heard before. It was a laugh in recognition of survival.

"You have been the most aggravating and effective fraudulent undercover law enforcement officer I have ever encountered. By the way, you know that telling Maria you were a policewoman is a crime. I could send you to jail," he said.

"You don't have proof that I did that. Plus, we aren't in Montenegro. It doesn't count."

He smiled. "Of course it counts."

He told me that Dimitri had been badly hurt by the women. He'd gone into the galley first and they held him accountable for their situation—and he was accountable for it. But for the eventual arrival of the police, they might have killed him.

"It was tough to see him so cut up. After all, he kept his part of the deal and protected me and you," he said. "It turns out that he was coerced to participate in this operation when he couldn't pay back a business loan from the Italians."

"How about the captain and first mate?" I asked.

"Your woman had a dead aim, right in the center of the head. She killed both of them. It was like an execution."

Davor said she claimed self-defense. The captain and his mate had hurt both her and her sister. He wasn't so sure it was self-defense, but he said she'd have to live with her decision.

"We both know that under the circumstances, no judge or jury would ever convict her."

It turned out that she didn't kill the cook. He was shot by the police but would live. The two idiots trying to escape the police in the lifeboat had been shot too.

Davor said that he was told Sam was the one who spilled the beans. He'd seen the Romanian waiters give an overdose of drugs to the woman who was found dead in Herastrau Park in Bucharest. She was being kept in the back of the restaurant and had tried to escape. The Italians told the waiters to subdue her, and they overdid it. Dimitri also said it was Sam who mistook me for Candi in Bran; it was he who had tried to stop me from leaving.

I winced at the memory of Scout attacking Sam.

"Who were the guns for?"

"They were the captain's. He was selling them to the Italians. It's his stock-in-trade. The women were for the Italian businessman Rocco Luigi. He has several seedy hotels in Italy that are known for prostitution, and he prefers eastern European women. He also owns that restaurant in Bucharest in the park. I think the police finally have enough proof to arrest him and the other men involved in this operation."

We were silent for a while, and then Davor spoke again.

"So, Jeni, as a result of your hardheadedness, a speedboat and a yacht were seized, weapons were recovered, and a human trafficking ring was broken up with multiple arrests already made, and more to come. I have to admit it's pretty impressive." He refilled his scotch and raised his glass in a toast.

"It wasn't just me. It was all the women. They had been pushed too far, and they finally had the opportunity to use their brains and their anger to turn the tables. You know, Davor, although I wasn't in favor of the plan to kill the captain, I didn't try to stop it. I don't regret it now, but I feel sure I'll wonder about my culpability or acquiescence later."

"You were at war. It was the right decision," Davor said. He remained silent to let me consider his words.

I hoped he was right. We both sat in quiet relief as we heard the engines finally turn over. Then we began our journey to Durres's dry land.

Chapter Forty-Two

LATER THAT NIGHT we all quietly converged on the iconic Adriatik Hotel in Durres, the antithesis of Porto Montenegro. It was where the ordinary Montenegrin, Macedonian, Albanian, or Bulgarian could afford to take a vacation to the beach and have a wonderful time doing so. It had history, Roman ruins, and deep character. It was warm and friendly, and I loved it. The whimsy of the place, damaged yet beautiful in its own right, was just what I needed.

Candi's eyes teared up when she saw me in the lobby, but she smiled through the tears. Everything was okay. We could talk tomorrow. Zach held me tight and told me he had already sent an email to Sue saying that we were all fine. Sue had sent me her love and gratitude.

Zach didn't let go of my hand, not even for a second. When we were all given our room keys, we were the first to head upstairs. We were both unusually quiet. My mind was reeling as we lay down in bed, but Zach held me close. Soon enough I fell into a dead sleep, safe and secure.

We awoke refreshed and renewed, with the early morning sun of a new day in our eyes. The troubling events and emotions of the last four days were finally behind us. As I looked out our balcony at the poetic scene that greeted me—calm waters, cerulean-blue skies, and the colorful slow-moving carts of beach vendors as their owners quietly prepared for a busy day—it all made me wonder if the night before had ever happened.

Breakfast with our colleagues, on the other hand, was anything but quiet. The conversation around the table in the main dining room, complete with white linen tablecloths and an unobstructed view of the Adriatic, was already loud and raucous when we appeared.

Zach was still upset about my participation on the yacht, but once Davor and Jean-Claude deferentially apologized to him, he joined in the banter.

"You ought to have been me in the helicopter when I saw my wife hanging under the boat like a piece of seaweed. I couldn't believe it." Then he turned to me. "What were you planning on doing if they turned on the engines?"

The talk went on like that until our breakfast was served. The conversation then turned to the future.

"I used Zach's phone and called my friend Anna before we came down. She said her private charities will take in the Moldovan women. I think that's at least five of them," I said.

"The woman who shot the captain and first mate is from western Ukraine. She said that with their passports and some money, she and her sister can take care of themselves. I wish they would get some professional help, but they are determined to make it on their own," said Davor. "I'll give them Anna's card in case they change their mind. The rest of the women will stay here in Albania and be helped by an NGO similar to Anna's."

"One last thing," I said, pulling out a laundry bag containing the Versace dress, which appeared to be none the worse for one day's wear.

"Oh, merci!" Jean-Claude said. Once he inspected it, he smiled and said, "Très bon!"

I then took out another bag and handed it to him. He was a bit confused when he reached in and pulled out the wet mess of straps and leather.

"Oh, non!" he exclaimed, horrified as he held the remains of the Jimmy Choo shoes away from his body so as not to make wet stains on his clothes. How would he explain this to his boss? Mindful of his duties, he dejectedly placed what was left of the shoes on the floor beside his chair and stoically pulled out a plastic bag from a pocket to begin the painful process of accounting for the inventory I had destroyed.

"Now mine," I said. Jean-Claude was confused for a moment, but then he smiled. He went outside to his car and returned with a small plastic bag containing my wedding ring and a receipt for me to sign. Once the French paperwork was complete, Jean-Claude made a move to place the ring on my finger.

"No, not you. That's for Zach to do," I said.

Jean-Claude dropped the rings into Zach's hands, who then ceremoniously bent on one knee and took my left hand.

"Jeni, do you promise to have and hold me, never, ever go anywhere else again in danger, and always throw the life ring in first before jumping into the sea?"

"I do!"

Cheers erupted. Soon the table's occupants began paying their checks and saying their goodbyes.

Candi and I separated ourselves from the group and took a stroll on the beach—our first time alone.

"I'm not sure Uncle Zach told you, but as soon as we left Montenegro I emailed Mom, and then she and dad called back to me on Jean-Claude's phone. Thank goodness they're still on the cruise."

"That's great news," I said, every bit as relieved as she was.

"I still can't believe I thought I could be a model in Italy! I'll never forgive myself for being so stupid. Even worse, I almost ruined Mom and Dad's trip, and I put your life at risk," Candi said.

"It's all over now," I said, signifying she was totally forgiven, "but I have to ask." I paused. "Did they hurt you?"

"I've wondered how to answer that question when it came."

She paused and told me that Dimitri didn't hurt her and had tried to protect her from the captain as much as he could—in his own way.

"I'm okay," she said. "Still, what I saw and what I heard was so awful. Aunt Jeni, they took away my innocence. Maybe that's not in itself a bad thing, but it was a horrific way to do it."

I knew that one day she would tell me what the captain and first mate, as well as their friends, said and did, but today was not that day.

Candi paused and looked toward the sea.

"The entire experience changed me and then brought me back to who I am. This is me," she said, pointing to her white shorts, T-shirt, and flip-flops. "I had all the yacht-set intrigue on the *Taku* to last me a lifetime."

"So now we go back, and you can recover in Romania."

"Will we be in time for the Diplomat Games?" she asked with a smile.

I groaned. Until that point I had totally forgotten about them.

"Yes, unfortunately, just in time."

Chapter Forty-Three

I RETURNED HOME to find 128 emails on my computer, almost all related to the impending competitions. They varied from general inquiries like "Where are you?" to specific ones, such as "Did you order the pizza?" I had been forwarded tweets sent out by Moira, such as "Jeni may be organized crime," and responses like "I thought she was CIA." There were emails from the embassy such as "We had a delivery of golf clubs" and "Are we really supposed to field a full soccer team?"

Where would I begin?

I decided to call Anna. She told me not to worry about the details—the games have a life of their own, and nothing ever goes according to plan. Plus, she said Moira had made more people mad than imaginable. I decided to wing it and not respond to any of the emails, tweets, or phone messages. I would just show up with my newly minted tan.

The truth is that the games were never a real competition. The Romanian Foreign Ministry was in charge, and the Romanians would win most of the games. I compared it to the US State Department planning games like baseball and football in DC and then expecting the other embassies to compete in them. Thailand's embassy wouldn't have much of a shot.

So why did we play every year? We played because we always had way too much fun. The event was quirky. The club itself was *so* retro 1950s. They had free beer. Even the name "Diplomat Games" was cool. I had to keep reminding myself that this year's games, just like in the past, would be fun.

It wasn't just emails that greeted us when we got home.

Collin was sitting in the shade outside our gate the day we returned. An incredibly clean and well-mannered Scout sat beside him. Collin had taught Scout to heel and fetch and play dead all in a matter of a few days, but all the training in the world couldn't keep the intrepid canine from jumping into Candi's arms and covering her with slobbery kisses. Once he had sufficiently showed his affection to Candi, he trotted to me and Zach to pay his respects, but thoughtfully he bestowed no kisses.

Candi warmly thanked Collin for helping, and told him how amazed she was at his dog-training skills. We all chatted awhile until Collin said we probably needed to get into our apartment and rest. He handed Candi the new leash he'd bought for Scout. As their hands touched, the ordinarily reserved Collin suddenly seemed emboldened.

"Candi, how about pizza tonight?" He blurted out the question, taking us by surprise. It was if he had rehearsed it all day and wanted to say it before he lost his nerve.

"Sounds wonderful! Will you pick me up?" she replied.

Wow, that was a change. An enthusiastic yes without any reservation? I exercised rare restraint and made no comment.

I was happy for her to go out that night. We didn't have to worry about Collin. Plus, I had tennis practice the next day and needed all the rest I could get. I would be playing in less than two weeks.

The weather was mild and sunny the morning of the Diplomat Games. A large bouquet of red, white, and blue flowers with a Good Luck USA sign had been delivered to us the night before, compliments of Sue and Bob. I had bought the perfect patriotic tennis skirt—with pockets. Zach and Candi had their golf clubs and shoes cleaned and ready. We were all prepared and pumped up.

My first tennis match was at nine o'clock in the morning. Other competitions were staggered throughout the day.

Nadia and I went to the tennis courts about twenty minutes early in order to warm up. We were assigned to one of the two amazing well-manicured clay courts in the far back corner of the club, practically hidden by old flowering shrubs and a wooden shed.

As soon as we went to volley, a tiny man pushing a wheelbarrow filled with rakes, brooms, and buckets ran up to us on the court and yelled for us to leave, saying the special courts were for members only. It was the only English he knew. He then began shooing us away with a broom, like we were wild dogs. Nothing we said made a difference since he knew no English and didn't care anyway. The foreign minister wasn't his boss.

Eventually a club manager came over and backed him down, just as we realized that our first opponents from some tiny country had not shown up.

I high-fived Nadia. As far as I was concerned, the forfeit was a win. Our next match would be at two o'clock.

Our first medal came later that morning in rowing, when Victor took second place. I told him I owed him dinner. We were totally annihilated in Ping-Pong by the Chinese, and in volleyball by the Swedes. Moira was happy because the Romanians had won in rowing and were likely to get medals of some sort in soccer, men's tennis, and Ping-Pong. She also coveted a win in women's tennis. I found myself not caring after Anna told me that Moira had worn out her shelf life with the committee and that the International Ladies were ready for me to be back in charge. Moira's quest to win at everything had backfired.

My tennis match at two o'clock was against a Japanese diplomat and her daughter. They were civilized and played the type of league tennis that I enjoyed. I was jealous of their cute matching tennis outfits and their whole fan club of husbands, children, and friends dressed in white sitting at the edge of the court in folding chairs with umbrellas for sun protection. Their ambassador even stopped by to wish them well.

Sadly, it wasn't even a real match. Although it was fairly miserable in the midday heat, we breezed through the first set without the Japanese women taking a single game or us working up a sweat. Actually, I didn't do anything. I just ducked out of my partner's way, and she was all over the court returning anything on our side. Nadia was going to get her desire—a final match with her nemesis. Soon enough the fan club was quiet and the mother and daughter demoralized, but we continued to played through without relenting in the least. We wanted a win that badly.

It was all well and good until the middle of the second set, when two young "umpires" who told us that they'd volunteered to help the Foreign Ministry for their résumé enhancement walked right into the middle of the court and interrupted our game. They said that it appeared to the officials, whoever *the officials* were, that we were likely going to win and they wanted us to know that the star Romanian players wanted to play the championship match not that night but the next day, which was a Monday.

"What? I can't," I said. "I have mandatory security training and then additional remedial training from the RSO for avoidance of international incidents, or something like that." I was dreading a day with Matt and his litany of State Department rules covering everything I'd done wrong in Montenegro, Albania, and Croatia. But it had to be done. The agenda for the one-on-one meeting was very long.

"You have to tell them we must play later this afternoon like it's always done."

They came back in a few minutes, heads hung down low.

"The foreign minister said that if you win, then you will have to play the final game tomorrow." No ifs, ands, or buts.

"Okay," I said. I knew it was a fruitless argument at that moment. I turned to Nadia and told her that we'd worry about what to do if we won later. "For now let's finish this game."

It was Nadia's serve. I could see her face harden and her eyes narrow in anger. She then threw the ball high into the air and swung her racquet with such force that the ball shot across the net like a bullet, whizzing within inches of our opponent daughter's small face. Had Nadia aimed perfectly, she could have taken her head off. Everyone gasped at the sudden ferocity.

For a few seconds we all stood in place, wondering what to do. Nadia assessed the situation and then shook her head. She took a deep breath and spoke.

"Sorry, my bad." Then she began to rub her right elbow.

Still, no one moved.

"Uh, I think I hurt my arm," she said, feigning an injury. "Jeni, you will have to serve."

At that point I realized that it had dawned on my partner that winning wasn't everything.

I shrugged my shoulders and said "okay," although I still had little confidence in my ability to serve. The "umpires," who were already bored and ready to go home, gave us the traditional Romanian response to everything: "Why not?" I was pretty sure they had no idea what the rules were.

Our opponents just sighed in relief.

In the end we played the league tennis that I knew with pretty strokes and lots of goodwill. We ultimately lost, but it was crazy. The Japanese fan club had become our fan club as well, cheering on those rare occasions when I got an ace. In the end it was an honorable loss for the Americans. We made great friends and planned to get together for lunch the following week.

Collin ran into Nadia and me as we exited the tennis courts.

"They won! First place!" He was exuberant. "There were some great golfers and shots, especially from Zach, but Candi's hole-in-one on the final par three was simply miraculous. It stunned the whole field. The Scottish twosome was in a tie with them until that moment, at which time they lost their composure and bogeyed the final two holes. Zach and Candi ending up winning by three strokes," he said, pumping his fist in victory for our side.

So, this time there was no choking by Candi. Despite a crowd of spectators and a really bad month, she had come through for Team USA.

Collin talked about the golf match as we ambled back to the clubhouse.

"The only bad news is that once Candi hit the hole-in-one, they almost had a stampede to the bar. All the golfers wanted to be first to order their free drink. The club manager finally offered to help the bartender handle the crowd."

I was a bit confused by this information, which fact made Collin smile.

"You do remember that Candi is obligated to buy a drink for all the golfers in the clubhouse because she hit a hole-in-one?"

I looked toward the clubhouse and groaned at the line of cheerful golfers at the bar, all ready to order.

Chapter Forty-Four

BUT FOR THE fact that it was dusk, I would have described the sky on Candi's last weekend in Romania as a tequila sunrise. The Black Sea horizon was washed in pale pinks and vivid oranges, enhanced by a layer of fluffy clouds above that absorbed the hues and were reflected by the water. Zach had finally managed to rent a sailboat in Constanta on the Black Sea, and Collin, Victor, and Candi were taking an overnight sail with us. Soon enough Victor and Collin, like Candi, would board planes and head to the States to prepare for new assignments. Even Scout joined the cruise in his new life vest and safety harness.

Zach was in his element at the helm, and Collin and Victor were on the bow hanging their feet over the edge, enjoying the slow speed of the sailboat and the occasional cool spray of the waves over their toes.

I popped the cork on the bottle of French cabernet I had stowed in Candi's suitcase and poured some into two plastic tumblers before reclining back on the bright blue cushions in the small cockpit. It was only a 32-foot sailboat, as opposed to a 320-foot yacht, but it was pure bliss. It was my observation that people seemed to have more fun on a 10-foot rowboat with a cane pole and a cold bottle of beer than on a $10 million yacht.

Candi came and took her tumbler, snuggling up next to me in order to ward off a bit of the cool wind from the edge of the mainsail. Just for a moment she was the little girl I'd once babysat.

"You know, I talked to Mom today and told her that I wasn't going to grad school for sports broadcasting or sports anything. I thought she'd be furious, but she was actually really happy. Go figure. You know they took that long trip to celebrate my graduation and no more tuition, but she said she would have gladly paid for grad school—only not a dime more for golf or anything like it. She said it doesn't make me all that happy. I never thought I'd say this, but she's right. It has no real meaning for me. I could never be a pro, and I didn't want to be on the sidelines. Collin says I ought to take the foreign service exam. We've talked a lot about it. He's convinced I can pass it. You know he's going to be in DC learning a new language for his next posting, and he said he would help me study for the exam. He's incredibly smart. Did you see he has new glasses? Plus, did you know he's going to Montenegro next? It's wild, but I'm pretty sure that I know more about Montenegro than he does ..."

I smiled, listening to her ramble on while I watched Zach at the wheel, trimming sails and adjusting course, soaking up the last of the sun. Soon enough life would be just the two of us again. I looked at my wedding ring and smiled. Given our renewed nuptials, maybe it was time for a honeymoon.

Printed in the United States
By Bookmasters